LOVE ON A SPRING MORNING

A PINE HARBOUR NOVEL

ZOE YORK

WWW.ZOEYORK.COM

Single father and widower Ryan Howard has zero interest in the movie being filmed in Pine Harbour or the high maintenance stars staying in the cottages at the end of his lane. He's just barely holding on to the raw remains of his life and the fantasy world being concocted around him is, as far as he's concerned, a complete waste of time and energy. The one bright light in his life is an intern on the set, and their quiet conversations at the end of the day on his back porch.

Hope Creswell hates her life, too, which is entirely unfair because she's blessed beyond measure. She's at the top of her acting career, a Hollywood A-list star, and surrounded by people that mean well. But Ryan makes her laugh, and cry, and before she can explain her double life, he kisses her.

the best family is the one you choose

For Rachel, Natalie, Andraena and Hannah, my first and most constant cheerleaders

CHAPTER ONE

SCHOOL FIELD TRIPS were invented by the devil.

Ryan Howard scoured the Scenic Caves gift shop for pain killers. Or a heavy mallet. Anything to make the piercing headache go away. He came up empty.

"Dad!" Gavin yanked on his arm, and Ryan pasted on a smile.

"Yeah, buddy?"

"There's this really cool dinosaur. You gotta come see it. Can I get it? Please?"

"Is it under the ten dollar limit?" Ryan followed his seven-year-old son to the display, knowing already that it wasn't. And Gavin had already had his eye on the same clay mould kit that his friend Ben had grabbed. He was going to ask for both, and that was Ryan's fault, because he'd been giving all three of his kids everything they asked for and more for four months.

The sharp stabbing pain behind Ryan's eye reminded him he didn't want to think about that right now.

Maybe it was time to call the counsellor again.

"So what do you think? Could we get it?" Gavin waved the giant box in the air.

"Your teacher asked that everyone stick to a ten dollar limit. Right? So how much is that?"

Ryan watched as his son traced his fingers over the dollar sign and numbers.

"Three dollars?" Gavin stretched out the words hopefully, then sighed in resignation and put the box back on the shelf. "Thirty dollars. More than ten."

"Yeah. Sorry, bud. Thanks for understanding, though." He ruffled Gav's hair. "Put it on your Christmas wish list."

"It's March. Christmas is a million years away."

"Birthday, then."

"Same deal." Gavin stomped away, and Ryan had to bite his tongue to keep from saying something else. *He's allowed reactions.* And by the time the seven-year-old reached his friends on the other side of the gift shop, he was happy to look at the clay mould kits again, the momentary disappointment forgotten.

The bus ride back to Pine Harbour was loud and noisy—a chaotic end to a chaotic day. At least they were almost home. He got a text message from his friend Olivia Minelli that she'd picked Maya up from preschool, no problem, and they were waiting together for Ryan's oldest, Jack, to get off the bus at home.

Suddenly becoming a single dad meant he was having to learn to rely on others. His friends were trying to make it easy. For the first few months after Lynn's death, he'd had his in-laws just down the road, but they'd recently headed south to escape the end of winter—and to free up their home so it could be rented by a film production company.

Hollywood was coming to Pine Harbour.

Well, one movie, with a big deal director and A-list actors and everything.

The stabbing pain returned, and with it that irrational fear of exposure that had itched at the back of his neck since November.

"What should we have for dinner?" he asked Gavin as they walked across the school parking lot to where Ryan's pick up truck was parked.

"Spaghetti."

"Deal."

But when they got home, Maya melted down when he only had the wrong kind of pasta in the cupboard, and Jack stomped off in search of the tablet—aka the glowing God. Ryan had a love-hate relationship with the damn thing. He knew his nine-year-old hid behind it, but it also helped him read and learn and, frankly, sometimes hiding was how the kid coped.

Ryan sometimes wished he had a device to hide for coping, too. That was something the counsellor had said after Lynn was shot—they had all been through something traumatic, and it was okay to escape from the pain. But other than re-reading *Hitchhiker's Guide to the Galaxy*, Ryan didn't really have anything. He wasn't a technology guy, and he didn't have the attention span for new books right now.

He couldn't even get a decent dinner together.

Fuck it all. "Peanut butter and jam sandwiches?" They all quieted down and climbed up to the table. He exhaled roughly and grabbed the jam. "Tomorrow we're eating a real meal, no complaints, got it?"

"Sandwiches are healthy," Gavin said. "Peanuts are a meat alternative, jam is fruit—"

Ryan laughed. "Jam is not fruit."

"Then what's the red stuff?"

"Sugar."

"Maybe we should make our own jam," his middle child retorted again. Right, because what they needed to add to the mess of their life was a canning production line.

"Maybe," Ryan said as he slathered peanut butter on bread.

"Is that a maybe that really means no?" Jack asked.

"Yep."

His oldest rolled his eyes. "Then you should just say no."

"If I say no, someone will cry." Ryan sighed and put down the knife he'd been using. "Look, guys, I'm just trying to get you fed, okay? I'm not trying to be a bad guy about making jam. Got it?"

"Got it," three little voices said in chorus, although Jack's voice wasn't so little anymore.

Had his voice started to change in the fall, Lynn? Did you get to hear that? Ryan shoved away from the counter and went to the fridge to get the milk and refocus. He needed to stop talking to his dead wife in his head. It took him to an ugly place.

His pulse thudded in his neck, like his veins were full of hot mud. Hot, *angry* mud. *Damn it all to hell.*

He wasn't going to yell at the kids. He didn't, most of the time, but it was in his nature to bark when he was upset, and it had been four long months of being upset.

Shaking his head, as if it was that easy to get rid of his demons, he pulled three cups out of the cupboard. "Milk to drink. No complaints, no whining, or I'll cancel Christmas."

"Yay, milk!" Maya cheered, and Gavin snickered, then echoed her, which made Jack laugh.

And watching his kids laugh, even if it was at his own expense…that made Ryan laugh. "Love you guys."

"Love you too, Daddy," Maya said, waving her hands in the air as he set her sandwich in front of her.

As they dug in, he stretched his arms over his head, trying to find the right angle to get rid of the tightness in his back. His new normal: wound tight and on the edge of being pissed off, constantly.

Ryan wanted a lot of things—happy kids, drama-free days, everyone sleeping through the night. But right along with all of that other stuff, he also wanted a fucking break, more than a few hours. His stomach turned at his selfishness. And it was impossible—it wasn't like he trusted anyone else to take his kids overnight.

He had to make do with the tiny bits of freedom he got each week for the few hours of work he did.

"What are you having for dinner, Daddy?" Gavin tapped his leg, and Ryan realized he was still standing beside the table.

"I'll have a sandwich, too." What he really wanted was a steak. With mashed potatoes and green beans drenched in butter. Three foods his kids would never touch in a million years.

So he made himself a PB&J, and ignored the twinge in his back.

Bath time was uneventful, but as it often did, the sadness snuck up again as they all cuddled in his bed for story time.

"I miss Mommy," Gavin whispered, the wobble in his voice tearing Ryan's chest open.

"Me too, buddy. So much."

Maya crawled onto his chest, burying her face in his neck, and from the foot of the bed, where he'd been reading a chapter book on a tablet, Jack turned. He kept his face ducked, not making eye contact with Ryan, but he scrambled for the empty arm space and hugged on.

They lay like that until Maya's breathing grew steady and Gavin rolled to the side.

"Come on, kiddo," he whispered to Jack. "I'll lay with you in your room until you fall asleep."

Not for the first time, he considered saying screw it and just buying another double bed for his room, but that wasn't a good forever solution.

At some point, they needed to move on, and part of that was learning to sleep on their own.

He left Maya in his bed—one battle at a time—and, picking up sleeping Gavin, followed Jack across the hall to the room the two boys shared, leaving both doors open. They read a short story together, then turned out the overhead light. On the wall, the moon lamp he'd gotten Gavin for Christmas glowed dully.

"I need some water," Jack whispered.

Ryan was halfway out of bed before he remembered to ask if Jack wanted to come with him to the bathroom to get it. His son shook his head, but the question mattered.

The routine was so precarious, the stability so fragile. *Because* we're *still fragile*, Ryan thought bitterly. When would bedtime be easy again? When would they all stop being so brittle and edgy and one wrong step away from tears?

When he returned to the boys' room, Jack took one small sip from the cup and handed it back.

"Want a song?"

Jack closed his eyes, nodding.

Two refrains of "The Wreck of the Edmund Fitzgerald" later, and his oldest was finally asleep.

He lay there for a few minutes, soaking up the gentle warmth of a snoozing kid before Maya cried out in the other room. He tucked the blanket securely around Jack, made sure the door was wide open and the nightlight was on in the hall, then crawled in beside his youngest again, Maya wrapping her arms around his neck so hard it almost hurt.

His four-year-old daughter, clinging to him for dear life while unconscious. Jesus Christ.

I've only got two arms, Lynn, and three kids who need to be hugged to sleep. That familiar hot burn seared his eyelids. He wouldn't actually cry. He was all out of tears. Crying would be easier—cathartic, at least. But he couldn't, even if he sank into all the sadness in his head. Even if he wallowed in it, turning the bitterness and regret over and over again until he was filled with a growing blackness.

Still, tears wouldn't come. His eyes would just get hotter, itchier, until he went downstairs and poured himself a glass of scotch.

He didn't always drink it. It had become this bizarre ritual, where he stared at the glass and thought, if only this washed it all away.

It wasn't that he wanted to be an alcoholic. *Fuck.* Even the thought of addiction made him want to pitch the glass across the room. But he wanted escape, if only for a few minutes, in a controlled fashion. And maybe by sinking into an almost addiction, maybe he could understand Lynn's pain.

Fuck.

There wasn't enough booze or harsh language or tears in the world to ever make him understand the mess that had been inside his wife's head.

It wasn't long before he heard sleepy footsteps, and

Gavin was back, crawling in next to him. The boy hadn't even really woken up.

Ryan tucked the boy in again, giving up on the idea of having a side of the bed to himself tonight. He tried to make enough room to lay fully on his back, but as soon as he gained a few inches on the left, Maya crowded into him on the right.

Ryan's thoughts drifted to his earlier wish. *Fuck that steak dinner,* he thought to himself. *I want to fast forward until all this pain fades away.* Somehow it didn't seem any less selfish to want to speed over some of his kids' childhood. But he was so close to falling to pieces himself. He couldn't get a real dinner on the table or shepherd his kids through a day without tears. Grief sucked donkey balls, and if he could lessen that load for his kids—and for himself—then he'd damn well do it.

Even if meant missing out on some good stuff in the process.

CHAPTER TWO

THERE WASN'T any good reason for Holly Cresinski to be heading to the tiny blip on the map of Pine Harbour three days early, other than she couldn't bear to stay in Los Angeles a second longer, and she didn't have anywhere else to go.

She reconsidered her plan many times on the four hour limo drive from Toronto, but as the driver stopped in front of a diner as instructed by Olivia Minelli, the local liaison person Holly had emailed after landing, all her worry slipped away.

This place looked *nice*. Could a town look kind? Because Pine Harbour did. A thick forest separated the little town from the highway, and the diner was in the middle of a gravel parking lot that butted up to that natural barrier. Across the road was a farm implement repair barn, and then the street continued down a hill toward what looked like a quaint main street. Sparking in the distance was the dark grey blue of Lake Huron.

Some of the buildings were new, others were older. Almost every vehicle in the lot was a pick-up truck, most covered in a generous layer of dirt. The entire thing was perfect. Real and unpretentious and probably not a pool boy or personal trainer or a mother who gets naked with pool boys and personal trainers within a hundred miles.

Because she was definitely done with nonsense like that.

Maybe she'd move to New York. Leave the L.A. house to her mother, and buy a nice one-bedroom apartment on the Upper East Side. *"Sorry, Mom. Couldn't find anything with a guest room. You'll have to stay at the Plaza." On your own dime.* Of course, Holly wouldn't say the last bit. No point in saying something she didn't have the guts to actually back-up with action.

A short, pretty brunette bounded out of the diner, looking dangerously chipper. She waved as she approached the limo, and the driver got out and spoke to her briefly before opening the door and gesturing for her to join Holly in the backseat.

"Hi! I'm Olivia. We emailed."

"Hope Creswell," Holly said in her smooth, practiced way. Sliding into her stage name—her non-stop public persona—was second nature now. "Thank you for accommodating my early arrival. I trust I'm not interrupting anything?"

"Not at all." Olivia gave her a warm smile. "Okay, so that's Mac's Diner. The owner is Frank. No Mac, that's just the name. I thought you might want to see where it was. You won't have a car, right? So if you need food delivery or something until everyone else gets here, you can call the diner and someone will drop off a meal for you. But I've stocked the kitchen at the cottage, so you should be okay until everyone else arrives on Sunday. You've got those numbers, too, there's a binder on the counter. I'll show you." She took a breath and looked around. "You came alone? I thought you were bringing an assistant with you."

"Emmett will come up next week. He and his partner are expecting a baby at the end of the summer, and the first OB appointment is this week, so I told him to come up after that."

"Oh, wow! That's exciting for him. Well, if you need anything before he gets here, I'm happy to help." Olivia filled the short ten minute drive south of town with more chatter about the local amenities—not many—and Holly stared out the window. She was being a bit rude, but she was bone tired after a five-hour flight and four-hour drive, even if all she had to do was sit the whole time.

Maybe she could go for a run once she got settled.

And then sleep for days.

The limo slowed at Olivia's instructions, then turned at a farmhouse, heading down a slight hill into a grove of trees. "That's Ryan Howard's house," her de facto guide said, pointing to the home on the corner. "He's the son-in-law of the Fenichs, who have rented these cottages to the production company. He's the property management, so to speak."

"So to speak?" Holly took in the pile of kids' bikes on the deck and the minivan parked next to yet another pick-up truck.

"It's complicated." Olivia smiled, her expression professional but guarded. "He's a great guy, just a bit gruff because he's on his own with three kids now. But he will help you out if you need something."

The limo snaked under the canopy of trees, revealing first one small cottage, than another, then a few more slightly bigger ones, all in a row. "So the other cast and senior production team members will be staying in these cottages," Olivia said, then pointed out the opposite window. "And that's where you and Emmett will be staying."

That was not a cottage.

The beautiful lakeside home was no more a cabin than she was a movie set intern. It was a *home,* and for the next three days, she'd be all alone in it. It was perfect. By the time everyone else arrived, she'd have her head on straight and her first week's lines memorized.

She gazed up at the modern, spacious house with the large wrap-around deck and smiled to herself.

This is what she needed. Work and solitude.

She murmured her thanks as the other woman led her inside, handing over a key before pointing out the kitchen and the bedrooms upstairs.

"All the fireplaces are natural gas, and they give off a good amount of heat. We're heading into spring now, but it's still quite cool at night." Olivia led her back onto the open landing, overlooking the great room below. "And your exercise room is set up downstairs. I'll show you that."

Her contract stipulated a workout room, set up just so. It felt a bit prima donna, but the reality was that if she didn't burn eight hundred calories a day, she gained weight. There was no diet in the world she could stick to for longer than two weeks—and that was only when the carrot at the end of the stick was pretty damn big. Like the Oscars.

Which you haven't been nominated for in years. She'd only managed one nomination, ten years earlier for best supporting actress. Since then she'd done everything right —time on Broadway, which she'd loved, and taken projects that stretched her in a million directions. None of them had resonated with the Academy.

At least her agent had a nose for good co-stars, which meant that the projects always did well. Like Joshua Pearce, best known for being hot and starring in raunchy comedies, who'd signed on to play a complete asshole here in *Unexpected*. Everyone in the film had a stake in making this one *good*. Take-their-breath-away good, get-noticed-and-boosted-to-the-next-level good.

Wipe-away-the-stress-of-being-one-missed-contract-away-from-nobody kind of good.

"Everything should be as you expect it," Olivia said softly, breaking into Holly's thoughts.

"Thank you," she said with a smile. Always with a smile, even when tired. Always with her hair brushed smooth and lip gloss firmly in place. Preferably with sunglasses on. Hope Creswell was cool as a cucumber and slightly aloof. She didn't spend a second worrying about her career being two missteps away from over.

But as soon as Olivia left, promising she was just a phone call away if Hope needed anything, the movie star went away for the night and Holly pulled out her running gear. Sweatpants, sports bra, t-shirt. Hair up in a messy ponytail. There was nothing cool or calm about Holly Cresinski. She worried and ran, and ran and worried. Every night, for at least an hour, no excuses and no exceptions.

Because people were counting on her. Emmett and his baby-to-be. Her agent, manager, publicist…although they'd all find other clients. But still. And her mother.

The woman child at age fifty. Maybe because she'd been a child herself when she had Holly, or maybe because she'd never gotten comfortable in that role of mother and adult woman.

Holly had been supporting them both since her early teens. At least now they didn't need to live in the same house, not that Maggie Cresinski respected property boundaries.

Her therapist would say this kind of dwelling was unhealthy. *Is she here? Is this an immediate problem? Is there anything you want to do about this?* No, no, and no. Holly increased the speed on the treadmill.

An hour later she dragged herself upstairs to the master bedroom, turned on the shower in the attached bathroom, and waited for the room to fill with steam.

And waited.

She stuck her hand in the water, cursing at the ice cold droplets hitting her skin.

Downstairs, she flipped open the information binder and picked up the phone to call Olivia, but her gaze fell on the name at the top of the page. *Ryan Howard, property support*. Letting out a deep breath, she typed in his phone number.

Busy signal.

She tapped her finger on the numbers on the page. She could call Olivia. Wait, and try this Ryan guy again. Or she could just walk up the lane and knock on his door.

It was just getting dark outside—not too late. And she needed hot water.

Grabbing a sweatshirt from her bags, still piled in the living room, she headed outside, not bothering to lock the door behind her.

The farmhouse at the top of the road was lit up, and through the big window at the back of the house she could see a man moving around the kitchen. She climbed the three steps to the small deck attached to that part of the house and knocked on the door.

A child of maybe seven or eight answered, and before he could say anything, he was joined by two others, one smaller, one bigger. Two boys and a little girl.

From behind them, a man bellowed. "What did I tell you guys about just opening the door? You can't do that!"

The tallest kid shrugged at her before stepping out of the way, making room at the door for a tall Viking of a man. Big, burly, and, as promised by Olivia, a little gruff. "Can I help you?"

He couldn't possibly mean it less. He said it because that's what you say when someone comes to your door, but she'd obviously caught him in the middle of something, and this had been a mistake.

Except she didn't have any hot water.

Her hair wasn't brushed and she wasn't wearing any lip gloss, but she put on her best Hope smile anyway and tipped her head to side. "Are you Ryan Howard?" When he nodded, she steamed ahead. "I'm sorry to bother you, but I'm staying in the house down at the lake—"

"That's my Grandma's house," the little girl piped up from where she was twirling around her father's leg.

Holly grinned at her, sensing a possible ally. "Well, it's a beautiful house. But there isn't any hot water, and that might be because the cast isn't arriving until Sunday. I'm a few days early."

"Ah. Okay." The back-lit giant turned, urging his crew of mini-Vikings to return to the table.

Holly stood in the doorway, unsure if she had an invitation to enter the home or not. After a moment, she decided to take the chance and stepped inside, closing the door behind her.

"Olivia said if we had any problems, we could ask you…"

He stood at the stove, his back to her. "I just need to finish dinner," he tossed over his shoulder. "We'll all walk down in ten minutes or so, if that's okay? It's just the hot water heater that needs to be turned on."

"Oh." Maybe she should have thought of that before coming up here, although she didn't have the faintest clue where she'd find that. "Is it something I can do myself? Is that in the bathroom?"

He froze, the extra-wide shoulders stiffening momentarily before he turned off the stove and set the spoon he'd been holding on the well-used stovetop.

"Look, miss…" He turned and Holly got her first good look at him. His solid jaw was covered in a few days growth of stubble, and his light brown hair had a decidedly unfashionable curl at the ends, but the sum total of his parts was unexpectedly attractive. Actually, each of his individual parts were appealing, too, but that still didn't explain her immediate attraction. She worked with good-looking men every day.

But this wasn't about seeing a good-looking man. This was about seeing one doing something as mundane as cooking his kids dinner. *He's like the town,* she thought to herself. Real and normal and unlike anything she'd ever had before. And as strange as it seemed to describe such a masculine man as cute, that's exactly what she thought. *So cute.*

He gave her a pained look which promised that her fascination with him was most definitely not returned. "It's not in the bathroom. It's in the furnace room."

Holly tried like hell to keep the stupid look off her face, but on this front, she *was* stupid. "Furnace room?"

He just looked at her, like he was waiting for her to realize this was beyond her, but if it was *just* the water heater that needed to be turned on, surely she could do that.

"Let's try this again." She flashed another smile, because that always worked. "Is this something I can do myself?"

He looked like he desperately wanted to say no, but maybe he equally didn't want to come down to the house, because after a long beat, he nodded. "Sure, yeah."

"I don't want to inconvenience you."

He let out a sigh. "No, I need to get used to stuff like this. I guess when those fancy Hollywood types get here, this won't be anything compared to the drama they'll bring with them."

Those fancy Hollywood types? "Uhhh..." Holly nodded. What else was there to do? "Right. This is pretty straight-forward, so I can do it. If you could just give me some instructions, maybe?"

"Yep. Hang on a second." He pointed at the little girl, who'd hopped out of her chair again and was spinning in circles in the open space between the two grown-ups. "Table, Maya."

Maya laughed as she scampered into her chair, but quieted down as her father set a bowl of macaroni and cheese in front of her. Two more bowls, with larger portions, were set in front of her brothers, and then the mountain man with the curly hair and perma-scowl grabbed a pad of paper off the fridge and sketched something out really quickly.

He handed over the paper, and pointed at it with his pen. "The furnace room is in the basement, through the door beside the laundry." She'd seen that; it was across from the workout room. "There are two units. The square one is the furnace. The round one beside it, here, that's the water heater. There's a knob on it. Turn it to the left. Call me if you have any trouble."

About that. "I tried to call before I walked over, but the line was busy."

He swore under his breath and stomped out of the room, returning shortly with a handheld phone. He pointed it at the little girl, who didn't seem cowed in the least. "No phones. Not a toy."

"Sorwee, Daddy," she said in an exaggerated little girl pout.

"Maya."

"*Daddy.*"

The entire family paused for a second before cracking up, and Holly covered her mouth with her hand, trying in vain to hide her own amusement.

"Seriously, kid, people need to get in touch with me now. I'm sure those movie stars won't be as understanding as…" He trailed off and looked in Holly's direction. "Sorry, what did you say your name was?"

There was only one answer here. *Hope Creswell, one of those awful Hollywood types. Sorry to be a bother.* But she couldn't bring herself to be that person tonight. "Holly. Holly Cresinski. And I'm sure everyone on the film shoot will be very understanding that we're all crowding into your lives for a few months, really. They're not so bad, those movie stars."

"Ryan Howard." He extended his hand, and she took it, enjoying the way he gripped her fingers, his skin warm and dry and rough against hers. He squeezed her hand more than people usually did, and she felt the stern shake all the way up her arm.

Who knew she'd been missing an honest handshake in her life?

He let go and crossed his arms over his broad chest. She looked up at him—way up. She was average height for a woman, and he still towered over her. In his plaid shirt shoved up to his elbows and his faded jeans, he looked every inch the rustic lumberjack she thought might live here—except for the cute part. That was unexpected.

And inconvenient, because this particular lumberjack had a family. She needed a clone of him back in Los Angeles, although she suspected that maybe something would get lost in translation.

"Thanks for the instructions. I'll call if I have any questions." She waved the paper in the air as she blindly reached for the door behind her.

He nodded, his face showing none of the distraction that rioted through her midsection. Of course not. She was a random nobody, sweating and flustered, who'd showed up in the middle of a late dinner demanding help.

But she could help herself, armed with the piece of paper in her hand. It was a little thing, but was hers.

He grabbed the door as she swung it open, closing it quietly behind her as she headed back into the night.

Holly Cresinski, maybe you should pretend to be yourself more often.

CHAPTER THREE

IT TURNED out the celebrities staying down the road from Ryan's house were pretty easy guests, because they were never home.

Olivia had promised being the property manager would be a relatively easy task, and other than the young intern coming to complain about the hot water heater before everyone else arrived, he hadn't had any other maintenance calls. So maybe his friend was right.

Everyone else in town was fascinated by the movie being made in their backyard. On the first day of filming, the cast and crew had finished early and thrown a barbecue for the community, but Ryan hadn't bothered to go. None of his kids were interested and it had been a school night. And even with the distraction of famous people, there would be the inevitable looks of concern and murmurs of so-called helpful advice.

But even if he didn't have to run the gauntlet of well-meaning intervention, he still wouldn't be interested in the fantasyland extravagance of making a movie. The amount of money they were paying his in-laws for the cottage rentals alone was crazy. *What a complete waste.*

So when his first counselling appointment in three months started with small talk about the filming, which had been under way for a week, he was a bit harsh.

Maybe more than a bit.

"So you're not a fan," Gayle, the counsellor, said drily.

"Sorry," Ryan said, then cleared his throat. "I'll be happier when they're gone, that's all."

"Even though the movie has brought you a bit of work?"

After a lengthy back-and-forth, Lynn's life insurance policy had paid out, and he lived mortgage-free in the home Lynn had grown up, that his in-laws had moved out of when they built the house at the other end of the lane. For the immediate future, he didn't need to work more than his very part-time reserve Army schedule required. "If I wanted to work more, I'd go back to being a paramedic."

"And you don't want to do that?" She looked at him gently. She had a way of listening that made these sessions tolerable. Ryan wouldn't go so far as to say he *liked* Gayle, but she was a good counsellor—better than the first one they'd tried as a family.

He'd do anything to protect his kids—from invasive questions for which they didn't have answers, for example, or other risks. Harder to pin down ones, like leaving them with other people, even if that wasn't rational, because he was okay with them going to school or being watched by Olivia or his other friend Dani for a few hours.

But he still couldn't leave them overnight, with anyone. Not their grandparents, not any of his well-meaning friends. Definitely not a hired babysitter or nanny. "I'm happy being a full-time dad right now."

She waited just long enough to let him know that she knew that wasn't a complete answer. "How are the kids?"

"Sad. Scared. Acting out a bit."

"How does that make you feel?"

"Seriously? You couldn't ask a more clichéd question?"

She laughed. "Sorry. Why don't you tell me what you wanted to talk about today?"

He shook his head. "I don't really know. The kids, I guess. Coping strategies for when they act out, when we have bad days."

"Ahh." She reached behind her and grabbed a sheet of paper. "Maybe this support group would be more your speed."

He took the information sheet to be polite, but he wasn't comfortable with his own grief—he definitely didn't want to deal with other people's sob stories.

"Ryan…" She trailed off, waiting until he looked at her. Her round, slightly lined face was dangerously close to sympathetic. He didn't want empathy or sympathy or anything. He just wanted to know how to get his life back on track. "Okay. Maybe not an entire group. But the coor-dinator…her name is Faith. She's a widow, about your age, and she's not big on feelings. She's a survivor. Email her and tell her you're looking for tips on helping your kids, and she'll give you just that, nothing more."

———

HE DIDN'T EMAIL the woman from the support group, but he didn't throw out her contact information, either. He took his kids south to Windsor for the weekend, for a visit with his parents and siblings and their spouses and children. His three sisters, all mothers, fussed over him. His mother and father were a bit better, knowing he still needed some distance. But the only real bright moment, other than seeing his kids happily playing with their cousins, was when his brother Finn came into the city from Wardham, the small lakeside town he'd moved to for love.

"How's Beth?" Finn's new wife was eight months pregnant with their first child. They'd met through his work as a marketing expert, and fallen in love when he did some consulting work at the winery she managed in Wardham.

"Good, working like crazy. She's hired two people to replace her at the winery for the next year."

"She didn't let you take over?"

Finn gave him a baleful look. "I know better than to offer. Go West is her domain. Besides, I've got my plate full with other consulting work."

"So that's going well?"

"Really well. Might hire someone this year to help me."

"Awesome, man." Ryan grabbed two beers from his parents' fridge and nodded to the side door leading to the driveway. It was after dark, and the kids were all in bed, but their parents were around and he didn't want to *talk*, exactly, but if they did wander into any touchy subjects, he wanted to be able to vent without judgement.

Finn waited until their beers were half-drunk before asking if Ryan was okay. But he didn't do it the same way as their sisters, or the counsellor, or any of the well-meaning residents of Pine Harbour. No, his brother just slid him a sideways glance and asked, "Don't you ever want to get laid again?"

Damn. He laughed, because that was the point of the question, to shake him out of his funk. But it had quietly poked at him for a few weeks. The answer was complicated. *Yes.* No. Yes, in abstract, and no, not when he gave even half a thought to the logistics of that. "I wouldn't even know where to look."

"Dating sites?"

Ryan recoiled at the idea. No, he definitely wasn't ready for dating. And since he wasn't his brother, who'd been a bachelor-extraordinaire until Beth had tipped him sideways into unexpected monogamy the year before, that meant that de facto, he wasn't ready for sex, either. "It's more complicated with kids." He closed his eyes, not wanting to see the look on his brother's face when he admitted the next fact. "And it's not like Lynn and I were super active in that regard, anyway. This hasn't been the longest stretch of celibacy in my life."

Finn didn't say anything, and when Ryan finally looked his way, his brother was staring into the distance.

"What?"

"I don't want to say anything ill of the dead, man."

"I know you weren't her biggest fan."

"For *you.* She was nice, and a good mom, but you guys had trouble."

"Sure we did. But I still loved her. And not just because we had three kids."

"Okay."

"What?"

Finn shook his head. "Nothing."

"Don't handle me with kid gloves. I may be battered and bruised, but I'm not fucking fragile."

"She's gone. You don't have to keep being faithful to her."

"That's not what I'm doing." And if it was, that wouldn't be a bad thing—he was still talking to her as if she wasn't gone. She was still in his heart. "The God's honest truth is that I'm just getting through the fucking day. I don't have time to think about cologne and flowers and bear skin rugs and seduction. Or whatever the hell voodoo magic it was you worked to make women get naked with you. That's all."

"You don't have any misplaced guilt?"

"No." His guilt wasn't misplaced, so the answer rolled right off his tongue.

His brother gave him a long, doubtful look before tipping his bottle back and draining the rest of his beer.

"It's not about being faithful to Lynn, okay?" Ryan sucked in a painful breath. "It's about being distracted from them." He gestured to the house, where his kids slept in a pile in the guest room. "Lynn did everything for them. Lunches, homework, kissing sore knees…I was just the guy who would wrestle with them for a bit before bed, if I wasn't at work."

"You've always been more than that to them."

"I've never been their mother." As it always did, the thought closed up his throat and made his eyes itch.

Finn clapped his hand on Ryan's shoulder. Ryan wasn't sure if it was supposed to be comforting, or if his brother was holding him in place for a lecture. "It's not your fault she's gone."

Lecture. Right. He twisted his neck, staring into the darkness. "It's my fault she wasn't happy."

His brother sighed. "She wasn't killed because she was unhappy. She wasn't at that grow-op because she was unhappy. It's more complicated than that. And none of the blame for her death rests on your shoulders."

"But—"

"No fucking buts." Finn shoved him away, spinning

him so they were face to face. Finn wiped his mouth with the back of his hand, his eyes narrowed. "I will kick your ass if you wear that. Because your kids will sense the guilt. And if you think you're responsible, what's that going to teach them? Is it their fault their mother couldn't cope with a medical diagnosis? That she was an addict, and had been her entire adult life?"

A red haze blurred Ryan's vision. "Don't talk about her like that."

His brother stepped back. *Out of smacking range.* But Ryan had never been a fighter. "She was."

"She smoked pot. You make her sound like she had track marks on her arms."

"I didn't say it in judgement. It's just a contributing factor that had nothing to do with you."

But Ryan judged. He hated that Lynn's choices had put her in harm's way, even if it was unexpected and mostly just terrible luck. And then he felt a whole new wave of guilt for that thought, blaming a dead woman who, separate from her faults, had been a wonderful mother and a loyal wife. "We never would have separated. I would have stood by her, supported her through whatever the illness looked like." But maybe Lynn hadn't known that. And the fact he'd never know ate him up inside. "I'll never get to tell her that."

"I know. I'm sorry."

Ryan swallowed the rest of his beer, drowning out the rest of the useless words that didn't matter anyway. "Tell me something good, Finn."

His brother turned and faced the yard. The confrontation was over, and the tightness in Ryan's chest eased.

"Beth bought the baby a tiny suit." Finn grinned in the

darkness, his happiness palpable, and Ryan couldn't help but laugh.

"Jesus, let him be a little kid."

"Babies like calculators and PowerPoint presentations, right? Tiny briefcases and investment accounts?" Finn hopped backwards as Ryan swiped at him with his foot. "Definitely wine, right? Helps them sleep?"

"You've got so many sleepless nights ahead of you, brother. I can't wait."

"Same." Ryan recognized that look in his brother's eye —the love and pride of a father-to-be. And hell, Finn didn't know the half of it.

"Let Beth be the boss, okay? She calls the shots on feeding."

Finn nodded as he rubbed his knuckles along his jaw. "We've taken these classes, but yeah, there's so much I don't know."

"You'll figure it out. Shit has a way of working itself out." Even as he said it, Ryan knew the reminder was true for himself as much as his brother. "Yeah, shut up. I know."

Finn bumped his shoulder as he stepped toward the door. "Good. Let's have another beer."

That conversation with his brother rolled around in Ryan's head for the rest of their visit.

The next night, once his kids were in bed, he powered up the computer and sent an email to the Bereaved Spouses group coordinator.

Then he went to the kitchen cupboard and poured himself a finger of scotch.

———

HOLLY TOSSED her script across the empty living room. Emmett had gone up to his room to call his partner. She could text him and ask him to come down and run lines with her, and he would. But that would just be torturing them both, because she knew her scenes for the next day inside out—this nervous energy was about something else. The subtle strain of unspoken discord on the set, maybe. Everyone could feel it, but the source hadn't yet made itself known. They were still in the early days of pleasantries and negotiating alliances.

The politics of a film set were something Holly would happily never experience again…except that would mean not acting. And despite the drama, she loved nothing more than sliding into the skin of another person and bringing a role to life.

Just thinking about being Kathleen made her legs tingle. She'd spent weeks in the wheelchair in L.A., working with a paraplegic choreographer to really nail what she could feel and do and what she couldn't.

She'd already worked out tonight before dinner. But all last week, as they'd driven away from the cottage before dawn and returned after dark, she'd thought the slightly inclined lane up to the highway would be perfect for hill repeats. She hadn't had the energy to actually do that, instead letting the elliptical drag her through her hour of mandatory calorie burn each night.

Tonight would be her last chance for the week, because she knew herself—hill repeats weren't going to happen after a fourteen-hour day of filming.

She grabbed her shoes.

The first climb she kept her speed under control, but after walking back down, she let herself sprint hard on the second go. This wasn't a workout, she didn't have a trainer watching and judging, and it didn't matter if she kept any energy in reserve.

And it felt *good* to pound against the gravel, pump her arms hard to drive herself faster, and hit that point where everything burned from the inside out. She'd been wound tight all week, waiting for something to crack on set—and now after a single day off, which was hardly enough of a break, they'd do it all over again. Long days of work, trying to make the vision of a crazy man happen.

At least, she assumed James Spencer was crazy. Her shoulders hunched together and she forced them to relax. The movie director was known for being difficult, but he created art. She needed to focus on that promised end result.

The house at the top of the lane was lit up again, after two nights of darkness. The Viking family had returned from wherever they went. She glanced through the kitchen window, but nobody was in there—the lights upstairs probably meant the kids were going to bed.

What would it be like to be tucked in? Have someone draw you a bath and read you a story?

Maggie must have done that for her when Holly was *really* little. But her earliest memories were of already being self-sufficient at ages five and six. Babysitters and roommates had been just as responsible for overseeing little Holly's teeth brushing and face washing as much as the pretty young model who didn't want to be a mother because being a party girl was so much more fun.

She sprinted hard on the last ten metres, jumping up to tap the stop sign before turning and walking back down the hill.

One more, she told herself. *One more sprint, one more look inside the happy house.* And then back to being the secretly sad rich girl who had no right to such feelings.

But this time, when she got to the top of the hill, she realized she wasn't alone outside.

Ryan Howard sat on the steps, in the cool shadows of the house, the porch light not on. At first she wasn't sure he was there and not just a figment of her imagination, but as she drew closer to the crest of the hill, he looked up and their gazes locked. She couldn't pretend she hadn't been looking at him, watching him in his private moment.

"Hi," she panted, slowing to a stop.

"Running in the dark, that's not safe," he said. His voice had a roughness to it that rubbed at her. It wasn't unpleasant.

"Not a lot of traffic. Everyone's tucked in for the night." There weren't any other houses on the lane, just his house and the cottages running down to the lake.

"Guess so." He stood, turning to go inside.

"Wait." She didn't know why she said it—she was mid-run, and he obviously wanted to be alone. But as soon as the words were spoken, she knew why they'd burst out of her—she wanted a little bit more of this gruff, intriguing man. She'd thought of him each day as they drove past his house on the way to the film set and now that he was here, alone in the dark with her, she wanted to know more about him. "We're not bothering you too much?"

He looked at her, brows drawn together, then shook his head. "Been pretty quiet all week, actually."

"That's good."

"The cottages all seem to be in working order?"

She nodded. "Definitely."

He lifted his glass to his mouth but didn't take a sip. Instead he just held it there for a moment, then set it on the railing. "How'd you score a room in the biggest house, anyway?"

It took a few seconds for Holly to process the question and realize he didn't know who she was. *Tell him.* But if she confessed she was the star of the film, this conversation would be over, she knew that in her bones. Because this man—private, grumpy, wary—didn't want anything to do with Hollywood types. "Reward for good behaviour?"

He didn't laugh—didn't even smirk. But he sat back down on the step and gave her a long, appraising look as he finally took a sip from his glass. "Doesn't seem likely."

She shrugged, acknowledging his doubt as valid. "I have an assistant, and we work together in the evening. It's just how the assignment worked out." *Not a complete lie.*

"An assistant?"

"Sounds fancier than it is." Emmett mostly kept track of her tea and fielded calls from her agent and manager. "How about you? How did you get saddled with taking care of us?"

"My in-laws own the cottages, and rented them out to the film. You're sleeping in their house."

Oh. "We booted them out?"

His lips twisted in a humourless smirk. "I think they're being compensated well for the inconvenience."

"So if your in-laws own the cottages, how did you got stuck with our complaints?"

"Well, the plan was..." He sighed and shifted his gaze into the distance. "The plan changed. They've headed out of town for a bit. Anyway, so far, you're the only complainer."

"Ah, but I fixed the problem myself!"

He lifted both brows at her declaration. "After I drew you a map to the furnace room."

"Right. Thank you for that."

"That's my job."

"Are you a full-time handyman?" She was babbling now, and couldn't stop herself. Normally she could do this, talk to anyone and draw them into a conversation, but she'd lost that reserved poise she usually managed as Hope. She felt off-kilter and flustered. *Get over yourself and leave the poor man alone.*

He laughed, for real this time. "No."

She wanted to poke him for more information, but who he was and what he did wasn't any of her business. She stepped backwards toward the road. *I'm going*, she told herself. *Damn slowly*, her better half responded with a solid dose of snark.

Maybe that was because he was watching her. Even as the space between them stretched to meters, he held her gaze.

"Well, thanks again," she said, lifting her voice.

He nodded, a small smile almost curling the corners of his mouth. "No problem. You see me again out here, feel free to stop and say thanks whenever you want. I don't hear it often from my regular bosses." He notched his thumb back toward the house. *His kids.*

Right. She had no business flirting with this man, even by accident.

She turned on her heel and joggled away, not looking back, even though she really wanted to.

CHAPTER FOUR

WEDNESDAY WAS ALWAYS THE KIDS' favourite day of the week. Ryan paraded with his Army reserve unit in the evening, which meant the kids had a rotating pizza date with either Olivia or her sister-in-law, Dani—Ryan's former co-worker from when he was a paramedic. Both of them were like family to the kids, the best kind of adopted aunts—pizza-serving, secret-keeping, and always fun. Their respective men were both in the infantry reserves with Ryan, and he appreciated the continued efforts of all his friends to shove him out the door, forcing him to be moderately social and productive.

And the kids really liked pizza.

As Wednesdays were also pre-school days for Maya, it usually meant that Ryan could leave mid-day and get some extra work done at the armouries, but this particular week was a school break.

They'd had four days of non-stop family time, and by mid-morning, Ryan was already sick of pizza talk.

"You guys want to get rid of me that bad, huh?" he asked, hurling Maya in the air as she squealed.

"Well, Uncle Rafe does have an X-Box," Jack pointed out.

As he did every time they asked for a video game system, Ryan pointed to their running shoes. "Outside we go."

They didn't complain, because they all loved the trail that ran through the woods. It opened into a clearing at his in-laws' house, then turned south along the lake for a good long while. It was tough going in places, but the kids had been hiking it since each of them learned to walk.

The boys ran ahead, sprinting back whenever they got close to being out of sight. Ryan stuck close to Maya, listening to his daughter's meandering narration about the fairies in the forest and the magic spells they used.

"What happens if you meet a real-life fairy, Daddy?"

"I don't know. What do you think?"

"Maybe have a tea party with them."

He smothered a laugh. "Oh yeah?"

"If they have tea."

"And if they don't?"

"Maybe play tag."

"That sounds like fun." He tapped her on the shoulder. "Want to play tag with me?"

She heaved a big sigh. "You're not a fairy, Daddy."

"I could be."

"No. You're a Daddy. Fairies are magical. Daddies are real." She looked ahead on the path, toward her brothers, and gasped. "I see one!"

Ryan just saw two boys covered in mud. "Okay, go get her then!"

Maya sprinted ahead, almost tripping over a root, but though she skidded sideways in the mud, she kept her footing. He followed, giving her some distance for the imaginary play, but when she ran past her brothers and disappeared around the bend, he took off after her.

"Maya Howard, get back here," he yelled.

From around the thick overgrowth, he heard her little voice saying, "Tag! You're it."

And damned but if someone didn't laugh. A woman. Since fairies weren't real, that meant that Maya had just poked a stranger.

They'd have to talk about *that*.

But when he caught up to her a second later, he lost all his words, because Maya was having a tag stand-off around a tree with Holly Cresinski.

And even though it was unseasonably warm, it wasn't warm enough for what she was wearing—or rather, what she wasn't.

The first two times he'd met her, she'd been wearing layers of sweats. Today, she was in a sports bra and tiny shorts. And shoes, probably, although his eyes couldn't seem to stray that far south. *Stop looking at her*, he ordered himself, but it was hopeless.

It wasn't like he'd been oblivious to the fact that she was pretty before, but he'd noticed it in the absent way one thought about a nice sunset or a particularly good cup of coffee—for a second, and then he'd moved on with his life, because pretty women and grieving single dads didn't really mix.

It had been a week and a half since their chat outside his house. He'd watched her disappear into the darkness that night, her long blonde ponytail swishing through the air, and for a few moments, he'd held on to the curve of her smile and the flash of her eyes. Then he let it go, and he hadn't seen her since.

Now she was right in front of him, and he couldn't

stop looking at her. She had so much bare skin. And it was all *gorgeous*. Long, strong legs. Slim calves, curvy hips, and a tiny, tight waist that he could span with both hands.

And her breasts. Holy shit, he could see her breasts, and they were like an oasis in the desert. Round, high, tight. Everything about her was tight. She was a fucking wet dream, and she was on his path—not that he owned it —and his kids were there too, which made his reaction totally inappropriate on top of the regular level of inappropriateness. And he still hadn't said anything.

He couldn't. He was reeling from his physical reaction, trying to process it and be neighbourly and remember his wife all at the same time. The abstract notion of having a sex life again was something totally different than actually having a sexual response to a woman while his children— the product of his love with Lynn—sprinted circles around him. It was enough to make him permanently mute.

"You're one of the movie people," Gavin said, apparently not having his father's problem with speech. Holly nodded, still laughing.

Jack jumped up and grabbed a branch on the tree Holly was standing next to. "Are you hiking today, too? We have the week off school."

She grinned at the nine-year-old. "You're lucky. I have the morning off work, but I need to go back this afternoon. So I was just finishing up a run."

"Do you want to see how fast I can run?" Gavin asked. Ryan couldn't see his face, but he could imagine the glint in his middle kid's eye. He was going to be a lady killer, and from the smile playing on Holly's lips, maybe he already was.

"Sure," she said, and off he went, his brother and sister hot on his heels.

Ryan took a step forward, flicking his attention back and forth between his kids and Holly's bare skin. *You mean Holly.* But as he watched a bead of sweat curve around her collarbone and slide down the middle of her chest, he was having trouble with that distinction. So he stepped to the side, looking way down the trail, physically forcing himself to look away.

"Fancy seeing you here," he said, his words straining to sound normal, but since he never said *fancy*, he'd clearly failed.

"Ryan, hi." She said his name softly, and it did something funny inside him. Made him want to lean in and lower his own voice, but he didn't, because what would he say?

She crossed her arms, covering her mid-section, but even out of his peripheral vision he could see the gesture just propped up her breasts. And that bead of sweat disappeared into her cleavage.

She cleared her throat. "Nice day for a hike."

And his first hard-on in months, apparently. He nodded, madly doing the ten-times table in his head. "It is. Do you usually get mornings off work?"

She shook her head, her long blonde ponytail swishing over her shoulders as she turned to follow his gaze. "Unexpected break, thank goodness."

"Unexpected?" They were standing almost side-by-side now, and while she looked ahead, he stole the moment to look at her—at the curve of her ear and the long line of her neck. Her delicate, strong jaw and...

"Not a big deal." She waved her hand in the air, brushing it off at the same time as she interrupted his cataloguing of her features. "And it looks like your kids are taking off on you..."

"Hey, stay where I can see you," he yelled, then made an apologetic face as he stepped past her, reluctant to say goodbye. "That's only going to hold them back for like ten seconds."

"Good luck." She grinned and waved as they moved in opposite directions. "Hey, Ryan?"

He glanced up the path. The kids were climbing a tree. He turned around, letting himself have one last selfish look at her. "Yeah?"

"Nice to see you again." She winked before jogging away, and once again, he found himself watching her—and this time, he wasn't left wondering why.

Danger, his inner voice of reason warned. *She's not going to be around for long.* But maybe that was good. Hell, it's not like he ever had any privacy. He couldn't sleep with her, but he could look, right?

Nothing bad ever came from looking.

———

BY THE END of the week, Holly could no longer deny that she wanted to see Ryan again.

It was the most ridiculous school-girl crush, but after running into him on the path, and seeing the way he looked at her, she was done pretending she didn't want more of *that.* Because when was the last time anyone wanted *Holly*? And okay, maybe the fact that she was in tiny shorts and a tight top helped—but Holly's boobs were the boobs of a total nobody. And he liked the look of them just because they were there, and maybe because they were attached to her—most importantly, not because they were insured for a million bucks.

"Are you muttering about breasts to the salad?" Emmett asked, sliding next to her in the kitchen.

"Boobs, not breasts." Holly shook her head. "Is it silly for me to be thinking about having a fling while we're here? Someone I can't actually ever get involved with? Is that cruel?"

"To him, or to you?"

The answer was probably yes, to both. "He's just... unlike anyone I've ever met."

"Who is he? I haven't seen you try to eye-fuck anyone on set." Her assistant leaned in and swiped a crouton. She handed over the bowl. It wasn't like she ate carbs anyway.

"He's not on the set, exactly. And don't say eye-fuck, it's crude."

"Crude can be fun. Wait, you don't go anywhere else. Who is this off-limits man that you can't..." Emmett's eyes got really big and he took a step back. "Hope Creswell, you don't dare try to seduce me."

She giggled. "Honey, could I even if I tried?"

"I've slept with women."

"Willingly?"

"Sure. I was confused and lonely...it was a difficult time."

"Uh-huh. And what time was that, exactly?"

"Twelfth grade. And part of the first year of college, but that was more threesomes than anything else."

"Awesome." She grabbed her salad back and stabbed it with a fork. "No, I'm going to seduce you. And that's the end of *that* awkward conversation. Make yourself a sandwich, then come run lines with me, okay?"

"You could do worse than me, though," he hollered as she skipped away.

"You're married," she yelled back. "To a man I happen to love more than you!"

When he followed a few minutes later, Emmett's eyes were soft, like he was still thinking about how lovely his partner was. Holly didn't want to re-open the conversation about her crush, so she stuck to work, but she couldn't shake the feeling that she wanted that. She wanted what her assistant had, what a lot of people had, that had always seemed nice enough, but maybe not for her.

Her dating history was limited and unimpressive. She'd long given up the idea that those magical feelings were real for wounded people like herself.

Well, screw that. Why couldn't it be for her?

And maybe the single dad in the middle of nowhere wasn't the safest or most logical step in the direction of finding love, but he liked her boobs and he didn't know she was a movie star. Right now, he was her only option.

A practice-run, so to speak.

No harm would come from flirting a bit.

———

THE NEXT NIGHT, Ryan put all the kids to bed in the boys' room.

"I like Daddy's room better," Maya pouted, even as she snuggled into Gavin's bed.

"We need to be brave," her brother whispered, and Ryan almost threw in the towel. But now that they were settled, the two youngest in Gavin's bed, and Jack in his on the other side of the window, it felt good. Right. About damn time.

"You are all the bravest," Ryan said gruffly, rubbing Maya's back as he tucked them in. "And you remember that being strong has many faces, right? You can cry and you can be happy. You can miss Mom and want to talk about her. Or not. It's up to you."

"I want to talk about Easter," Jack said.

Ryan laughed, and they did. They talked about making a big ham dinner and going to church and doing an egg hunt. Before long, three sets of eyes were slowly blinking shut.

He flipped on the baby monitor on his way downstairs, where he poured himself a drink and headed outside.

Absolutely not because he'd hoped to see a pretty blonde runner. Not because he'd noticed she liked to run the inclined road at night, and wanted another chance to talk to her.

When he found the lane dark and quiet, and rough disappointment surged in his chest, he told himself it was for the best. *She's out of your league, buddy.* Well, no shit. Young, pretty, sexy, with an exciting entertainment career…she'd be slumming to be interested in the stay-at-home dad from Pine Harbour.

Lusting after Holly was an exercise in self-flagellation.

And then there was the guilt. He swirled his around in his glass, staring down at it. Breathing it in like the vapours might connect him to his wife. *I miss you, Lynn.* He squeezed his eyes shut. Damn it. *I'm sorry.*

If she were alive, he wouldn't think twice about another woman, not like this. *Am I a total shit for being lonely, baby?* Fuck. He stood, fingers tightening around the glass. The urge to toss it against the wall of the house was almost overwhelming. He didn't want to use loneliness as an excuse.

He didn't *need* an excuse to have a healthy reaction to a beautiful woman. He was single. Grieving, yes. For all he knew, he might always feel torn between the wife he lost and any other woman he might share a bed with.

Not that he actually had a bed to share at the moment, or any time in the foreseeable future.

He stalked into the house, pissed at himself for having any of these thoughts. And that's all they were, innocent thoughts. But if he couldn't handle thinking about it, how the hell would he ever move on with his life?

And how fucking unfair was it that he had to move on at all?

Setting his glass on the desk tucked into a nook in the living room, he fired up the computer.

He checked Facebook first, where his mother-in-law had taken to messaging instead of sending email. He sent Gloria a quick reply, letting her know how the rest of March Break had gone for the kids, and that everything was fine with the cottages.

Then he checked his email, not expecting anything new, but there was a message from Faith Davidson.

`Hi Ryan,`

`Sorry about the delay in getting back to you. I was on vacation. I'm back now, and would be happy to meet up with you. Our group meets on the first Thursday of every month, at the United Church in Lion's Head. But I've got flexible work hours, if you want to meet for coffee. My son goes to kindergarten, so daytime works best for me.`
`No pressure—email chat works fine for me, too. God knows it's hard enough for us`

solo parents without trying to fit in yet another thing.

All the best,
Faith

He read it twice. Not a single uncomfortable hair stood up on his neck, and he didn't feel like sprinting for the door.

Taking a deep breath, he hit reply.

CHAPTER FIVE

THE WEEK before had been exhausting, and Holly had spent her entire day off napping, exercising or running lines.

And then Monday crushed her soul. She never dealt with conflict well, and this project was full of it. The fighting between the other principal players was too close to the knock-down, drag-out fights her mother would have with her boyfriends and sugar daddies.

It had been a long day of Parvati Spencer struggling under her husband's direction, and the leading actor, Joshua Pearce, being distracted by his phone blowing up every break until James banned phones from the set entirely, an order which only lasted five hours, but had a lingering effect. They filmed right up until dusk, when James threw a hissy fit about the lack of light, and the assistant director called it a day.

They were filming at a private cottage north of town, on the other side of the provincial park. It was a twenty-five minute drive to the cottages they were staying in, which some people griped about, but they all had trailers on set. This was their home away from home, and it was good that it was also away from work. Living right on top of the film set was never a good thing, in Holly's experience.

She let out a heavy sigh of relief as they pulled onto Blue Heron Lane, and Emmett gave her a hug as they waved goodnight to all the others.

"You want pizza for dinner, my lady?"

She really did. "Don't tease me with carbs."

"I could make you that cauliflower-crust pizza."

"Really?"

"Of course, really."

"Yes, please."

He kissed her temple and headed for the kitchen. She shook off her lonely funk, had a shower, and emailed her manager instructions to give Emmett a bonus and a few extra weeks of parental leave when his baby arrived. Then she went back downstairs and poured them each a glass of wine to go with their almost-pizza.

The almost-normal meal made her think of Ryan. A guy like him probably only ate Chicago-style deep dish pizza. With extra cheese and bonus meat.

Once the lights on the row of cottages started to dim, Holly changed into nighttime running gear and instead of hitting the treadmill to burn off the cheese, she grabbed a reflective jersey and headed up the hill, doing the now familiar incline repeat training. On the third uphill sprint, she saw him sitting on his deck, the porch light now on.

In one hand, he was holding a glass of amber liquid. In the other, he held out a bottle of water. "You looked like you could use this," he said with a weak, wry smile. It didn't last long, and her chest tightened in a way that had nothing to do with being out of breath when it disappeared.

"Thanks," she gasped.

He stood, slowly stretching to his full height, and took a wide step in her direction, handing her the water before retreating to the step again. "They're not working you hard enough on that movie set?"

She stepped back herself, unsure of where to stand, of just how long this conversation might be or if she was even really welcome. "Not like this."

He nodded in that absent way that acknowledged what she was saying without confirming understanding. Of course not. She was being deliberately vague.

She turned the conversation back to him. "How was the rest of your week with the kids off school?"

"I survived." He shrugged. It wasn't much of an answer, but it was more than she had a right to. She unscrewed the water bottle cap and took a sip, then another, rocking side to side to keep her legs warm.

"You gonna keep going?" He tipped his head at the stop sign, and she realized he must have watched her complete at least one climb. Watched her jump and high five the sign.

And in that moment—the dawning recognition of one lonely person being watched by another—she said *screw it* to the last fifteen minutes of her workout, and shook her head. "Nope, I'm good."

"Are you in training for something?"

Being eternally beautiful was a stupid answer. It was the truth, but also futile and ridiculous, and not something she wanted to admit to this man. She didn't know much about him, but she instinctively understood two things: he wouldn't have a lot of time for stupidity, and he wasn't shallow. So she went with a different truth. "I run marathons."

"Yeah?" He shifted over a bit on the step.

She moved closer. "Only one or two a year, depending on my schedule."

"I had to run every morning for PT when I was on basic training, and I hated it. I can slog my way through 5k if I have to, but give me a heavy kit bag and a rifle for a ruck march any day of the week."

"You were in the military?"

He nodded. "Still am. Reserves now."

"That's amazing. Anyone who wears a uniform is doing a good thing." Holly stopped a few feet away from him. *Leave him alone,* she told herself, but the warning didn't carry nearly as much weight as the warm feeling in her middle that got hotter and sweeter the closer she got.

He was wearing a long-sleeved t-shirt tonight, the sleeves pushed up past his elbows despite the cool of the night air. Heavy muscles corded his forearms and she wanted to reach out and stroke the golden light brown hair covering his skin.

Down, girl. Do not pet your neighbour's arms.

"You want to sit?"

She jerked her gaze up to his face, and the inscrutable look there. "Um, sure." She smiled as she joined him on the step. As her bottom hit the wood, she realized she was almost close enough to touch him, but her body wouldn't listen when her brain told her to shift over. "You do this a lot, sit out here and have a drink? It's nice."

He hunched up a bit, leaning forward. "It was a long winter inside, I guess. Just me and the kids. As soon as the snow melted, I started coming out here after they went to bed."

"This is the first winter…you've been on your own with them?" She asked it slowly and carefully. Trying not to pry, but not wanting to ignore the bit that he'd shared, either.

He just nodded, a short, terse jab of his chin.

"It's nice out here." She turned her face up to the sky. "Lots of stars."

"I hated the quiet at first." He scuffed his heel on the lower step as he braced his hands behind him, joining her in looking up. His upper arm brushed hers, leaving a lingering warmth as they talked.

"You're not from here?"

"Nope. I was a city kid. Married the country girl. Never thought I'd end up loving it here."

"I love getting away," she said quietly, still counting stars. "I spend most of my time in L.A. and New York. Last year I went to Sundance and I almost—" She cut herself off. She'd almost bought a ranch. "I thought about moving there. It was beautiful."

"Sundance, eh?"

She shrugged. "I took my mother. That was a mistake."

He laughed. "Drama there?"

"As long as I can remember, I've been the parent in the relationship."

"Ouch."

"Yeah. And I can't say no. So she came and tried to snare a movie star husband."

He gawked at her for a minute. "Just like that?"

Well, it wouldn't have been the first time. "My mother's incredibly beautiful and used to getting what she wants."

"Ah." He looked up and down her face for a moment

before changing the subject—in the wrong direction. "It's gotta be fun, rubbing elbows with the rich and famous."

Uhh… "Less fun than you might think."

He laughed. "Well, constantly dealing with those Hollywood types sounds like hell to me, but I'm more private than most people."

So awkward. "Am I not one of those Hollywood types?"

With a small laugh, he glanced her way with an unexpectedly soft expression on his face. "Sorry."

But something danced in his eyes, something that told her he wasn't sorry in the least.

She slapped lightly at his arm, trying not to notice the solid mass of his biceps or the warmth emanating from beneath his thin shirt. "Well, I guess I am, so that's fair."

"You're not so bad," he said, his lips turning up in the slightest of smirks.

God, she wanted to stay and see more of that smile, but if she stayed, she'd keep touching him and that would lead to nothing but trouble. She bumped his shoulder once more, because how could she not, then stood. Reluctantly. "Well, thanks for the water. I'm off to bed."

"Come back again some time, this was fun." He raised his hands when she cocked her eyebrows at him. "What can I say? I don't have much of a life."

She could feel her smile transform her entire face. "Me either, so I think I will."

———

THE NEXT MORNING, after the boys got on the bus and Ryan dropped Maya at preschool, he headed up the peninsula to Tobermory, where he'd arranged to meet Faith at the Tim Horton's coffee shop.

He parked his truck in a long row of trucks and headed inside. Scanning the room, he quickly found a petite woman with honey-brown hair, pulled back in a loose ponytail, watching the door, and she waved as soon as his gaze landed on her. His first impression was that she was young—his counsellor had said they were about the same age. These days, Ryan felt ancient, but this woman practically glowed with happiness and youthful vitality. She offered him a big, friendly smile.

"Are you Ryan?" she asked, standing and holding out her hand. She wore a t-shirt that said FRESH MILK right over her breasts, and ripped jeans. The tiny diamond stud in her nose was…different. Definitely not what he expected.

"I am." He returned her firm handshake, then gestured to the counter. "Do you want a coffee?"

"Sure. I'll come with you."

She left her backpack at their table, just grabbing her wallet from the big pocket.

"I can get the coffees," he said, but she just waved him off.

"It's okay. I'll get us this time, and that way you'll feel obligated to talk to me again, and next time you can pay. Deal?"

"That's sneaky."

"I'm a mom. I hide veggies in chocolate muffins. Sneaky is my middle name."

He laughed at that, and was surprised to realize he was still grinning when they returned to their table. There was something about Faith that immediately set him at ease— an instant sense of camaraderie. Like she might be the one person on the entire peninsula who got him. It was a strangely comforting thought.

"So what do you want to know about me?" he asked after taking a sip of coffee.

Faith wrinkled her eyebrows together. "Nothing."

"What?" That was the last thing he expected her to say.

"I'm here for you, not the other way around. You can tell me as much or as little as you want, but I don't *need* to know anything about you. I mean, I'm a curious human being, so I'm wondering about your story, sure, but I'm not a counsellor. Just someone who's been through something that might be similar to what you've been through. Although probably totally different." She laughed. "Everyone's story is different. That's something that I've learned, for sure."

"Okay." He took a sip of coffee and shifted, trying to find a more comfortable angle to sit in the formed plastic chair.

"How about I tell you about *me*, and what I struggled with?"

He nodded. "If you don't mind?"

She shook her head and took a deep breath. "My husband, Clark, died in a boating accident three years ago. It was a freak thing, and it took me a long time to really process the fact that he wasn't going to come home. I find myself looking at the door, thinking I hear his car...still today. My son was just a toddler when his father died, so he doesn't remember him, which makes me sad. And my life has changed a lot—I was going to be a stay-at-home mom. We wanted to have two kids back to back, and we'd just started trying for the second when Clark died. So everything that I thought my future would look like changed in that instant. I still replay the visit from the police, over and over again in my head."

Their stories weren't the same, but some of the similarities shook Ryan to the core. "Yeah. I do that, too. The replaying."

She smiled softly. "Most of us do."

"Does your son have nightmares or act out?"

"Not about his dad, no. But only having one parent…I think he worries more than the average four-year-old. Sometimes I think I've projected that onto him, that he's more of an old soul than he otherwise would have been because he saw me crying for so long."

"So I'm not the only one worried that I'm scarring my kids for life?"

"God, no." She sighed, and boy did Ryan recognize the emotions heavy in that sound. "Tell me about your kids."

"Jack is the old soul. He keeps everything inside, trying to be the responsible one. He's nine going on forty. Gavin's seven, and Mr. Loud, always wanting attention now, which he never did before. I don't know if that's his mom's death, or his age, or being the middle one. And Maya…she just turned four, and she doesn't have the words to tell me just how much she misses her mom, but she does. They were inseparable. I worked a lot and…" He shook his head. "Gavin and Jack will hopefully always remember Lynn. I worry that Maya won't, or that she'll just have the fuzziest of recollections, and wonder if that will be worse."

Faith nodded, and as she listened, Ryan kept talking. He told her about his in-laws and his friends, work and the kids. She chimed in from time to time with little suggestions and thoughts, but for the most part she just sat there and let him go. And then slowly the conversation turned, and he listened as she talked about therapy pros and cons for the kids, and ways to help them remember the parent that is gone.

Before he knew it, his coffee was gone and Faith's phone was beeping. She grimaced. "I'm sorry, I have a lunch-time phone call with my editor, that's just a calendar reminder."

Ryan looked at his watch. They'd been talking for almost two hours. "I should get going, too."

"Was this helpful?" Faith asked. "Sometimes it is, sometimes it's too much."

"No, I appreciate it. This was…good. Sort of."

"I'm heading to Owen Sound next week, if you want me to stop in Pine Harbour…you do owe me a cup of coffee, after all."

"Nicely played." He took a deep breath as he stood and stretched. "Maybe. And if not, I'll think about coming to the group session. But thank you, either way."

He thought about their conversation the whole drive home, and how easy it was to talk to Faith. Maybe because she was a stranger, and maybe because she'd shared first—he was so tired of feeling like the broken one in a circle of well people. Maybe he should go to the support group, after all.

Over dinner, he brought up Lynn to the kids, something he'd realized after talking to Faith that he didn't do enough. All he had to do was bring up a single memory and Jack and Gavin ran with it. They all got a little teary, but they laughed, too, and most importantly, they smiled.

And when he tucked them into bed, they did it again.

CHAPTER SIX

RYAN WAS ALREADY in a pretty good mood when he got outside and found Holly strolling up the lane, carrying a thermos and two cups. The shy smile on her face as she stopped a few feet short of the deck filled him with a curious warmth he hadn't felt in a long time.

"Hello there," he said with a grin.

She flashed him a brilliant smile and held up her offering. "I thought I'd take a chance and see if you wanted tea."

"Sure."

She sat down on the steps and he joined her, leaving a foot and a half of space between them for decency sake, but he wanted to be a lot closer. She wasn't in running gear tonight—she wore dark jeans and an oatmeal coloured sweater. Her hair was braided and hung halfway down her back, and he had an overwhelming urge to tug the elastic band off the end of the braid and work his fingers through her silky strands.

After watching him get settled, her eyes bright and

curious the whole time, she pointed her finger at his chest. "You're…happy."

He laughed. "I know, it's an unusual state of being for me."

"That's too bad." But she looked at him like she knew just how precarious joy could be.

"You too?"

She shrugged. "I don't have anything to complain about. Not like you. You've got a lot on your plate."

More than she probably knew, although maybe Pine Harbour gossip had drifted to the film set. Even if it had, the last thing he wanted to talk about was the sad reality of his life. "You look like you're in a good mood, too. Better than yesterday."

"Yeah. Yesterday was drama-city. Today wasn't so bad. And now we're having tea," she said with another smile, handing him a cup of…not tea.

He took a tentative sniff. "What is this?"

"Chamomile. Good for sleep."

"Interesting. In my world, tea is black. Maybe green if I'm eating sushi."

"Well, in my world, I need to be up every morning at five, so this is what I drink at night." She winked at him and took a sip.

"Five? Damn, that's worse than the Army. Or kids."

"It's all I've known for a long time. I do love sleeping in, but it rarely happens."

He took a sip of the flowery liquid. It was hot, that was something. "Tell me something fun about your job."

She pressed her lips together, the corners fighting to turn up.

"What?"

"You don't need to make small talk."

"I'm being polite. Wait, no." He laughed, then groaned. "I'm not great at this being social thing. I mean, I'm genuinely curious about what you do."

She gave him a skeptical look. "You really want to know?"

"I do." He grinned. "What was the most entertaining thing that happened today?"

She made a pained face. "Okay, you can't tell anyone this."

"Cross my heart."

"The director and his wife, who is one of the lead actors, had a screaming match over lunch about how they don't have any emotional intimacy in their marriage."

"You're kidding me. In front of people?"

"The entire cast and crew. She's lovely, but he's a piece of work." She gave him a wary side-eye. "Do you want to hear more?"

Ryan groaned. "No, not even a little bit."

"Tell me something fun about your kids." She sipped her tea, then swiped her lower lip with her tongue, leaving her mouth wet and shiny.

He stared at her mouth for a moment, then lazily drifted his gaze back to her bright eyes. He didn't really want to talk about his kids all of a sudden. Somehow they were closer now than when he'd first sat down.

She stared up at him, slowly blinking. Once. Twice.

"Maybe you don't want to talk about anything at all," she finally whispered.

"That's probably true." He cleared his throat, pushing away his thoughts about her mouth. "Maybe I need some more tea."

———

HOLLY'S CHEEKS flushed as Ryan turned and stared into the darkness. That had been a stupid thing for her to say. She must have read him wrong, thinking that he wanted to kiss her.

"I've got lots of tea," she said, desperate to pretend she hadn't just hit on him—and been rejected. At least he hadn't gotten up and run inside.

She took his mostly-full cup and added a bit more from the thermos, then turned and settled her back against the newel post where the railing met the stairs. She wanted to show him that they could still keep talking and she wouldn't launch herself at him.

"So all those people down there—" He gestured toward the cottages. "Are they all too tired out from being crazy all day to hang out at night? I never hear wild parties. Isn't there a movie star staying in that house with you?"

All the air vanished from Holly's lungs. *That's why you can't kiss him.* She stared at him, stricken. "Um…"

"I know, you can't say anything bad about them. I shouldn't have asked."

"No, it's okay…" Her voice was weak and ragged. It wasn't okay, at all. But she was lonely and he was lovely and she'd just wanted to escape for a little bit. "I should go."

"Stay." He held out his hand, then put it down on the step between them. If she hadn't moved over, it would have been on her knee. She felt the burning loss of that touch that she had no right to want, and wanted to cry.

Instead, she told herself to stop being a baby.

So she didn't get everything she wanted in life. She still had more than most—even if she didn't have anything that felt as valuable as what this man had, or what he had lost.

"Help me out here," he said quietly, his gaze pinned on hers. "I'm out of practice. What should two new friends talk about?"

She had no idea. When was the last time she'd made a friend? Probably Liana, and that was years back. "I had cauliflower-crust pizza for dinner last night."

He laughed at her *so-so* face. "My kids love pizza—with regular crust, I mean."

"And you?"

"I like steak."

"Let me guess—your kids do not?"

"Nope." He sighed and took a few more sips of his tea. "This isn't that bad."

"Yeah." But that was her life. A string of compromised choices, all because her biggest choice of all—her career—made everything else complicated.

"What would your last meal be?"

"Pasta," she said without even taking a second to think about it. "Like, ten bowls of it, until I had a belly ache."

He made an amused face. She wanted to twist around again and sit side-by-side. Wanted to stay late and talk about everything under the sun, but if she did that, she'd also want to kiss him.

Instead, she'd go home and dream about what his lips would feel like on hers. Yet another thing that Holly Cresinski would never taste.

"Speaking of the tea, I'm getting sleepy." She smiled at him. "Thank you for the company."

"Anytime."

She stood up, and he stood as well, his arm brushing

her shoulder as they walked down the steps and out to the lane.

"I mean that, Holly. I've got great friends, but they don't come and visit me at night. I'm lonely, too."

"I'm not—" But she was lonely. She just didn't think she had any other choice.

"Then come back and keep me company, for my sake?"

She nodded. "I'd like that."

"I have to work tomorrow night, but I'll be home Thursday. Come over, if you can."

She hugged the thermos close to her body. "What time do your kids go to bed?"

"Eight, usually. Knock on the door if I'm not out here."

———

TWO NIGHTS LATER, there was no excuse, no pre-text. Holly just walked up the lane and sat on Ryan's porch with him, talking about nothing and everything for more than an hour.

"I can't believe you're surprised I like country music," she said, laughing as he blushed a little.

"You just seem so…urban."

"I like all music, actually. But I became a die-hard country fan when I spent a few months in Nashville a few years ago."

"Working on a movie there?"

"No, I was between jobs at the time." She'd been prepping for a role in a movie that got canned. "I was only supposed to be there for a few weeks, but I met my best friend there. We bonded like sisters right away, and when the job I was supposed to do fell through, I ended up staying with her for a while."

"I never did that couch surfing thing."

Holly hadn't exactly slept on Liana's couch—the singer had a six bedroom house and a separate pool house, too. "Well, I've never done the settled down thing, so there you go."

"Is your life pretty nomadic?"

"They do a good job of making us feel at home on location. But I dream of working in New York, living in an apartment and walking to a theatre every day. Or even Nashville, although I only have a passable singing voice. But in another life, maybe I would have been a songwriter or something."

"Songwriting, eh? So would that be your dream job?"

She frowned. She didn't want to lie to him—but he was right, those weren't realistic job options for a lot of people. "The singing thing is just a fantasy, I promise you."

"I'm sure you've got a lovely voice."

"Oh no, I sound like a strangled cat. Totally tone-deaf. How about you?"

He shrugged. "My kids like it when I sing to them."

"I bet." He had a lovely baritone voice, rich and warm. She took a deep breath and shook that off. "The New York thing is more likely though. I'm thinking of moving there in the fall."

"Now that's the kind of city I picture you in. More your speed than Los Angeles."

"I hope so. I don't love cities in general, but that's where the work is. Have you ever been?"

He shook his head. "I haven't been anywhere like that. Grew up near Detroit, joined the Army as a medic, did a few years, then met my wife when I was at college. Moved here, had three kids. We drove to Chicago once."

"I've never been to Chicago!" she exclaimed, and he laughed.

"Glad I could balance out the life experiences a bit." His voice took on this gravelly tone when he went sarcastic, and it made all her girly bits sit up and take notice. "What else haven't you done?"

"Hmmm. That I want to do, or would never do?"

"Either." His eyes flicked over her face and he smiled. "Maybe the never would do. What are you scared of?"

"Spiders. And snakes…I went to Australia once. Beautiful country. Deadly fauna."

"Jesus, you've really travelled everywhere, huh?"

"It's a perk of the job. You never went overseas with the Army?"

He shook his head. "I was in the reg force between conflicts, and have always been exempted from tours since I joined the reserves. I'm one of the grumpy old guys now, yelling at the new privates. I'm a company quartermaster, so that means I run the unit's supply room."

"Interesting."

Huffing a little laugh, he just looked at her.

"What can I say, I find everything about you quite interesting."

They shared a little smile. Before she could ask him something else, a faint, animalistic scream pierced the air. Holly nearly jumped out of her skin, but Ryan reached out and pressed his hand to her leg. "It's okay, it's just a coyote."

"Holy crap!" She stared into darkness, unsure of the direction the howl had come from.

He squeezed her knee before removing his hand. "There are some farms to the south. Might be there. If you hear a gun shot in a bit, don't be alarmed. Licensed hunters are allowed to shoot coyotes on sight."

"Are they dangerous?"

"Definitely for livestock. Not for you, not right here, although I wouldn't want to meet a pack of them. You don't have coyotes in Los Angeles?"

"I don't know. Probably in the foothills, but I've never heard one before."

"Well, there you go. Pine Harbour's given the world traveller a new and unique experience."

More than one, she thought as she shifted closer to him.

———

FRIDAY NIGHT she brought chamomile tea with her. Saturday night he made her hot chocolate, and they talked about her running.

"Are you in training for a marathon right now?"

She shook her head. "I can't do that while I'm working, it takes too many hours out of the week."

"You do the long runs that go for hours?"

She looked at him in surprise, and he laughed. "I'm not a runner, but a lot of guys in the army are. I listen well."

He definitely did that. She kept waiting for him to tell her he'd figured out she wasn't just working on a movie— what did he think she was doing, anyway?—but he never did. It was like he didn't care about that. He was listening to all the other things she was saying.

The Holly parts.

On Sunday night, she did her hill repeats, and when she was done, he had a foam roller and a protein bar waiting for her along with the bottle of water she'd expected.

"You didn't have to do this," she said, as she balanced on top of it and rolled out her hamstrings.

"But this way, you might stay a bit longer," he said, kind of gruffly.

If she hadn't been all sweaty, she'd have hugged him.

Once she'd scarfed the protein bar, she asked him about why he had the roller.

"I pulled my right hip flexor on a military training exercise a few years back. Got that for physiotherapy after. The kids like it."

She laughed. "I bet."

The next day, Monday, was another killer start to the filming week. After spending an hour with Ryan the night before, it was like dysfunctional whiplash and it made Holly unbelievably grumpy—especially when they didn't finish until almost ten.

She thought about not going up to his house. It was late and wake-up would come early.

But as they turned onto Blue Heron Lane, she saw him sitting on the steps, and she knew she couldn't stay away.

She'd already showered at her trailer on set, so she just grabbed a sweater and slipped out the side door when Emmett was on the phone. It was weird, sneaking around when she was his boss, but she wasn't ready to deal with his questions yet. And he was a smart, attentive assistant. He'd put two and two together really quickly. She could trust him, though—he'd proven that time and again with her mother.

"I wasn't sure if you were coming," he said as she slid onto her spot next to him. His sleeves were rolled up and her forearm pressed against his. Hot skin and soft hair imprinted on her before she could shift away, and when she did, she ached to slide back.

"We had a long day." She tipped her head to the side. "I'm sorry."

"Nothing to be sorry for." He licked his lips. "You didn't bring your tea. Do you want me to make you something?"

She shook her head. "I can't stay long."

"Early morning, right." Ryan leaned back on the hand closest to her. She couldn't break away from his gaze. At least a foot separated them, but they'd both twisted their bodies and now they were facing each other.

Don't do it, she warned herself. *Don't you dare kiss him.* She leaned in, because she wasn't that great at taking direction from her moral compass at the best of times, but at the last minute, she dropped her forehead to his shoulder. Staring at the worn grey boards of the deck beneath them, she took a deep breath, then let it out. "This is a really bad idea, isn't it?"

He shifted, wafting an irresistible combination of laundry soap and man scent in her direction. "I don't know," he said quietly into her hair. "What is *this*?"

"Me bringing tea in a thermos. Running up and down in front of your house when there's a perfectly good treadmill in the house I'm staying in." Nervous energy coursed through her as she confessed. She turned her head just a bit, just enough to see his Adam's apple bob up and down.

"Not just a treadmill. One of the stars demanded an entire exercise room."

Oh, bugger. "Ryan, I need to tell you—"

"No, don't." He cut her off, his words low and private. He reached across his body for her hand and she gave it to him, lacing her fingers through his as he moved a bit, settling back on his free arm, closest to her. They were practically cuddling, and it felt better than anything in the world, the hot press of his side against hers, his cheek against her hair. "I don't care if this is a bad idea. I like it, and I don't have a lot of things I like about my life right now."

But there's no way he'd snuggle up, side-by-side, with a celebrity. "I know your privacy is important to you, and I'd never do anything to—" she started again, but again, he cut her off.

"I can't date, Holly. I have nothing to offer you, so before you say anything, you need to know that this is all I've got. A few minutes after my kids go to bed. The rest of my time has to be about them. When I say that I'm a private person, I mean I've got some messed up fears about exposing my kids to the world—even other people. I don't want them to have to deal with any upheaval. I need to protect them, and I can't do that if I'm distracted."

She ducked her head. He definitely couldn't do it if he was entangled with someone famous, either. She needed to walk away from him, but she couldn't.

"My kids are everything to me, so there's no room in my life for something just for me right now. And I don't know when there will be. I don't know when I'd be able to take you out for coffee or to a movie. And you're a beautiful woman, Holly. You deserve all of that and more. You deserve a heck of a lot more than sitting on my porch, and that's all I can offer."

She wanted to tell him it was okay, that she understood —because she did. But it wasn't okay, so she sat there silently, her heart aching for him.

"I don't have any illusions about what you might see in me, but if you're thinking of telling me there's no future, I promise you I already know that. I just..." He dragged in a ragged breath, and she realized this wasn't just about logistical difficulties of single parent dating. This was emotionally challenging for him.

She wanted to crawl into his lap and make it all better —and she didn't even know just exactly what was wrong. "This can be whatever you want. I'm…" She trailed off, too, because this conversation was harder than she expected. "I think we have a connection. You said we're friends. All I know is that spending time with you at the end of the day this past week, that's been something special. I don't want to give that up. So if all we can be is friends, I want that."

"I don't think I want to be your friend." He huffed a laugh. "Sorry, that came out wrong."

"I know what you mean." She turned into him, wanting to hug him. Actually, she wanted to climb him like a tree, but that probably wasn't an option. No, it definitely wasn't an option. Hell. She twisted away. "I should go, before I do something stupid like kiss you."

Ryan held on to her hand, not letting her go very far, and when she stopped, he tugged her arm until she looked back at him. He smiled, but it didn't reach his eyes—they were somber and sad. "If things were different…"

"I know."

"Will you come back?"

Say no. Tell him you're Hope Creswell and nothing about your life is simple. "Maybe."

But she knew she was lying. There wasn't a chance in hell she'd be able to stay away from him.

CHAPTER SEVEN

HOLLY DIDN'T GO up to see Ryan the next night. She wanted to, so much, but if they were just friends, nothing more, then maybe every single night was too much.

She needed some space.

So when Emmett asked if she wanted to get out of Pine Harbour on Wednesday evening and go shopping in the slightly larger town of Wiarton, she agreed.

As if the universe thought she needed to be taught a lesson about hiding from her problems, Ryan walked out of the Tim Horton's coffee shop just as they were about to walk in. Emmett had gotten hooked on the raspberry-jelly filled donut holes he gleefully called Timbits like he was a born and bred Canadian.

"You go ahead," she said to her assistant, avoiding his curious gaze.

"This is a surprise," Ryan said, stepping out of the way of people heading inside, but he kept his gaze on her face. She turned her back as much as she could, praying she wouldn't be recognized.

"You're going to work," she said, looking at his

uniform. Seeing him all jacked up like that was not good for her unrequited desire for the man.

"I am," he murmured, leaning in a bit. "But I've always got time to talk to you."

She told her fluttering stomach to stop being such a teenage girl. "Good, you've saved me from having to look at donuts I can't eat. My assistant is addicted to the ones covered in white powder."

He held up his own brown paper bag, his eyes dancing like he knew he was being bad. "He's crazy. You gotta go for the fritters. I could share."

"So tempting," she breathed, before reluctantly shaking her head.

"I know," he said, his eyes dropping to her mouth, and maybe it was because they were in public, and nothing could happen, or maybe it was because forty-eight hours had eroded her self-control, but she decided to allow herself a little flirt.

"I like the uniform, by the way. You look good in it," she'd said as she looked him over again. He looked more than good—taller, broader, stronger in green camouflage. "I mean, you always look good, but you look especially good in that."

His grin flashed bright in his face, but before they could say anything else, Emmett came out and Ryan excused himself before she could make introductions— which was for the best.

Emmett gave her a look, but he didn't ask and she didn't offer any explanation for the conversation.

She stared out the window as they headed to a local gallery, wondering where in town Ryan's armouries was located. Where did he go in these few hours of work, when he got to be someone other than Dad?

Even though he never complained about being a non-stop parent, it still seemed to take its toll.

She knew a fair bit about his life now, although he never shared anything specific. They mostly talked about hypothetical situations and bucket lists, but every so often he'd reference people in his life, and she'd stitch that piece into the secret patchwork of facts. She thought about that pieced together picture of Ryan Howard a lot when they weren't together.

She also thought about how careful she'd been not to give him quite the same access. *Soon,* she thought. She'd tell him soon.

———

THE NEXT NIGHT, she almost did, but he'd had a bad day, and she was heading out of town for the weekend, going to Toronto for a press junket… she told herself she didn't want to dump her career information on him and then run away, but deep down she knew she was just being cowardly.

So instead of coming clean, she let him tease her about her big city ways and her attachment to hot flower water. She poked him to think about where he might like to take the kids when they were older, and how awesome it would be when they all liked steak. It was a nice visit, but his black mood persisted.

"You sure I can't offer you some of my tea?" she asked as she yawned, holding out her cup.

He growled good-naturedly under his breath.

She yanked the thermos back. "Okay, it's not your thing. I get it."

He winced. "Sorry. I'm poor company tonight."

"Today's shoot didn't go well, either. Maybe it's a full moon or something, everyone's off kilter."

"I'd believe it," he muttered, but above them the moon was just a sliver. "Of course, my kids go crazy a few times a month, so it's likely sugar hangover more than anything."

"Mmm, sugar."

"Now you're wishing I'd shared that donut with you, eh?"

She laughed and leaned against him, and he put his arm around her.

And when she stood, reluctantly, needing to get to bed because she had an extra early makeup call in the morning, he pulled her in close for a hug.

That's all it was, just a hug, but an awareness pulsed through her entire body that she wanted more.

"I'm going to Toronto for a few days," she whispered into his neck, trying not to get lost in the scent of him and the warmth of his skin.

"I'll be here when you get back." He tightened his grip on her and she closed her eyes.

Had any man ever hugged her for this long? Any arms ever been this strong around her? And still he didn't ask for anything else. Didn't want to be seen as her plus one or take a selfie with her after she'd fallen asleep in his bed.

What cruel irony that the only man who didn't want her for anything other than herself was the one man she'd probably never have a chance with. She didn't need him to explain that he wasn't ready to bring a woman into his house. She'd tried hard not to listen to the rumours, but she knew his wife had died the previous year. And the house she was staying in belonged to his in-laws, so it wasn't like she could invite him into her bed, either.

And you're lying to him. That weighed heavier on her every time they came together. But if she—no, *when* she told him, it would be over. She knew that without a doubt. She was going to hurt him, badly, because she'd kept this secret from him.

But she couldn't tell him, because she wasn't ready to let him go yet. It was awful and selfish, but Holly had never had anything like this before. She'd dated another actor for more than a year, and never shared a tenth of the intimacy she'd already shared with Ryan.

She'd learned in the last week what a true connection was, and it had nothing to do with sex. It gutted her to think that she'd never get a chance to deepen that connection with him.

"You okay?" he asked quietly as he let her go, his gaze raking over her face.

She gazed up at him, willing herself to just focus on *him* and let go of her feelings. She looked at his face, barely covered in twenty-four hours of stubble. His hair, just creeping over his ears, and longer, scruffier on top. She smoothed her hands over his chest and down his sides to his solid, thick waist. "There's a lot about me you don't know."

"I know you aren't asking me for anything, or looking at me with pity in your eyes. I know you understand I don't have anything to give. That's all I need." He squeezed her hands in his, his fingers curling all the way around her smaller fists. "You're shaking. Are you cold?"

"I'm..." She took a deep breath. "We've never talked about your wife, and—"

"And I don't want to," he interrupted her roughly.

"Okay. I wasn't going to. But I think—"

"Don't. Don't think about my life." He dropped her

hands and shoved his fingers through his hair, shadowing his face.

She froze. How had their conversation gone so sideways, so suddenly?

She reached out, her fingertips brushing his forearm. "Ryan, I'm sorry."

"You don't have anything to be sorry for." His voice, gruff and heavy, sounded like an entirely different person to the one who'd just spent an hour teasing and asking her questions. He looked down at her hand, and slowly twisted out of her grasp. "This…thing between us. It was a break from reality for me, okay? And if you can't be on board with that, if you insist on talking about me and my feelings and all the stuff I don't want to talk about, then I need to ask you not to come over."

Shaking now for an entirely different reason, she took a step back. All the gentleness was gone, and in its place was a defensive shield. She knew that's why he was barking at her, but it still stung. "Did you ever think that maybe it was a break from reality for me, too?" Even though her voice was trembling and she was totally showing her hand, she kept going. "And what about that talk of friendship? I c-care about you. I thought we were getting close enough to talk."

"I guess it's not that easy to escape my demons." He looked at her again, but it wasn't just that his gaze was hooded and dark. An entirely different man stared at her for a second, and in that instant, she thought it might be possible that she was seeing more of Ryan than she'd ever glimpsed before.

But he didn't want her to see that side of him—how broken he was. And maybe that was fair. She'd just wanted to play at being normal, too. Her demons paled in comparison to his, she was sure, but they'd both been pretending.

She bit her lip to keep from crying. No way would she let him see how deep he'd gotten under her skin. But she had to make sure he knew she got that this was hard for him. "I'll go. But if you change your mind, you know where I am. I'm sorry if I've overstepped."

"I'm the one who should be sorry. And I am, but this is for the best." He exhaled roughly, and for a second she thought he was going to reach for her. Instead, he hardened his mouth and nodded. "Goodbye, Holly."

She watched, speechless, as he disappeared inside, leaving her standing on his porch all alone.

———

RYAN DIDN'T SLEEP WELL that night, unable to get the look on Holly's face out of his mind. The next night was even worse. He'd been a complete asshole to her. He'd known what he was saying, but it had been like he was watching himself push her away. The worst part was that he still wasn't sure he was wrong to do it, which made him feel shitty all over again.

Proof he wasn't in the right headspace to have a casual flirtation or anything else. He'd thought Holly was a safe choice to start taking some little moments here and there for himself, but he'd forgotten there was still another person involved there.

On Saturday, he took to the muddy trail again with the kids, happy for the excuse to pass the cottages, but the big one was locked up tight. She'd said she was going away for a few days, but he regretted that he hadn't had a chance to apologize again before she left.

Again? He'd done a piss-poor job of it on Thursday night.

He kept telling himself it was for the best that he realized it was going too fast before it actually went anywhere. If he couldn't handle a hug and some pretty basic questions, he had no right to keep flirting with her. There was no such thing as an uncomplicated crush with his emotional baggage.

On Sunday night, a dark SUV rolled past his house, and he went outside, watching through the trees as a light flicked on in the lake house.

She didn't come over.

He ignored the ugly slide of emotions through his gut as he realized that signalled the end of his doomed infatuation with Holly Cresinski. *It's fine,* he told himself. *Bound to happen eventually. Just a matter of time. Better now than later.*

None of the platitudes worked, and when he went back inside, he kicked a kitchen chair across the room. It was what he'd asked her for. What the hell was his problem?

Swearing under his breath, he returned the chair to its rightful spot at the table, and went to the cupboard. *No.* He didn't need a drink tonight. He needed…

He couldn't put what he *wanted* into words, not even in his head. As he turned out the lights and locked the doors, climbed the stairs and slowly undressed, he fought against the whispers in his head. *You want her. You missed a chance to kiss her and hold her and take her, like you've wanted for weeks. And you're mad at yourself.*

Yeah, he was mad at himself. Because while yes, he wanted those things, that barely scratched the surface. Would kissing Holly make anything better?

Or would it just be an escape? Would he be using her to forget about his life the way that Jack used his tablet?

But he couldn't dig deeper than that. He could feel a headache coming on and he leaned his forehead against the tiles.

Cranking on the shower, he stepped under the steamy spray, and without thinking about it, he took himself in hand.

Jerking off in the shower used to be an almost daily thing for him. He'd maybe done it once or twice since Lynn's death, and it had made him cry—there was something fucked up there, but he wasn't going to bring up masturbating to the counsellor, so it just sat in the back of his head as something that triggered feelings he didn't want to deal with.

His poor balls. It had been a long five months.

But this was different. As he stroked himself, it certainly brought up feelings. Frustration. Desire. Anger. But not sadness. He could feel guilt niggling on the edges, but right now, alone in the shower, he blocked that out and focused on letting himself have just this moment.

One fantasy. He pressed away the ache and let himself imagine.

Holly, spread out on a blanket somewhere. Not here. Outside, under a setting sun. Naked, turned on, and ready for him. He wanted to cover her body with his and lose himself in her for a night.

He couldn't have her. Not now, definitely, but not even before. He wasn't ready. But he could have that fantasy. And maybe in time…

Maybe there will be someone else. He'd thought he'd love one woman for the rest of his life, and fate had other plans.

So Holly couldn't be it for him, either. In time, there would be other crushes.

If there was one lesson Ryan had learned over the winter, it was that whether he liked it or not, life went on.

She'd be gone in a few months.

Until then, he'd watch her from afar. The long swing of her hair, a dozen shades of blonde from the palest white to golden sunshine. Her expressive mouth, pouty and wanting in one moment, wry and whip-smart in the next. Her long legs, toned and taut.

The way she ran like she was being chased by the devil. Like she was all alone in a fight against something.

Damnit. His erection faded. Wow, he really was an asshole.

He didn't know why Holly pushed herself so hard, but for all that he'd liked sitting next to her and talking, had he really found out anything about her? He'd been too distracted by the softness of her skin against his fingertips and the scent of her hair, brown sugar and the beach, to really get to know her.

He'd used her.

For escape and fantasy.

All because he knew she'd be leaving.

He had to make it right. Even if it was just as a friend or because he wanted to maintain his record as a decent human being, but mostly because she'd given him a tiny bit of hope that life would eventually return to normal and he'd smashed it to pieces because he wasn't ready.

In the process, he'd smashed her, too.

———

FAITH FOUND him in Mac's on Tuesday morning, where

he'd been sitting and drinking coffee for almost an hour. Dean Foster, a local provincial police officer and a fellow Army reservist—and the oldest of the Foster brothers, all friends of Ryan—sat with him for the first fifteen minutes before thumping him on the shoulder and making a wisecrack about Ryan talking his ear off.

He wasn't really in a talking mood, which meant accepting Faith's offer of another coffee date had been silly, but somehow in their emailing back and forth, she hadn't taken no for an answer.

And now she was in front of him, wearing a t-shirt with the *Periodic Table of Beer* on it.

"Beer?" He nodded at her chest.

She grinned. "And I don't really drink it."

"You're interesting, Faith Davidson."

"And you're grumpy. What's up?"

"Bad weekend."

"Yeah, me too. Do they have good coffee here?"

He waved at the waitress and leaned back in the booth, crossing his arms. "You don't look like you had a bad weekend."

"Well, I did. My son has figured out that I don't know everything, and he's translated that to doubting most of what comes out of my mouth."

"Ah." Ryan knew that feeling well. "It's just a phase."

She arched an eyebrow at him, as if to say *really? Tell me something I don't already know.*

"And it only gets worse," he grumbled.

She threw a sugar packet at him.

"What made your weekend sucktastic?" she asked, changing the subject slightly as the waitress arrived with the coffee pot, and Ryan took the interruption to really look at this woman. Funny, pretty, and slightly geeky.

For whom he felt nothing but kinship.

Why couldn't he have a crush on Faith? That would be convenient.

She lifted the steaming cup to her lips and paused, breathing in deeply.

"It's not *that* good," he grumbled.

She took a sip and set the cup down, her eyes twinkling. "Does it bother you that I took a bit of pleasure in a hot cup of coffee?"

"Yes." She just nodded as he processed his unexpected answer. "I mean…"

"You meant exactly that," she said softly. "You're still at the point of being pissed that other people are happy, or even just chill. Because you think you've lost that forever, and it's not fair."

Ryan stared across the diner booth. "How do you— that's a super-creepy psychic ability you've got going on there, Faith."

"Because it was true for me. And most people I've met. Some linger in that *phase* longer than others." She rolled her bottom lip between her teeth, pausing before she added, "And you're super grumpy. Put two and two together…"

Ryan rubbed his jaw. "Damn. I don't want to be like that, you know? I don't want to set that example for my kids."

"Grief is selfish. It's gotta be that way. But it can also be like quicksand, and that's when you need to reach out and get help."

"And move on?" Just saying the words made his skin feel tight.

She shook her head. "Not necessarily. I haven't moved on, not really. But finding some peace is a good first step."

"No offence, but you look pretty Zen right now. I'd kill for some of that."

She laughed as he realized the ironic inappropriateness of that statement. "It comes with time, and in layers. I'm still not over a lot of things. I haven't started dating yet, for example."

The still-fresh memory of holding Holly close slammed into him, and he squirmed on the vinyl cushion. Faith kept talking, oblivious to his discomfort.

And finally, he couldn't hold back the question on the top of his mind any longer. "Is there a timeframe that's too soon for dating?"

She blinked at him. "Too soon? That would be different for each person."

He stared at this near stranger and told himself to keep quiet. He didn't know her from Adam. But he couldn't talk to anyone else about this…and while he didn't know her, she didn't know him. She didn't carry the weight of the community's judgement for his lustful thoughts. "It's not really dating, exactly. There's someone who has come into my life, and won't be around for long, and I'm… attracted to her."

That was such a weak way of explaining how he couldn't stop looking for Holly every time he was outside. That his pulse had picked up at the thought of her coming over each night, and how gutted he was now that she wouldn't be doing that anymore.

A curious look came over her face, and she bit the side of her lip before quietly saying, "It's not me, right?"

He laughed. "No. Although it would be easier if it was."

"Good, 'cause I'd have to tell you to lock that shit

down." She grinned. "It would make the whole support group thing too awkward."

He grimaced, then finished the last bit of his coffee. "I guess I should come out to that, eh?"

"Yeah, don't think I didn't notice that you missed our April meeting last week. So you'll come to the May meeting, right? Or else..."

He shook his head. "You're kind of scary, you know that?"

She nodded. "That's the thing about loss, Ryan. Out the other side of it? You discover just how tough you really are."

CHAPTER EIGHT

WHEN HOLLY HEADED BACK to the cottage for a few hours in the middle of the day, and they took the slow turn onto Blue Heron Lane, she couldn't keep herself from looking through the tinted windows at Ryan's house.

His truck was gone.

It shouldn't matter—she wasn't going over there. Their ill-fated connection had ended maybe before she wanted it to, but it had to end— better that he hurt her than she hurt him.

Her heart didn't agree, but then it rarely got a say in how things went for her. She closed her eyes and rolled her head back against the seat, stretching her legs out in front of her.

"Do you want a massage? I can arrange for an RMT to come over." Emmett asked from the driver's seat. Sometimes they used drivers when they filmed on location, but with all the breaks, Emmett had rented an SUV so she could come and go at will.

"No, I just want a nap." They would be shooting into

the night, a difficult confrontation scene between Kathleen, her character, and Cameron, Joshua's character.

"Do you need anything from town? There weren't any greens in our grocery delivery, so I thought I'd go shopping. I'll be back in plenty of time to get you back to the set."

She'd kill for a pint of ice cream. "Maybe popsicles?"

"Sure thing."

Emmett pulled up in front of the house and she wearily climbed out. Instead of heading inside right away, she walked across the deck and looked out at the lake. She wasn't one of those actors who could channel her own feelings into a character. It was exhausting keeping Kathleen's sadness and sense of betrayal separate from Holly's regret over Ryan. For one thing, they weren't the same, at all—and she needed Kathleen to be *angry*.

Let him go. If only it was that easy. She didn't even know what she was clinging to—a fleeting connection? A fantasy flirtation?

"You look like you're thinking hard about something," the object of her thoughts said from behind her, his voice rough and deep.

"Ryan," she gasped, whirling around.

He stood at the top of the steps, taking up far too much space for her comfort. He was larger than life and getting bigger by the second, it felt like, filling up her world. He wore a plaid shirt loose over a t-shirt that stretched tight over his chest, dark jeans and work boots. He looked big and burly, and her arms ached to wrap around him. A part of her fantasized that he felt the same way, because his thumbs were looped into his pockets and his hands clenched in fists. *Don't hold back,* she wished she could say, but that would be heading in completely the wrong direction. So she pressed her lips together instead. Silence being golden and all that.

"I owe you an apology," he started to say, his shoulders hitching up a little more with each word. "I didn't have a great hold on my emotions last week." He blew out a breath. "I don't want to make excuses. There's no justification for yelling at you. I'm sorry."

He stepped a bit closer and pulled something from his back pocket. "I wrote you a note saying as much. I was going to leave it for you. I didn't know you would be here."

"Oh." Of course not. He wasn't here to see her. She straightened her back and held her head high as she glided across the porch. Holly Cresinksi couldn't handle this, but Hope Creswell could. She pasted on a smile. "That wasn't necessary, but thank you."

He frowned at her. "Of course it was necessary." He extended his arm, holding out a neatly folded piece of white paper. "Here."

She glanced at it, but didn't take it. "I appreciate the apology. Really. We can just move on."

"Holly…" He dropped his hand and moved closer, into her personal space. She could feel the faint warmth of his body and see his jaw clenching and moving. She dropped her gaze from his face, but he filled all of her senses anyway. His now familiar scent, the rough rub of his sounds as he cleared his throat and sighed. And even though they weren't touching, she could feel his solid strength beneath her palms.

She pressed her hands to her thighs, pulling herself in tight, trying to hold herself together so he wouldn't know how close she was to falling apart.

"There's more," he said roughly. "Maybe I should just read it to you."

At the whisper of paper unfolding, she snapped her head up and reached out without thinking, wrapping her fingers around his wrist. "Don't."

Beneath her fingertips, his pulse thumped under warm skin. Ever so slowly, he relaxed his grip on the note, and it fluttered to the ground. He repeated her name, his voice more strained and she looked up, meeting his gaze.

The heat she found there was enough to melt her frosty exterior ten times over. Enough to burn her to a crisp at the same time. It matched the restless ache she'd carried inside her for a week now. "Stop looking at me like that," she whispered.

"I can't." He swayed toward her, and it took all of her will power to look away. "I missed you this weekend."

"You pushed me away."

"I know."

"Nothing has changed."

"I've changed a little. Enough to know I don't want to push you away again." As he spoke, his words spilling naked between them, he brought his face almost to her cheek. So close. So far. Still in the safe zone.

"There are still things you don't know about me." Her voice cracked as she said it and he groaned, pressing his face into her hair. "And things I'm going to ask you…"

"We'll talk."

It didn't feel like they were going to talk. She couldn't think straight and he smelled so good, felt so warm, and her mouth watered to know how he tasted.

Come inside. "How much time do you have now?"

"Not enough for talking."

"We shouldn't do anything else…" She trailed off as he

ghosted his lips over her temple, unable to stifle a weak moan, and she tightened her grip on his wrist that she still held between them.

"I know that, too," he muttered, slowly twisting his arm inside the circle of her fingers. He pressed their palms together as he shifted her backwards, pressing her against the wall of the house. As he loomed over her, her world narrowed to the two square feet they occupied together and the unsettling electricity sizzling between them. When he pressed one of her hands by her head, holding her in place, she gasped—then he stroked his other hand along her jaw, cupping the back of her neck, and her brain short-circuited. "But then you touch me, and I can't remember why this is a bad idea."

"Because it was only a good idea as long as it was an escape from reality," she breathed, trying hard not to press onto her tiptoes and close the gap between their faces.

"This feels pretty damn real," he ground out. "And I'm not running."

"You will."

"Maybe. Or it might be you. As long as we both know…" He swore under his breath and covered her mouth with his, swallowing her next noise and the one after that.

———

RYAN HADN'T MEANT to kiss her. He'd planned on not even seeing her, but his cowardly plan had backfired—thankfully—and as soon as he saw her leaning against the rail, looking over the lake, his course had been set. When that polite mask had dropped over her face, something inside him had pranged—he'd hurt her, and he needed to show her how wrong that was. Show her how much he valued her. When she grabbed his wrist, the mask dropping away, his primal instincts took over.

He'd pinned her against the wall, going from zero to sixty because this was a kiss that had been days in the making. That he thought would never happen.

She was right. They should talk.

But right now her tongue was stroking against his and she'd slid her hand into his hair. Thinking and talking were for some other guy, or some other time.

She tasted like warm lemons and her skin was dewy and soft. And she made the most amazing noises, like it had been a while since she'd been kissed, too, which made him feel like the luckiest man in the world.

He brought her palm to his chest, because *oh God* he wanted to feel her touch, but she did him one better. She stroked her fingers down his torso and around his waist, blazing an electric path he felt through his t-shirt.

He kissed along her jaw, to her ear, exploring all the spots that made her sigh and squeeze him tighter. Down her neck, breathing in her sweetness. Tasting it.

When she gripped his hips, sliding their pelvises together, he let her rock against him before sliding away with a rueful laugh.

"Not pulling away, just slowing down," he said roughly as he licked his way back to her ear. "Or I'll lose what little control I have left."

"You've still got some control?" She sagged back against the house as he braced his hands on either side of her. It was impossible to miss her chest, heaving between them, and those beautiful breasts. His dick thumped at the thought of how good her nipples would feel in his mouth.

"Hanging by a thread." He kissed her forehead, and

she looked up at him. "This isn't why I came here," he whispered.

"I know," she said, kissing his jaw with featherlight brushes of her lips. "I'm okay with that. Sometimes the best things happen by accident."

"I need to get the kids in fifteen minutes. We should continue this later."

"We're filming late tonight, that's why I'm here now. Break time."

"Oh. How late?" She laughed and he nipped at her lower lip. "Okay, I won't push my luck."

"I'll be exhausted when we get back. Wouldn't be good company in the least."

"I doubt that, but I get it." He groaned as he thought about his own calendar. "And I work tomorrow night."

She cupped his face and rubbed her nose against his before dropping a breathless little kiss on his lips. "Soon. And until then…"

He wrapped his arms around her and pulled her close. "I really am sorry about last week."

"Me, too."

He kissed her again, tasting her lips and teasing her tongue as she opened for him again.

"Okay, I really need to have a nap," she said, shoving him away with absolutely no conviction after a few more kisses. She smiled, pressing her lips together in a secret kind of way, and he held her gaze for as many heartbeats as he could handle before it felt weird and sappy.

"Would it be too forward to ask for your number?"

She laughed, leaning into him. "God, no. But it's an L.A. number, so maybe email, too? And we can text. Do you have a smart phone?"

"Yes, the country boy has an iPhone." Not that he used

it that often, and his email hadn't been syncing regularly…
but he'd fix that for her. He pulled it out of his back pocket
and they exchanged email addresses and phone numbers.

"Hey." She squeezed his hand, making him look at her
after he finished typing in her details. "I like the country
boy. A lot."

"Good. He likes you, too."

He gave her one last, quick kiss before reluctantly leaving. When he did, though, his steps were light and easy.

———

THAT NIGHT, Holly could feel her character humming
through her veins, and when the cameras started rolling,
she nailed it on the first take.

Unfortunately, Joshua was a freaking robot opposite
her, so James growled for the room to be reset. People
scurried around them, righting a lamp that Joshua
knocked over, fixing her collar where she'd worried at her
shirt, reapplying her nibbled lip gloss. No little detail was
left untouched—even the carpet was vacuumed after she
wheeled across it in the wrong direction.

Holly didn't pay the stage hands any attention. She'd
slipped into the zone, and all that mattered was chan-
neling the character and telling the story.

Too bad her co-star wasn't in the same zone. It could
have been an early night.

Twelve takes later, she was blissfully excused after
nailing her close-ups in a single round of short takes.

Leaving Joshua with James's bluster, she scurried to
her trailer, where she found Parvati talking to Olivia.

"You done already?" Parvati asked her, and she slowed
to a stop, joining them.

"Done for now. We'll see if he calls for me again."

"Want a glass of wine?" Parvati tipped her head toward her own trailer.

She almost said no, but actually… "You know what? Yes, I would. Half a glass, in case I get summoned by your husband. And white, so it won't stain my lips." Parvarti's lips twitched at the list of demands and Holly sighed. "I know, I'm sorry I'm such a diva. Olivia, do you want to join us?"

The local staffer smiled. "If you've got water, sure. I'm pregnant, so no wine for me. And neither of you are the least bit diva-esque, I gotta say."

"Seriously?" Holly looked her up and down. "I would've never known. You look fantastic."

"It's still early-ish. I'm sure by the time you guys leave I'll have popped right out and started waddling."

Holly felt a pang of…something softer than jealousy, but in that vein. She'd never gotten close to having the type of relationship one would bring a child into, having been trained from an early age to be distrustful of the dangers of motherhood. No better birth control than being raised by a woman who found children icky.

"I'm totally jealous," Parvati said, admitting what Holly couldn't. "James wants to wait until after I've elevated my career to the next level. And I'm terrified about losing my body." She made a face. "Now I'm the one who sounds like a diva."

"Really, I get that!" Olivia laughed. "I don't think there's anything either of you could say that would make me think you're drama queens or anything like that."

Holly slung her arm around the other woman's shoulders. "Oh, come, let's tell you stories."

They ushered her into Parvati's trailer, leaving the door

open so they could hear if either of them were called to the set.

"There's so much drama on a film set, isn't there?" Parvati giggled and shook her head. "Poor Olivia, seeing the worst of people."

"Oh, we've got our fair share of drama here, too. It's just human nature."

"Really?" Holly shook her head. "Pine Harbour seems like the nicest town."

"We're putting our best foot forward because this film shoot is one of the best things to happen here. But we've had tragedy and scandal and conflict that would rival anything in Hollywood." Olivia shook her head. "But enough about that. I want celebrity gossip, and you guys need wine."

While Parvati poured, Holly told Olivia who got wasted at the Oscars and who was currently living in a hotel because his wife had changed the locks, but they still appeared happy as a clam together in public.

By the end the night, Holly was giggly and slightly tipsy. The power of girlfriends, she thought as she crawled into bed. She grabbed her phone and sent a quick email to Liana, who was on tour in Australia.

`I miss you, sweat pea. Had a nice night with Parvati and one of the production company staffers, but I need my bestie. I'm coming to Nashville for a visit when this film shoot is over.`

After she hit send, she started another message. This one, to Ryan, took her longer to write, because she wanted to get it just right.

Tucking into bed after a long day of work. Thinking of you.

His response came in the middle of the night, and as soon as the phone vibrated, she had it in front of her face.

Best thing I've heard all day. And now I'm thinking of you. R.

So dangerous, she thought. How this man made her feel…and what he made her think, deep in the recesses of her mind. Fantastical things she never imagined would be possible for her. Ordinary, wonderful things she didn't dare speak, lest they not come true.

CHAPTER NINE

ON THURSDAY, Ryan dropped Maya at preschool and drove thirty minutes south to Wiarton to buy condoms.

Just in case.

He had no clue where he might have sex with Holly, or when, but he needed to be prepared, because he was pretty sure their first kiss would have counted as foreplay.

Blushing like a teenager, he handed the box to the cashier who couldn't care less, paid, and hustled back to his truck, paranoid that someone he knew might see him. Then he went grocery shopping, because outside his fantasy sex life, he still had three growing kids to feed.

Back in Pine Harbour, he dropped the groceries at his house, then decided to head into town and get lunch at Mac's. He found Rafe and Olivia Minelli having an early lunch at a booth.

"Rare day off together?" he asked as he approached.

Olivia waved a black and white picture in the air. "We had our first baby ultrasound this morning." She handed it over, and as he made the appropriate *cute alien you've got there* noises, she got out of the booth and pointed to her seat. "Here, you should join Rafe. I've gotta get back to work."

"I don't mean to interrupt…" he started, but she waved off the protest.

"Really, I was eating and running anyway. There's always a long to-do list when I get back on set."

"What exactly are you doing? I've talked to some of the people staying at the cottages—" One person, but they didn't need to know that "—and it seems really… involved. Complicated."

Olivia nodded. "It's busy, for sure. I do whatever needs to be done."

Ryan laughed. "You sound like Holly. She talks about work a fair bit and I swear, I still have no clue what she does."

"Holly?" Olivia frowned. "Wait, Ryan Howard, are you seeing someone?"

"What?" Grateful that grumpy came so naturally to him, he frowned at her. "No. Why?"

"Who's Holly?" She narrowed her eyes at him suspiciously.

"One of the movie set people. Don't make me say something rude about pregnancy hormones and memory." Ryan could hear himself talking, even as he tried to shut the hell up. But ever since that kiss, Holly was all he could think about. Still, he couldn't believe he'd just inanely managed to jam her into a conversation, and now he was stumbling in any direction he could think of that would change the subject. He rubbed his jaw—not really effective, but it was all he had.

"Okay, well, we'll ignore that crack because you've got three kids and even though I'm only a few months into gestating my first, I'm pretty sure they sap brain cells at a crazy rate. Actually, I'd been meaning to tell you, everyone is thrilled with the cottages. But Hope's assistant mentioned that the front step of the Fenichs' house is loose. Do you think you could check it out?"

It hadn't seemed loose when I climbed those steps a few days ago, he thought, but he nodded. "Sure thing."

"Thanks." She squeezed his arm, then stepped past him and kissed her husband goodbye. Her fingers lingering on Rafe's shoulder. He'd been shot in the same incident Lynn had died. Olivia's voice softened, the all-business approach dropping for a second. "Shouldn't be late tonight, but go to sleep if you're tired."

"I'll wait up for you."

Ryan slid into the booth as Rafe watched Liv head out the door.

"She still worries about me. I've been back at work for almost two months, and she stresses every time I'm about to go on a run of shifts." A provincial police officer, Rafe worked shifts, alternating three or four days or nights in a row.

"You going on days tomorrow?"

"Yeah, so I'll be up and gone before she wakes up. She was getting up with me, but the morning sickness is kicking her ass. You'd never know it, though. She's a rock star."

"Lynn was like that, too—strongest when she was pregnant. Super Woman, that's what I always called her." A familiar ache pulsed in Ryan's chest, the edge of it sharper than usual because of how his thoughts had just been distracted by Holly.

"You okay?" Rafe made a face. "Or some variation of that question that's more sensitive?"

"I'm good." Ryan grabbed the menu from behind the napkin holder. "Probably just hungry."

"Because you know if you need to talk or something…"

"I know." He definitely didn't want to talk about moving on with the man who'd tried to save Lynn's life. Pine Harbour was just too damn small.

He ordered a hot roast beef sandwich, which came quickly, and they ate in easy silence. Rafe finished first, and talked at Ryan about an Army training exercise—they were reservists in the same unit—until Ryan was done.

"You heading home?" Ryan asked Rafe as they headed out to their trucks.

"Gotta pick up some books at the library for Liv, then yeah. You want to come over?"

"Sure. I've got an hour to kill before I get Maya. I'll follow you."

He drove behind Rafe, and if there had been two parking spots in a row in front of the library, he might have missed the new banner stretched across Main Street.

But Rafe snagged the last spot, so Ryan drove down the block and turned around—only to see Holly's face flying high above him.

What the hell? He scrambled out of his truck after doing the world's worst parking job on the opposite side of the street from the library, and stared at the vinyl banner. Usually that space was taken up by one of a dozen signs the town owned. Seasonal celebrations, a couple of charity runs…and now…

"Pine Harbour welcomes Hope Creswell and Joshua Pearce," he read out loud twice, the second unnecessarily loud.

Rafe jogged across the street. "What's wrong?"

"What is that?" Ryan bit out, stabbing his finger in the air.

"The movie sign? I don't think the town paid for it. They got a promotional allowance or something from the production company. Liv just had it put up yesterday."

"That's not what I mean."

Rafe wrinkled his brows. "I don't think I follow?"

"Who is Hope Creswell?"

"Jeez, Ryan. I know you've got a lot going on, but how do you not recognize the movie star living at the end of your lane?"

Mouth hanging open, probably looking like a complete idiot, he scissored his head back and forth between Rafe and the sign. Up. Down. Up… "Hope Creswell."

"I know you said you haven't had a lot of complaints, but you seriously haven't met her?"

"I'm not sure who I've met and who I haven't," he ground out.

"She's nice. I met her when I visited Liv on set. And she's gorgeous, man. You're missing out if you haven't seen her movies."

Ryan knew full well just how gorgeous she was. *She glows when she runs.* Of course *she's a fucking movie star.*

"I don't watch a lot of movies," he said dumbly. "I have to go."

"I thought you had time to hang out?"

"Change of plans…" he trailed off, still staring at the sign.

"Okay, well, I'll see you later?"

"Yep." It came out as a harsh bark as he wrenched open the door of his truck, but he didn't care. He needed to be alone right now. Somewhere he could yell and rage and maybe punch something.

The pretty girl he'd kissed was a movie star full of secrets? *Fucking hell.*

When he hit the highway outside of town, he lingered at the stop sign. Home was to the right, but the private cottage most of the filming was happening at was to the left. On the other side of the provincial parks.

You can't storm onto the set and demand to see her. No, but he wanted to.

Instead, he turned right and headed home. He needed more time to process what needed to be said.

———

HOLLY PRACTICALLY SKIPPED up the lane after a quick, late dinner with Emmett.

As soon as he headed up to his room, she slipped out onto the deck, wrapping her sweater around her with both arms, hugging a thermos of tea tight to her chest. This time she didn't bother with the second cup.

They could share.

She grinned to herself as she passed the quiet cottages where everyone else was tucked in for the night, then she settled on his steps. There wasn't any movement in the kitchen, and the lights were still on upstairs, so she assumed he was putting the kids to bed.

She slid her phone out of her pocket and sent him a text message.

Holly: Sitting on your porch. No rush, I have tea and stars to look at.

Some time passed. She sent the same thing as an email,

then looked at the lights upstairs. First one blinked off, then another.

Her pulse picked up in anticipation and she stood. Through the window, she watched him move through the kitchen, picking up dishes and carrying them to the sink. He paused in front of a kitchen cupboard, his hand on the knob, and he stood there for almost a minute with his head bowed.

Holly's breath caught in her throat as he turned. He looked tired, but as he made eye contact with her, his face twisted and she realized with a jolt that he wasn't happy to see her.

For an awful, agonizing moment, she thought he might turn and walk back upstairs, but he slowly came to the door and opened it.

"Hi," she whispered, not daring to speak any louder than that. "Are you okay?"

"I hate that question." He stepped out and yanked the door shut behind him, but didn't move far onto the deck. Just stood there in front of the door, hands shoved into his pockets. Not looking at her. "I'm never okay."

A stuttering noise burbled in her throat. "I'm sorry," she finally blurted.

"Yeah."

"What's going on?" But she thought maybe she knew. *Say it first, show him you meant to tell him sooner.*

Hesitation had always been her Achilles heel.

"What's going on?" he repeated, ice dripping from his words. "'They're not so bad, those movie stars.'" He was breathing hard, his mouth pulled tight, the skin around it white. "That's what you said to me, that first night in my kitchen. And then every time we talked, you let me think you were just a girl who worked on a movie set."

Oh, shit. "Ryan..."

"No. You don't get the right to look at me like that."

Like she'd do anything to back up and do this differently? Like she'd come to need him, like he was the best part of her day? Holly had no idea if all of that was on her face. She hoped it was, hoped something might make him see that she hadn't *meant* to hurt him.

"I never said that, exactly, and I *am* just..."

"You played me for a *fool*."

"I didn't mean to," she whispered, scalding hot tears burning her eyes.

"What the hell did you *mean* to do, *Hope?*"

She winced at the harsh bite of his words. "Holly. My name is Holly."

"That's not what the giant fucking banner in town says!"

Her stomach lurched into her throat at the pain and anger rolling off him in waves.

"Hope is a stage name." She took a deep breath, ragged on the inhale, burning on the exhale. Her hands shook as she pressed them to her midsection. She had to make him understand. "Nobody calls me Holly. Nobody tells me how to do things for myself, or looks at me like I'm an ordinary woman. That first night, it wasn't Hope who asked you for help. That was *me*. Nervous and lonely and not sure of myself. *Me*. And I liked the way you didn't know who I was, or treat me differently, so I gave you my real name. I didn't l-lie to you."

"No?" He shot her a hard stare and twisted away, staring into the dark. "I didn't think I was kissing a movie star. So call that whatever you want, but I feel lied to."

"I'm sorry."

"That's not good enough. Maybe this is my fault,

because I didn't want to talk about how fucked up my life is, but I can't…be exposed like this. I can't risk people peering into my kids' life because we're a freak sideshow."

"I tried to tell you…" She didn't go on because she knew that she hadn't tried hard enough. "We both just wanted to escape—"

"Stop!" He growled it, like he choked back a yell. "We are not the same. I'm sorry that you wanted to escape from your fancy life for a bit, but I'm not the guy for that. You can't be the needy one, Holly. I'm the needy one. I need stability and security for my family. I need *zero fucking drama* for my kids, you got that? You start kissing some single dad in small town Ontario, you don't think my kids won't have their picture in grocery store magazines? And then someone starts digging and finds out how their mother died? That. Cannot. Fucking. Happen. Got it?"

Each word was like a physical blow. He was right. She'd been beyond selfish. "Got it," she whispered.

"You want to be treated like a normal person? Here's a newsflash: normal people don't always get what they want. Sometimes they need to make sacrifices, and sometimes what they want just isn't available."

Even though she felt awful, that pushed one of her no-go buttons, damn him. "You don't think I don't know about sacrifices? Who the hell are you to judge me?"

He shook his head. "I'm nobody. And I'm not judging you. I'm just saying, I'm not available. Not to you."

"You're right here in front of me, Ryan. And I'm right here in front of *you*. I know I'm not going to be here forever, but we have a connection—"

"You're not listening." He glared at her and she took a half-step backward. "You don't always get what you want. Now leave me the hell alone."

"I never would have told anyone…" She pressed her lips together, holding back everything else she wanted to say, because she *was* listening, even if she didn't like what he had to say.

He nodded, looking at her without exactly meeting her gaze. "I know. Right now I'm pissed, but I'm not so angry that I can't remember you're a genuinely nice person. I'll be more reasonable about this in a few days."

The unspoken *but we're definitely done doing what we were doing* hung between them, and suddenly, it didn't matter if he'd be more reasonable later or if he still liked her as a human being.

It didn't matter that she'd hurt him, because this hurt her.

She'd foolishly fallen for someone who had warned her repeatedly that he wasn't available.

She'd done this to herself.

Mumbling further apologies, a long, never-ending stream of *alltherightthings* because she couldn't give him another chance to talk, to accidentally pierce her heart all over again, she backed up. When she bumped into the post at the top of the steps, she spun around and ran into the darkness.

CHAPTER TEN

"WHAT THE HELL is wrong with you?"

Holly took a deep breath. "I'm sorry."

She'd held it together for more than a week, but inside she'd been slowly unraveling, and blanking on her lines was the first crack that had made it to the surface. She hated Mondays.

James whipped his script binder across the room. "Take twenty minutes, and get your fucking lines down."

"I only need ten. I'm sorry."

"Save the fucking apologies, Hope. You're the professional one, remember? Stop fucking up my movie."

He stormed out and she released the breath she hadn't realized she was holding. Emmett held out a bottle of water as she slid past him, and she took a series of small sips as she headed upstairs to the bedrooms that had been turned into makeup and dressing rooms. He followed, and as soon as she was settled in her chair, he slipped the script in front of her.

"It's no more his movie than yours and mine," Parvati said quietly as she slid into the seat next to Holly.

Holly closed her eyes and took a deep breath. "It doesn't matter."

"Want to run the scene?"

She nodded, and they quietly ran their lines together.

Ten days had passed. A week and a half of self-flagellation and regretful rehashing in her head. When she woke up this morning, she'd thought she was finally fine.

Ha.

Fine was the last thing she was, apparently. Maybe numb and useless, but definitely not fine.

Emmett gave her a little hug as she headed back downstairs, but that just made her think of Ryan's solid warmth.

She didn't need him. Or if she thought she did, she was wrong, and in the meantime, she could damn well pretend she didn't.

You're an actress. Start putting those skills to good use.

"You get yourself unfucked?" James barked as he stomped back in.

She took another deep breath. "Yep. Let's do this."

———

ON THURSDAY, Ryan scowled at the privacy fence being erected between his house and the cottages closer to the lake.

"Stop making that face," Olivia said from beside him. She had a clipboard and a cellphone that kept ringing, plus a radio headset.

"You look like you're running half of the free world with all that gear," he grumbled. "I can't believe this is necessary."

"They're going to be doing some filming here next week. It's not a big deal."

"My kids like to play on that trail! Why couldn't this be put up after the weekend?"

"They're still welcome on the trail when filming isn't happening. We haven't turned your lane into a gated community or anything, and it won't be up for long." Olivia waved him off as her headset crackled. "Oh, and Emmett says that step is still squeaking!"

Ryan crossed his arms and scowled again for good measure. One sad benefit of being a widower—nobody thought twice about him being a curmudgeon.

———

ON SUNDAY, hammering woke Holly up at seven. *Bang. Bang. Bang.*

A piece of wood clattered a little louder than necessary, and then the hammering resumed.

She lay there, glowering at the ceiling for a few minutes. There was only one person who would be doing minor construction at this hour, since the set construction guys knew better than to do that on her day off. She listened to Ryan literally beat against her house. Okay, his in-laws' house. But still, it was her temporary cocoon and he was battering it. The imagery was clumsy and heavy-handed.

It was also painfully on point.

She put on her robe, went to the kitchen, made herself a cup of coffee on the one-cup machine, then pasted on her Hope Creswell face and opened the slider door. "Can I help you with something?"

"No, ma'am, just fixing the step."

"I don't recall there being anything wrong with it."

"Your assistant told Olivia that it squeaked. We

wouldn't want the fancy movie star to be annoyed by that."

"Seriously?" She almost spun around and glared at the house, but something about that didn't quite ring true, and Emmett maybe didn't need her wrath. "No other reason why you might feel the need to take a blunt object to the space where I'm staying right now?"

"Nope."

"You pushed me away, Ryan, not the other way around."

"You lied to me."

"And this is a very passive aggressive way to punish me for that."

He put down the hammer and glared up at her.

"What?"

"Nothing."

"Okay, then. I'm going back to bed."

Inside, she found Emmett making coffee. He gave her a surprised look. "What are you doing up? It's your day off."

"Ryan Howard is replacing the step. He wasn't quiet about it. I'm surprised you slept through it."

"Is that what that was?" He shrugged. "It didn't bother me."

Really? It had driven Holly out of her mind.

And for the rest of the day, she wouldn't be able to shake the memory of him looking up at her, practically vibrating with anger.

———

"GO AWAY."

Emmett sat on the edge of Holly's bed and smoothed his hand down her back. "Come on, up you get."

"I don't want to. I hate Mondays."

"I don't think that's an option, is it?"

No, it wasn't.

She'd pulled her shit together in the last week, as James would say, but he hadn't stopped picking on her. She was one day away from having her agent call the producer and run interference, because it was ridiculous. "I'm being punished for having a bad day. One single bad day. Joshua's a complete mess, and I'm—"

"I know. Into the shower you go."

"It's still dark outside," she whined as he hauled her out of bed and shoved her toward the bathroom.

"I'll make you a coffee smoothie."

"That sounds awful."

"It will be." He laughed as she groaned. "No, it'll be good. I've already had one this morning."

"That explains the chipper. Go away, chipper man."

He just crossed his arms and raised his eyebrows.

Fine. She shut the bathroom door and turned on the shower, but she didn't get in right away. Instead, she stared at herself in the mirror. *What's wrong with you, woman?*

What was really wrong was that Emmett woke her up mid-dream. Mid-*Ryan* dream. She was hopeless, because their little encounter on the porch the day before should have been the final nail in the coffin of her crush.

But it had done the exact opposite. Now he was in every thought, and even his anger was twisted in her head, like it was proof he couldn't shake her, either.

Stripping down, she stepped under the hot spray, but that only reminded her of him, too. How she'd wanted this shower that first night and how he'd helped her figure it out for herself.

Fast forward two months and she'd shattered his trust in her. Way to repay him. So dreaming about him? That must be her penance. It was so cruel that she'd only had one brief afternoon of kissing him. Had never had a chance to press against him naked. *Like that would make it better? That you didn't get to break his heart even further?*

But it wasn't just that she longed for what she'd never had with him.

It was also that she'd squandered what she *did* have.

Every time James yelled at her, or Joshua checked out during an important scene, she wanted to run to Ryan's arms and tell him about it. They'd spent six weeks flirting and talking about *nothing*, because she was scared he wouldn't want her as she really was.

A legitimate fear, since he hadn't.

Maybe if things had gone differently…

Unfortunately, wishing wouldn't make it so.

THE SUPPORT GROUP met in a church basement in Lion's Head, a ten minute drive across the highway.

He didn't have any reason not to go, although he tried to find one. He put off asking any of his friends to watch the kids, and Dani finally cornered him at Mac's on Thursday morning. She drove up in her own car, but she was in her paramedic standard-issued blue pants and shirt. "Didn't you say that bereaved spouses group was meeting tonight?"

Shit, had he told her that? "Maybe?"

"I'll take the kids. My place or yours?"

"Aren't you getting off a night shift?" He looked pointedly at her uniform.

"That's what naps are for."

So that's how he ended up sitting on a folding chair, drinking cheap coffee and listening to people just like him share their painful stories. It was all chest-achingly familiar.

Faith gave him a reassuring smile when it was his turn to introduce himself.

"I'm Ryan. My wife died last fall, unexpectedly…" As he talked, he stared at the linoleum floor. He didn't want to look up and see recognition on anyone's face. "I've got three kids, and we're all doing as well as can be expected, I guess. Some days are better than others. And me personally…I have these moments where I feel like I've got it together enough to move on, and then it all falls apart."

As it had with the others around the circle, a warm pause followed his introduction—it seemed like the group policy was to triple check that a speaker was done before carrying forward. Finally Faith cleared her throat. "Thanks, Ryan. As a reminder, everything we talk about in this circle stays in this circle. We mean that in two ways. One, this is a confidential group. But secondly, we don't need to carry each others' burdens away from here. We're here to unload in a safe space, leave those thoughts and fears and doubts and worries" —she pointed in the centre of the circle of chairs— "here, and hopefully walk out a bit lighter than when we came in."

"Before we get started with tonight's topic," an older woman said—Emily, according to her name sticker, "I have some general announcements. Next month's meeting will start a half hour earlier, to accommodate the church choir…"

As she droned on, he carefully looked around the circle. Nobody gawked at him. No excess sympathy. Most people looked similarly numb, in fact. *Grief is selfish*, Faith had said. Boy, was she right about that.

"Thanks, Emily." Faith grinned at the group. "Okay, so taking a cue from the changing season outside, I'd like to talk tonight about blooming. Opening up to others, finding another way to have our needs met—those things that our spouse used to do for us. Who do you talk to now when you have a bad day at work? Have you taken another stab at being intimate with someone? Are you relying more on your friends, or finding new people to fill the gap?"

"Nobody," was the first answer from a man across the way. "I've never been a talker. My wife pulled it out of me, even when she was sick. But now…I don't know. It's easier not to talk to anyone, I guess. Not that anyone wants to hear my grumpiness."

Ryan nodded. "I hear you on that. And I've got close friends, but…I just can't."

"I do most of my talking online," said Emily. "I was on a crafting forum before my husband was killed, and that's a huge community. Thousands of people. So that's where I found people like me, before I knew this group existed. There's something easier about talking anonymously."

"Where they can't see you crying at the other end of the Internet connection," Faith said softly. "And you can reply on your own terms and own timeline."

"Exactly."

"I did the same thing in online writing circles," Faith added, "but it wasn't enough. Particularly with my son, I felt like my real self was wasting away, and all my feelings were locked inside that virtual community. That's a danger for someone like me, who works in words all the time."

"That's what my doctor said, that's why I'm here," the first man said gruffly. "My blood pressure is too high. He said I need to talk about this stuff or I'll kill myself, too."

There was a long pause then, and Ryan wondered if everyone else was having the same thoughts as him—there was a part of him that wanted to die after Lynn was shot. And the guilt for those thoughts still ate him up inside.

"It's not so bad, living again," another woman, Jenny, said quietly. "I have a boyfriend. I actually thought about putting that in the announcements, it's such a big deal."

"Nothing wrong with not wanting that, either." Faith said after she finished giggling at the announcements comment. "There are other ways to take care of those needs without dating. But it's wonderful to celebrate, and hear when other people find that happiness, because there some societal expectations of mourning that are hard to negotiate.

You know in movies, how the dead spouse leaves a note, explaining how they want their partner to keep living and be happy? I didn't think my husband would want that for me. And that's held me back for a long time. It's complicated, figuring out how to move on."

The conversation continued, but that thought stayed with Ryan for quite a while. He had no idea what Lynn would think of his attraction to Holly. Or how he'd feel if the situation was reversed. They hadn't been particularly possessive of each other. No jealousy or any reason for it. They'd fought, about drug use and taking out the garbage, some minor parenting disagreements...but never about fidelity.

Which only made him feel guiltier about how easily

he'd slid into wanting Holly. Shouldn't he be more loyal to Lynn? Wouldn't she want that?

But it hadn't felt wrong in the moment. It had been too much for him to handle, but not for reasons of guilt. So why did he feel like he should be guilty now? Would that boomerang effect ever stop?

It wasn't Holly that he felt guilty about. He still felt like he'd failed Lynn, and it had nothing to do with what he was doing in the present, and everything to do with what he hadn't done in the past.

———

HOLLY TOSSED and turned in her bed for almost an hour before she padded downstairs and made herself another cup of chamomile tea. Back upstairs, she unfolded Ryan's well-worn apology note.

She already knew what it said, word for word. But she read it again, her eyes devouring the sharp points and harsh swoops of his handwriting.

Reaching for the notepad and pen she always kept beside her bed, she started writing. *Dear Ryan....*

———

RYAN HAD KNOWN it was just a matter of time before he ran into her again. She slept five hundred feet away from him and now the entire movie production had been moved into his backyard. But knowing that and experiencing it were two different things.

On Saturday, they were halfway through a road hockey game in the driveway—Jake Foster and Gavin playing the Montreal Canadiens versus the Vancouver Canucks, aka

Ryan, Jack and Maya—when Olivia pulled up. Instead of driving through the manned gate, she parked in front of Ryan's house and got out.

"Hey guys!" she said, far too cheerfully.

Everyone was far too cheerful for Ryan these days.

Maya abandoned the game and sprinted toward her friend. "Livvie! I want to see the movie!"

Ryan clenched his jaw. "Maya Howard, we talked about this."

Olivia just laughed. "It's fine...I'm actually waiting here for Dani, she wants to come for a tour, too. We can take Maya with us."

"Aw, come on! That's not fair!" Gavin threw down his stick and gloves.

"Hey!" Ryan whirled, pointing at his son. "First of all, I don't like that word. It's not fair that some kids don't have hot dinners and hockey sticks to play with. Go sit on the porch and think about what's truly fair and not fair in this world. Two minute time out." Shaking with unfair resentment, he took a deep breath. "Everyone just hang on a second."

Beside him, Jake frowned. "Should we go inside?"

Ryan shook his head, expelling that deep breath before taking another. *Don't freak out over a tour. That's a reasonable request. Get your shit together.* "I guess it's fine. I just...I'd prefer if people remember to ask me first."

Olivia winced. "Sorry."

"It's okay." He glanced at Jack, who was staring at the ground. "You want to go too, kid?'

Jack made a noncommittal noise.

"Hey, I'm sorry I snapped. I'm going to apologize to Gav, and if you guys want to go, you can."

Jack picked up his brother's hockey stick and gloves,

and stashed them away with his in the oversized plastic bin they kept next to the porch. Ryan gave his shoulder a squeeze as he made his way over to Gavin, who was blinking back tears on the porch.

"I'm sorry for yelling at you, bud." Ryan took a seat next to the seven-year-old and bumped his shoulder. "You got anything you want to say to me?"

"I'm sorry I said it wasn't fair."

"That's a big statement, right?"

"Right."

"You want to go with them?"

"Can I?"

Was he such an ogre that his kids thought he'd hold them back from something like that? "Of course. I just want you to be appreciative, not whiny. That's all."

Little arms wrapped tight around Ryan's waist and he squeezed his son close. "Will you come, too? It'll be fun."

"Playing hockey is more my idea of fun, bud."

"Please?"

And that's how he ended up awkwardly standing ten feet away from Holly, down by the lake, trying to look anywhere but at her decidedly-not-Holly made-up face. Her hair was shiny smooth and she was wearing makeup, a lot of makeup, although it was all carefully applied to make her look like she wasn't wearing anything at all.

Movies were weird.

Next to her, a ridiculously good-looking man flashed a pure-white smile, practically blinding the group. "Joshua Pearce, nice to meet you all."

Olivia's headset crackled and she leaned in. "Joshua, Hope…twenty minutes left on the lunch break. I have to go down to the dock, excuse me."

Ryan watched as she scurried away, impressed at how effortlessly his friend blended into such an alien world.

"I thought your name was Holly," Jack said, and Ryan jerked his attention back to his kids, who were now grilling Holly on her name. He took a step forward, but she shot him a look that said, *it's okay.*

"Most people know me as Hope Creswell." She paused and looked right at Ryan. "That's not my real name, though. Holly is."

Jack continued, totally oblivious to the undercurrent of tension zinging between the star and his father. "So you've got two names?"

"Yep." She smiled. "And most people don't know my real name, so that makes you guys special."

Gavin had to chip in. "You're just like Clark Kent and Superman."

She laughed, and *God,* had Ryan missed that sound. Which just pissed him off.

"I'm not that cool," Holly said.

"You can run fast and make movies. You're cool." Gavin held out his fist and she tapped her knuckles against his before kneeling to Maya's level.

"I need to get back to work now, but are you guys hungry? I think there's tons of food left in the catering tent. Should we go check it out?" She held out her hand and Maya slipped her fingers into Holly's.

Ryan hung back, watching as his kids happily traipsed along with the movie stars. Of course this made them happy. It was an escape from reality.

And isn't that exactly what you wanted for yourself?

But the happiness was fleeting, because it wasn't real. He gritted his teeth and followed, pissed off that for the rest of the day, they'd just talk about how cool this had been and how wonderful Holly was.

Of course, to his kids and the rest of the world, she hadn't actually done anything that wasn't wonderful. And even to him…even though she'd kept something big from him, at the same time she'd given him something big, too —friendship on his terms, no questions asked.

That just made him even madder, because while Ryan was starting to get the idea that he'd overreacted, he still felt wronged, too.

He didn't know what to do about that.

CHAPTER ELEVEN

HOLLY CLOSED HER EYES, hoping to steal a ten minute power-nap while the hair stylist reset her hair to what it should look like at the beginning of the scene.

The sliding door to the deck opened and closed, and footsteps approached. A voice cleared, and Emmett asked, "Hope, are you hungry?"

She hated how resentment prickled at that very reasonable question. This was this poor guy's job, to make sure her every need was met, and she'd never been such a bitch before, but the last twenty-four hours she'd been in the worst mood, and had taken it out on him more than once. Swallowing back the snappy response on the tip of her tongue, she nodded as much as the hair stylist would allow. "Sure. Tea and a muffin, please."

He slipped away again, and she took a deep breath, shoving away the feelings that didn't belong in her head right now. She wasn't Holly, or Hope. She was Kathleen, and she'd just seen her nurse out the window. *I know why she's here, and I'm torn between concern and anger.* Her lines for the scene ran through her head, and she breathed in and out, urging them into her bloodstream. One more take, and she'd nail it.

After the rockiness of the previous two weeks, she'd slipped into a new headspace. Still mad as hell in her off-hours, but when they called action, she was delivering performances that she *knew* were the best in her career. Rejection really had made her stronger.

Maybe she should thank Ryan for that. She snorted to herself. Doubtful that he'd care.

It had been so hard to be pleasant and upbeat the day before when he'd all but sneered at her and Joshua after Olivia had introduced them to her friends. Of course, it was awkward to be introduced to a man one had secretly kissed. But she did her best. And once she started talking to the kids, everything else had faded away. She really liked Jack, Gavin, and Maya—talking to them was a genuine pleasure. And as long as she focused on their faces, she'd been able to blur out Ryan's scowl.

Just like she'd been able to channel everything into Kathleen, blurring out the rest of the world.

But this new focus had come at a price—she wasn't that pleasant to be around, a state she wasn't comfortable with. When Emmett returned and slid a teacup onto the table beside her, she held out her hand. He squeezed it after hesitating a beat.

"Don't quit on me, Em."

He laughed. "You need to work on your apologies, Hope."

He wasn't wrong.

———

EMMETT HAD PASSED on the muffin request to someone

else, an intern probably, and when she was released by the hair and makeup people, she found a basket overflowing with enough baked goods to feed a small army—most of which she couldn't eat.

This is a sign, she thought as she looked in the direction of Ryan's house. When they took an early dinner break, Holly set aside the healthiest muffins that she might eat, rearranged the basket, grabbed her phone, and told Emmett to text her with a five minute warning when they were ready to get back to it.

Her heart in her throat, she tromped up the lane, all the things she might say spinning through her head.

A peace offering. Too weak. *I'm sorry.* No, not in front of the kids.

When he opened the door, just enough to see what she wanted and definitely not enough to seem welcoming, she just skipped all of the opening options and went straight for word-vomit.

"I asked for muffins at lunchtime and they brought me an entire basket of them. They'll go stale before I can eat them all, and some of them I won't eat anyway, so I thought the kids might like them. Here, you can just have them. I have to get back. Don't read anything into this. I don't have any expectations. Just blueberry buttermilk muffins. And bran. Warn the kids those aren't chocolate chips. Nobody likes raisins."

He stared back at her, his face hard and his eyes dark. Oh God, this was a mistake. She'd had a stupid, impulsive idea, but she was only making things worse. She took a half-step back, quite certain that fleeing would be the best option, but it was too late.

The door swung open the rest of the way and Ryan's

kids piled out the door around him. Gavin's eyes lit up and he pointed to the basket. "Muffins?"

She winced and shrugged a silent apology.

He waved his hand. "Come on in."

"I have to get back," she said quietly as she stepped in. "We're doing a night shoot tonight, so we're just on break."

"Well, thank you for the treats, right guys?" Ryan picked up Maya, who was reaching for the muffins, and Holly slid them onto the kitchen table.

Maya squealed in protest, and shook her head at Ryan when he shushed her. "No, Daddy. Put me down, your prickles are poking my face."

Jack rolled his eyes at Holly. "They aren't prickles Maya, it's his beard." He said it to his sister, but he said it for Holly's benefit. Telling her he wasn't a baby.

Gavin laughed, a silly giggle. "But that's a good name for them. Like Daddy's a porcupine."

From deep in Holly's belly, a laugh started and once it took hold she couldn't stop.

Maya looked at her, eyebrows drawn. "What so funny? You don't like Daddy's prickles either?"

Such an innocent question. She shouldn't have felt a stab of heat, deep inside her core, but there it was. And when she glanced up, her laughter fading from her lips, she saw an echoing fire burning bright in Ryan's eyes.

Damn it. "Okay, I need to get back to work. I just wanted to deliver these muffins. Be warned, the ones that look like chocolate chips are actually raisins."

"I like raisins," Jack said solemnly, so she gave him a high five.

She patted Gavin on the shoulder as he gave her a thumbs up, and waved at Maya. Ryan just watched her, and she got it—he wasn't available. But it hurt a little, knowing they had this chemistry between them and they'd never get to explore it. *He's right. I shouldn't always get what I want. It's made me spoiled.*

On the porch, she stopped for a second and took a deep breath, then jogged down the stairs, but she didn't get far before the door opened behind her.

"Wait." Ryan's voice was low and oh so sweet to her ears. "I want to hear the answer to that question."

She turned, taking in a nice, slow look at him. His broad shoulders were hunched up and his strong hands were clenched at his sides. He looked nervous, so nervous, and she wanted to make sure he really wanted to hear her answer first.

"If I like Daddy's prickles?" Another stab of desire pulsed inside her, and for a second she wasn't sure he'd actually have this conversation with her—or any conversation—but then he slowly stepped down the stairs toward her. His long, muscled legs quickly ate up the ground between them. "Seriously? What good comes of us talking about that?"

"Okay, I probably deserve that." He stopped a few feet away from her and crossed his arms, then shoved his hands in his pockets, like he couldn't figure out what to do with them.

Touch me, you idiot.

His gazed locked on hers and his voice, when he spoke, rasped out of him in a whisper. "Look...I'm sorry. I miss you."

"I miss you, too."

"I might have been too hasty in pushing you away. I was hurt and I reacted harshly."

And that was why she hadn't been able to bring herself

to seek him out and apologize sooner. "Twice. You pushed me away…twice."

"Okay, I may have been hasty and wrong…twice."

Hot, achey relief flooded through her body. "Just like that?"

Smiling, he nodded once, then twice more in fast succession. "Apparently so. I mean, not *just* like that. I've been thinking a lot about you, and me. We both could have done things differently. But I'm sorry, Holly. I'm unbelievably sorry that I hurt you."

She returned the smile, enjoying the tug between them and how her smile seemed to deepen his. "If you wanted any more muffins…I could bring some up later tonight."

Emotion clouded his face. He glanced back at the house.

"Hey, it's okay." She ignored the stab of pain in her gut. She needed to be the bigger person here. She pasted on a smile. "No expectations. No kissing. I just miss sitting on the porch with you. I really meant I'd bring you some muffins, it wasn't a euphemism for something dirty."

He frowned. "I'm not very good at this, but I wasn't saying I don't want something dirty…"

She laughed as he trailed off and turned red. "Wow."

"Um…"

"Maybe we should stick with being friends. And it'll just be our secret, I promise." Because she was leaving in six weeks. Because they came from separate worlds and what they'd had was fragile and temporary at best, imaginary and made of dust at worst. But what they might have again…that would have to be sensible. Realistic. And not dirty at all.

"I don't know about just being friends. But I do think we need a do-over." He shoved his shirt sleeves up to his elbows. He looked rumpled, over-sized, and irresistible. His big hand shot into the space between them. "Hi. I'm Ryan Howard. I live here. I'm the caretaker of the cottages."

She took his hand and shook it. "I'm Holly. You might know me better as Hope Creswell, but my real friends call me Holly."

"You've got a lot of those?"

"Nope."

"I know the feeling."

Heart hammering in her chest, she took a deep breath and confessed. "I wrote you an apology note. Like the one you wrote me."

Slow as molasses, he arched his eyebrows and gave her an appraising nod, his gaze never leaving her face. "Is that right?"

"It got a bit wordy. That's why I haven't given it to you yet."

"How wordy?"

"Ten pages."

He started laughing and she joined him. "That's a lot of saying you're sorry."

"Most of it was other stuff." God, that felt good to say. "I started rambling about my mother and work…"

He nodded as she talked, and when she trailed, off, he filled in the gap. "Stuff you weren't sure you could tell me?"

She swallowed and nodded. "We spent weeks making sure we were still strangers and I regret that so much. I don't know you that well. I want to…but the basic facts haven't changed."

"You're leaving."

Six weeks. "I want to say something here about jet

planes and flexible schedules, but…I'm scared." God, it felt good to admit that. "You're a special guy, Ryan Howard."

"Hardly," he muttered, but he was still looking at her.

"You're special because you do something that nobody else does. You tell me no."

"And you'd rather I be a yes-man?" he asked quietly.

"No. But knowing that I'm optional in your life…that's scary."

"You're not optional." He shook his head slowly, his voice raw and rough and perfect. "I don't know how you'll fit…as a friend or more, I don't know. But pushing you away hurt me as much as it hurt you. I'm sorry."

She licked her lips, all fumbling nerves now. "Do you think you might be able to tell me why you did? Not now, but soon?"

A slow nod was all the answer she needed as her phone vibrated. "Duty calls," she whispered as she waved her hand in the air.

"See you soon," he rumbled, his gaze locked on her mouth.

CHAPTER TWELVE

RYAN'S HAND shook as he started an email to Holly later that night.

If you aren't too tired, I can put on a pot of chamomile tea.

She knocked on his door ten minutes later. Her hair was damp and piled loosely on her head, her face scrubbed clean. She was wearing black running tights and an oversized hoodie.

"What are you smiling at?" she asked as he gestured for her to come inside.

"You look like you again," he said roughly. "Earlier today…the make up and the clothes. They weren't you."

"Yeah, I was in character. I should have shown your kids the wheelchair."

"Wheelchair?"

She tipped her head to the side. "My character's a paraplegic…wow, there's a lot we haven't talked about, isn't there?"

"I guess so." He pointed at the kettle. "Tea?"

"Yes, please."

When he turned around again, she was still standing.

"You can sit, you know."

"Um, shouldn't we go outside?"

He pointed to the baby monitor on the counter. "It's okay. I closed the kids' bedroom door." *So we can talk in private* was the unsaid promise, but talking was the last thing on his mind. He wanted to haul her hard against him and kiss her, over and over again. Slide his hands under that sweatshirt and explore every inch of her body. But she wanted to talk—and she was right, it was surprising how little they knew about each other.

"Do they all sleep together?" she asked as she curled onto one of his kitchen chairs.

"Yeah. For a while we were all sleeping in my room, but now—for the most part—Maya's in with Gavin and Jack. They have two twin beds in their room, she curls up with Gavin. And her room is where we pile all the laundry."

Her face crinkled as she laughed. "I love that."

"They sometimes fight like cats and dogs, but bedtime...they love to cuddle up." He watched as her laughter faded into a wistful expression. "Do you have any siblings?"

"Nope." She held her breath for a minute, then laughed nervously. "My mother didn't even want me. Once I was born, she was vigilant about birth control until she could convince a doctor to tie her tubes."

Ryan set the teapot he was prepping on the table and dropped into the chair beside hers. "Seriously?"

She lifted one shoulder and pulled her knee up in front

of her body. "I know, it's awful. I did a fair bit of therapy to deal with it in my early twenties."

He wrinkled his nose at the T-word.

"You're not a fan of talking about stuff, are you?"

"Nah. I just want to get better and move on, ya know?"

"Easier said than done."

"Yep. Turns out that's true." He shoved his hand through his hair.

She gave him a small smile. "You need a hair cut."

He laughed. "I need a lot of things."

She cocked one eyebrow. "Tell me what else you need."

Heat sizzled as, just like that, they slid from emotional conversation to innuendo and promise.

"Okay, I'll get a hair cut." Swallowing hard, he tipped back in his chair.

Her gaze heavy with barely restrained teasing, she nodded slowly as she dragged her lower lip between her teeth. Wet and shiny, the plump flesh begged to be kissed. Like his hair begged to be cut by her.

But they needed to take this slow.

"Tell me more about your mother."

Grinning, she shook her head. "Do you have clippers?"

"No."

"Really? You don't cut the boys' hair?"

Against his will, his mouth curved into a sloppy smile. "Yes, I have clippers. No, you can't cut my hair."

"Don't put off to tomorrow what you can do today."

"Fine. I'll cut my hair after you leave."

"I don't need to leave." Her gaze was steely, and part of him recognized she was talking about a lot more than a hair cut and tonight.

He didn't know what to do with that. He didn't want her to go, but she was a movie star who lived in Los

Angeles and he was a single dad with three young kids that needed to be kept out of the spotlight. She had to leave, as much as it would kill him.

"Yes, you do."

She shook her head. "Late call tomorrow, actually. But in general, I mean. I was thinking…" she trailed off, biting that lower lip again.

"I can't think about the future, Holly."

"I know." She shook her head. "For now, let's just focus on tonight. I don't have to leave *tonight*. I've got time to stay and talk, and cut your hair…and anything else. I'm all yours."

A million thoughts spilled between them as her eyes darkened with desire, but also something else—she wanted to do this. Cut his hair. Start something between them. That stirred a lot of previously smothered feelings deep inside him.

He didn't want her to go. He sank into that knowledge. It felt good to admit that to himself.

"You want to cut my hair?"

With a jerky nod, she leaned forward, stroking her fingertips down his temple. "Nobody lets me do stuff like that."

He grabbed her wrist, holding her hand against his cheek. Taking a ragged breath, he fought back the impulse to pull her into his lap and kiss her until she forgot all about his stupid hair. "Who else do you want to give a haircut to?"

"No one," she breathed. "Just you, I promise."

Good enough for him. "Wait here."

She grinned, a big, silly, happy smile as he shoved her back in her chair before sprinting upstairs. He grabbed the clippers, a towel, and after staring at the cupboard for ten agonizing seconds, a condom. Just in case.

Dirty bastard.

Yeah, maybe he was.

———

EVERY CELL in Holly's body hummed with anticipation. *You only wanted to talk,* said the angel on one shoulder. *Talking is overrated,* chimed the devil. The classic conflict.

But when Ryan re-appeared, his eyes were bright with desire. He stumbled over his words, telling her about the supplies he'd brought downstairs, and moved around the kitchen, closing the blinds on every window. Not really a conflict at all.

If anything, they'd both proven they were capable of restraint.

Too much restraint.

It was time to shuck the idea of what they should do… and just be.

"Where do you want me?" he asked.

"Here." She patted the chair he'd been sitting in. "And take off your shirt."

He froze, and gave her a look of concern that was beyond adorable.

"What?" She moved closer, taking the clippers and towel from his hands. The simple touch of her fingers grazing his was enough to light the room on fire.

He swallowed hard. "This is going to sound stupid, because I'm not normally a vain guy, but I haven't done a sit-up in like…six months."

"So?" She set the supplies on the table and reached for

the hem of his shirt. He didn't stop her, so she slid her palms under the fabric, touching the hot, warm skin of his abdomen. Her breath hitched as she absorbed his warmth and explored his body. He was big all over. Thick, muscled core, flaring broader up to his chest. No hair on his sides, but as her palms skimmed his body beneath his shirt, both of them breathing hard now, she found a vee of fur covering the centre of his chest, and she followed that line of hair down his midline to his tensing abs—maybe not six-pack defined, but strong and capable and panty-wetting all the same.

"Do you know how hard it was for me to avoid touching your nipples, there?" she asked, pressing onto her toes. She hooked her fingers into his belt and tugged his erection into the cradle of her pelvis. "Take off your shirt, Ryan. I want to sit on your lap and cut your hair."

"In that case," he said thickly before whipping his shirt off, giving her a first glimpse at his massive shoulders and chest. "You should take yours off as well."

Before he finished talking, she was wriggling her sweatshirt over her head, and as soon as she was free, his hands were on her, exploring her torso like she'd mapped his. Holding perfectly still, she felt the trail of goosebumps that followed his rough, calloused fingers as he teased the thin, criss-crossing straps of her sports bra. When he tried to tug one side over her shoulder, the many skinny straps in the back stopping him, he cursed and spun her around, pulling her hard against his front.

"What kind of devil bra is this?" He nipped at her neck and she sighed, stretching her head to the side. Offering herself to him.

"The kind that keeps us focused on a hair cut." Although she really liked his curls. They stood on end when he shoved his hands through them and felt like silk against her fingertips.

"I have scissors. I could cut it off."

She laughed and spun in his arms. "Sit down."

"Will you kiss me?"

"Over and over again, I promise."

Without letting go of her hips, he settled himself on the chair again, and she straddled his lap. In her tight spandex pants, she could feel every inch of how much he wanted her, and she rolled her hips, nestling his cock right at the apex of her heat. "Come here," she whispered, pulling his face to hers.

This kiss wasn't like the ones on the deck outside the lake house.

This wasn't just a kiss. This was heated foreplay and hunger let loose. She took her time, and he let her, but his hands were all over her back and her butt, and beneath her his entire body had turned to granite.

Her mountain man, in every sense of the word.

She pressed his lips open with hers, filled his mouth with her tongue. Slow, seductive strokes. Wet, teasing tastes. Breaths in and out, his air becoming hers and vice versa. All of it quieter than quiet and hotter than hot.

"How short do you want it?" she breathed after a time, as she kissed her way to his ear. She nosed at the yummy spot beneath his jaw, wanting to roll around in the perfection of his warm, tight skin.

"What?"

"Your hair."

"That wasn't a ruse for you to get in my pants?"

"Nope." She pushed back, bracing her hands on his shoulders. "I really want to cut your hair."

He blinked at her, his face blank with confusion, and she giggled.

"You kiss me like a porn star and then take a break to cut my damn hair?" Pressing his fingers into the small of her back, he urged her closer, and she almost went. Her lips were still wet from his tongue and her mouth was already lonely.

But she had a task, and she really wanted to get it done.

"And just how do you know how a porn star kisses?" She mock frowned at him.

"We have the Internet."

"For that, I'm going to take my time."

"I take it back. I'm an altar boy. You're an angel. Come back here with those angelic lips..."

She slipped off his lap, keeping her hands on his bare torso as she swayed around his body. "You look like a ruffian."

"Okay, let's go with that. I'm a bad boy." He reached his long arms behind him and possessively gripped the backs of her thighs, pinning her against the chair. "I'd like to corrupt you, come back to my lap."

"You're a reputable community member and a father and a member of the military. You need a haircut."

———

RYAN KNEW she was teasing and he thought he liked it. It was hard to tell, though, because his hormones were rampaging hard. "Are you doing this to take things slow?"

"Nope, although that's probably a good idea."

He was shooting himself in the foot all over the place. Well, no surprise there—this was the first time he'd needed to put the moves on someone in fifteen years. He was more than rusty. "Okay. I like the number two clippers around the side, and four on top."

He watched her studiously inspect the hair clipper and the comb attachments, then plug it in and approach him cautiously.

"Stop looking at me like that," she whispered with a smile as she mimed the action she'd do to trim the sides.

"I told you, I can't."

Knocking his side with her hip, she moved around him, then turned on the clippers. Small chunks of hair fell to his shoulders as she worked, her cool fingertips pressing at the base of his skull, then around his ear. Occasionally she swiped the hair off his shoulder with the flat of her palm, and each time she did, it took all his restraint to not pull her back into his lap.

Her hands on his skin? Pure, delicious torture.

"Okay, now I'm going to do the front," she said slowly, stepping between his legs. Her bare midriff was right in front of his face, and that proved more than he could handle. Before she could turn the clippers on again, he leaned forward and kissed the soft, trembling skin above her belly button.

"Looks good to me," he said, tasting her skin, not giving a fuck about his hair.

"You haven't seen it," she gasped.

"Wasn't talking about the haircut, Holly."

Rearing out of his seat, he picked her up and sat her on the table. His momentum rocked her backward and he followed, planting one hand on the wood top right behind her gorgeous ass, the other at the nape of her neck. Holding her in place.

And then he kissed her.

Like her kiss, it was full of intent and downright X-rated.

Unlike her kiss, there wasn't anything slow about how he stormed her mouth.

He couldn't get enough of her, and like a predator let off-leash, he didn't waste any time getting to what he really wanted—this woman, warm and soft and ready for more. Inside the tight confines of his arms, she wiggled closer, sliding her hands all over his bare torso.

Had he really worried about taking his shirt off? He'd never felt stronger, bigger, tougher. He sucked her lower lip into his mouth as he eased out of the kiss, rocking the pad of his thumb over the wet flesh as he pulled back just enough to catch her gaze.

"What do you like?"

She laughed, a slightly out-of-control shaky giggle that made him kiss her all over again.

"I like that," she said as she chased his mouth when he pulled away again.

"How far can we go?"

"Do you have a condom?" she asked in a quick, breathless rush.

He nodded, his dick surging full of blood at the promise of being put into action.

"I can be quiet," she whispered, rolling off the sports bra that had stymied him earlier, baring her breasts.

He wasn't sure he could be, but he would. Oh, God, he would.

Ducking his head, he breathed in the sugary sweetness of her skin, his mouth watering as he lost himself in her soft swells. Her breathy sounds turned to the quietest of groans as he tugged first one peak, then the other into his mouth. Her nipples were like raspberries, nubby and sweet on his tongue, and as she arched against him, grinding her pussy against his abdomen, he was struck with the need to know how she tasted all over.

Dropping to his knees, he curled his fingers under her waistband, shaking with the divided need to get her naked and not be a complete brute. She lifted her hips, giving him some clearance to slide her spandex pants down her legs, and then she froze.

From behind him, a whimper came across the baby monitor.

He dropped his head to her thigh, and she laughed, a half-hysterical, half-understanding giggle that made him like her all the more.

"I should go," she said with a groan, tugging him back to his feet. She kissed his chest, then looped her hands behind his head. "We'll do this again soon? And maybe do some of that talking we thought about earlier?"

"Yes, to both," he muttered, kissing her hard and fast before handing back her bra.

Over the monitor, another weak cry, this time calling out for Daddy, and she pushed him toward the stairs. "Go. I'll let myself out."

CHAPTER THIRTEEN

"MUST BE nice to just sit around and watch everyone else dig trenches and do section attacks all day," Tom Minelli drawled as he handed Ryan a hot cup of coffee.

"Yep." Ryan nodded to the back of the military transport truck, and they hoisted themselves up to sit, legs dangling above the still dew-wet grass. At the moment, the troops were getting breakfast from hay boxes set up on the other side of the command centre clearing. Ryan and his two quartermaster staff would eat after everyone else headed back into the field for the day's military exercise. "Speaking of which, has the CO talked to you about being the CQ next year?"

"Why do you think I brought you coffee? What's going on?" In their regiment, company quartermasters often stayed in that post for a number of years before being promoted out. Ryan had only been the CQ for a year, but he'd had a quiet chat with his commanding officer and the Regimental Sergeant Major about stepping back into a regular infantry grunt role at the next re-jigging of the command structure.

"I don't know. I've only got a few more years, ya know? I want to do the fun stuff. Blow shit up, lead a night raid."

"Kind of screws you up for promotion."

"I don't care about that." And he really didn't. Everything had changed with Lynn's death. "I'm going to have to find a new day job. Something with more regular hours than being a paramedic. If I stay in the Army, too, it's gotta be something for *me*."

"Wow. That sounds…healthy."

Ryan snorted. "Better late than never, right?"

"So who's got the kids this weekend?"

"Your sister and Jake. Good practice for them, she said." Tom was the third-oldest Minelli sibling. Zander, the oldest, was in the reg forces out west, the only one of their friends to go career Army. Rafe was the next oldest, and he was currently on the other side of the breakfast line, jacking up some young corporal for not shaving properly. Tom was a few years younger than Ryan, and his sister Dani had the misfortune of being the only girl and the baby. When she'd started dating Jake Foster, everyone had something to say.

Dani didn't care, and neither did Jake—who was also in the reserves, but he'd skipped the weekend exercise officially because of work, but unofficially, Ryan knew he was playing Uncle Jake, and he appreciated that more than his friend might ever know.

"God, I'm going to be an uncle again before too long, aren't I?"

Ryan grinned. "Probably. I think Dani's just vain enough to want to look good in her wedding dress, but…"

"Dude, that's my sister!"

"You started it. Besides, she was my junior medic. I don't want to think of her like that, either."

"So. Hockey?"

"Yep. Flames are doing well," Ryan laughed as Tom made a face—he was a Canucks fan.

"Their lucky streak has to run out sometime." Nobody in Pine Harbour was a Flames fan, although that would change when Zander came home.

"Let me guess, your brother is being insufferable about it."

"He's such an asshole. I told him he couldn't stay with me when he comes back this summer." Tom shrugged at Ryan's surprised look. "Yeah, I know, he's visiting a lot lately. Gearing up to get out, I guess. He's talking about starting a security company here, if you want to get in on that with him."

"Maybe." It didn't really excite Ryan, but work was work. He'd needed to step back and focus on his kids, but in the last few weeks—since Holly crept into his life—he'd been thinking hard about what the future would look like. At the moment he was coasting, but it wouldn't take much for that to turn into drifting, and before he knew it, he'd be a slacker without a job, with kids who were growing up and what would he be modelling for them?

He needed *something*. But it had to be regular day-time hours. "Yeah, I'll talk to Zander when he's back next."

"The Park Service might have openings, too…" Tom trailed off. He was a park ranger, which was a great job, but those wouldn't be the positions that would come up. Starting over again in his mid-thirties wasn't the same as looking for a job straight out of college. "Anyway, yeah, I'm good to take on the CQ hat. You gonna show me all the secrets?"

"Definitely."

They finished their coffee in silence, then made their way to the breakfast line. Ryan rubbed his chest, trying like hell not to think about his kids. Jake would probably be making them waffles right about now, before heading to work for the day. Dani had said something about baking cookies. They were having a blast and he shouldn't worry.

He did, though, and he felt a heavy ache of relief an hour later when Dani texted a picture of Maya, elbow deep in a mixing bowl.

Thank you, he messaged back.

Stop worrying, his friend responded, and he winced. Was he that obvious?

He spent the rest of the day making himself busy, and when night fell, he left the CQ in the hands of his storeman and went to find the enemy party commander. For most training exercises, they asked another regiment to provide a small attack force, and that group operated independently, providing a realistic challenge.

"Sir," he said, snapping to attention.

"Sergeant Howard, how can I help you?"

"Well, sir, I was hoping I could help you. Need another man for your midnight raid?"

"And how do you know we're going to do a midnight raid?" The captain grinned at him, and Ryan smiled right back.

"Lucky guess."

———

FROM THE DECK of the lake house, she couldn't actually see Ryan's place. The foliage on the forest was too dense, and the deck was just off-angle to see up the lane. But the row of cottages between the two homes was quiet today, everyone else either inside or away on this lazy Sunday. The security fence had been taken down the day before, as they'd moved to their last filming location, this time in town. So when she heard a big vehicle—a truck, maybe— her heart skipped a beat. And when her phone lit up a few seconds later, the most ridiculous grin split her face in two.

Ryan: Back from that weekend thing. Gotta get the kids in a few. Are you around?

Shoving her notebook and blanket into the Adirondack chair she'd officially claimed as her own, she dashed down the steps and up the lane. She was breathless as she skidded to a stop on his porch, where he'd piled a shocking amount of Army green stuff.

When he stepped out of the kitchen, slowing to a stop as he caught sight of her, she did geeky jazz hands because she was nervous. And it didn't help that he looked extra good. *Oh my God,* she thought. *Why does this man not walk around in fatigues all the time?* On the top, he was stripped down to just a green t-shirt, and his camouflaged pants rode low on his hips. The imposing black leather boots gave him an extra inch of height he definitely didn't need. In his regular clothes, Ryan was six-foot-something of down-home deliciousness. Now he was a warrior giant, big and bad and all hers...for the time being.

"So yeah...I'm around," she said, her voice doing a weird sing-song thing that made the jazz hands look totally normal. *Oh god.*

The look on his face made it all worthwhile. He held her gaze for a moment, his own smile slower and less nerve-twitchy than hers. "I'm filthy, I should warn you. But you're a sight for sore eyes."

She didn't care if he'd rolled around in a mud puddle. Three days without touching him was officially too long. *You're in such trouble, missy.* She knew it. The film would be done principal shooting in another five weeks. And Ryan was too fragile for a real relationship. She could practically see the timer on the end of their...whatever they were doing.

But knowing all of that didn't make a lick of difference to her over-eager heart. She nibbled on her lower lip as she moved closer, taking in the streaks of dirt and remnants of green and black camo makeup on his face. "I kind of like this rugged warrior look."

He held out his arms and she fell against his chest, squeezing tight as she moulded herself to his body. He smelled like hard work and metal, and if he didn't have to get kids and probably sleep for a week, she'd offer to help him scrub every last bit of olive-green paint off his lightly tanned skin.

"You got some colour this weekend," she murmured as she ran her fingers over his forehead and into his hair.

"Ever heard of a farmer's tan? Army guys have it just as bad." He grinned as he tugged down the collar of his green t-shirt, showing the paler skin she'd gotten fleetingly familiar with the week before. She pressed up onto her toes and kissed his collarbone where a light dusting of freckles blended the tan line into the soft curls of hair rising from the centre of his chest. *Rugged.* That was the only word for Ryan Howard. Big, rough, work-honed, and stronger than strong.

She'd never been more attracted to a man in her entire life.

"What are you thinking?" he asked, his voice rough and catching on the last word.

She closed her eyes and snuggled her face into his chest. "Inappropriate thoughts."

His hands had been resting on her hips, loosely possessive, but now he held her tighter, his hands splaying wide across her lower back, his fingertips branding the top of her ass. "Like what?"

That husky note in his voice did dangerous things between her legs. "Showering together."

There were a lot of bulky things on his utility belt—a knife, some pouches—but there was no mistaking the heavy erection growing against her belly. "I'd like that."

"I can tell," she whispered, rubbing against him. With a groan, he lifted her up, cupping her bottom as he carried her into the house. Holly laughed as she held on tight, but the laughter died when he set her on his kitchen table and slid his hands into her hair, holding her in place so he could slant his face over hers and tease her lips open.

"One of these days, we're going to have more than a few minutes together," he growled before tasting her, the tip of his tongue sliding against the sensitive flesh inside her mouth. The very thought of what they could do with endless amounts of time made her nipples tighten, and without thinking, she grabbed his hand and slid it over her breast. She needed his palm there, his heavy touch rough against the sensitive nub.

He did her one better, cupping and squeezing her overheated flesh as he tugged their cores together.

Face flushed, heart pounding a mile a minute, Holly whimpered as Ryan started to rock against her, deepening his kiss at the same time. This wasn't why she'd run over. But now that it was happening…

She gave herself over to the kiss and the caresses, the heat and the whispered words. Somehow she found the bottom of his shirt and tugged it out of his pants. The touch of his bare skin, hot and pebbled to the touch as her fingers raised goosebumps, was enough to melt her inside. Their connection astonished her—any love scene she'd ever acted out, any real kiss with previous men, they all paled against this desperate, honest grinding.

Ryan pulled back from her mouth, searching her face for something—permission?—as he rolled her nipple beneath his palm, then skated that hand down her shaking midsection to the button on her jeans. "Can I?"

Oh God. This man and his manners. She was going to die. "I thought you had to go get your kids."

His eyes darkened and he licked his lips. "I've got time to make you feel good."

The week before, she'd been one hundred percent ready to have sex with him. And today she'd literally raced over when he messaged her. So why was she balking now? "Um…" She dragged a stuttering breath into her lungs, then grabbed his t-shirt as he eased back, confusion on his face. "No, wait. I want…" She let out a watery laugh. "Okay, look. The list of things I want to do with you definitely includes whatever you were thinking. But like you say—we need more time."

"Time isn't something I've got a lot of," he said, smoothing his hands over her hips. He leaned in and she eagerly kissed him again, but this time it was calmer. More kissing-for-kissing's sake, less feverish-race-to-get-naked. She'd kick herself for this later, but before they went any further, she needed to make sure they were on the same page.

And before that could happen, she needed to convince

herself she wasn't falling hard for this man. They didn't need to talk for her to know that Ryan's heart was full-up with his kids and his grief, and she was—at best—a sexy distraction.

It wasn't a common role for her, but she could do fun and sexy. Taking a deep breath, she walked her fingers up the centre of his t-shirt, over the corded muscles in his neck, and across his cut jaw, ending up at his talented mouth. The guy could kiss, that was for sure. "Then we'll need to make time," she purred. "Stolen moments here and there. If you see me, you grab me and kiss me. And when the time is right, we'll make sure that it's good for both of us."

CHAPTER FOURTEEN

HE COULD FEEL her eyes on him, watching as he unloaded firewood. The cast and crew were having a bonfire on the weekend—some sort of team-building event that Holly wasn't looking forward to—and Olivia had tasked him with the site prep. Picnic tables assembled, fire pit dug out, hardwood stacked.

"Enjoying yourself?" he finally asked, ambling over to the deck where she sat, kind of reading a binder. Mostly just watching him, though.

His ego wasn't complaining.

"Definitely." She did a quick glance around, but they were alone. Her grin got bigger as she roamed her gaze over his body. Two days had passed since they'd shared that last scorching kiss, and she'd been working non-stop. Last night she'd called him from her bed, close to midnight, and they'd talked for a few minutes before going a couple of rounds on almost goodnights, then one regretful real one. She'd been the one to actually hang up, and he'd held his phone against his chest for a long time after, his cock half-swollen just from the sound of her voice.

Now his dick just needed one glance from her to bounce to that almost perpetual state. The Holly Effect.

She set down her work, but didn't get up. Her smile settled into a lazy twist at her lips, and it was sexy as hell. "You have to get kids soon?"

He nodded. "Bus will arrive in ten minutes. Maya's at a friend's house until dinner, having a playdate." The first one he'd accepted. He was getting there. Slowly. "You working on lines or something?"

"Yep, for tomorrow. I'm actually done for the day." She stretched out the last few words, and he wasn't going to pass up the unspoken request for spending some time together.

"You want to join us for dinner? We're having hamburgers, nothing fancy."

Why did such a simple offer light up her eyes like that? "Your kids won't wonder why you're having the movie lady over?"

He laughed. "As long as the movie lady doesn't kiss me, they won't think twice about it."

"Deal." Her eyes crinkled, and he bounded up the stairs. She tipped her face up as he got closer. "Hello, there."

"Since I can't kiss you later…" He leaned over and pressed his lips against hers. Hard yielding to soft. Brittle won over by sweet. She parted for him and he stroked her cheek as he deepened the kiss, wishing they had more than a few minutes. She stirred something inside him, a youthfulness that made him wish she wasn't disappearing in a few weeks.

There'd never be enough time with her. He'd been grappling with that surprising realization for a few days—however long he'd have with Holly, he'd want more. It was for the best they knew from the start that there was also an end.

Bittersweet was better than broken-hearted any day of the week. In theory. Each day he kissed her, though, was another day he thought about inviting her to stay for the summer.

But stay where, exactly? She was living in his in-laws' home. Sure, all their furniture had been put in storage—a ridiculously wasteful idea he'd scoffed at when Olivia told him that was the plan, although it made the idea of maybe sharing her bed a bit easier.

Sharing his wasn't an option. Not yet. Maybe not ever.

Jesus, he was all kinds of fucked up. And he was still kissing her. Sort of.

"You okay?" she asked softly, kissing the corner of his mouth.

He shook his head. Freudian slip, body-language style. "Yeah. No. I'm a bit distracted. Not your fault." He cleared his mind and kissed her again, with purpose, and when he pulled back she was smiling, a soft, tempting look he wanted to put on her face over and over again. "Okay, I gotta run. We should be back from getting Maya around five. Come over any time after that."

———

HOLLY WATCHED Ryan hop back into his truck and leave, then went inside.

Where Emmett was waiting, arms crossed. *Oh, shit.* "What?"

"So that's the crush, huh? Cute guy with the cute kids?"

"Yep." She could trust Emmett to be discreet. But that didn't mean she was going to give him any more than what he'd already observed. She went to the fridge and opened it.

"You going to be able to say goodbye to all that cuteness when we leave?"

She was glad her head was buried in a search for salad stuff so he couldn't see her face. *No, I'm not sure I'll be able to handle that in the least.* She was pretty sure she'd need to spend a month sobbing on Liana's couch in Nashville. *A month you could spend in Pine Harbour, instead.* So unhelpful, her inner psyche. She needed to just enjoy what time they were going to have together and stop trying to manufacture something impossible out of wishes and dreams.

Behind her, she heard Emmett shift off his stool, then he appeared over her shoulder. "What are you doing?"

"Looking for stuff to make a salad with."

"Hungry?"

She took a deep breath and flashed her assistant a winning smile. "Not exactly. I'm going to the cute family's house for dinner, and I want to take a salad."

"Oh, sweetie…" He gave her a sympathetic pouty-lip frown and she thumped him in the chest as they both stood up.

"Don't, okay? Don't make a big deal out of this or anything. Just…can you pull out everything I need to make a salad?"

"Do you want me to just make it?"

"No," she retorted more sharply than necessary. "I want to do it."

"But you need me to tell you what goes into a salad." He crossed his arms and raised one eyebrow.

"Hey. I know it includes lettuce. And other stuff. It's just the combinations that I'm fuzzy on. I can make a *salad*." Surely. She was a skilled professional, how hard could it be? Besides, she had her phone. She grabbed him by the shoulders and steered him out of the kitchen. "Actually, I'm good."

"Googling doesn't count," he hollered as he skipped away.

"Yes it does," she muttered under her breath, turning back to the fridge. Strawberries. Kids like berries, right? Pulling out her phone, she typed **strawberry salad** into the search bar and said a silent prayer to the Internet gods.

An hour and a half later, she knocked on Ryan's door, pretending she wasn't nervous as hell. The sight of him swinging the door open eased that just a bit—until his gaze caught hers in that slow-down-the-world kind of way that made her mouth dry and her heart hammer extra-hard against her chest.

"Hi," she breathed, and he just nodded, a slow smile curling up the corners of his mouth as he stepped back to let her in, his eyes never leaving hers. She broke the contact to greet the kids.

"I brought a salad," she said, holding the bowl out. "It's not muffins, but it does have strawberries in it."

"I don't like salad," Maya said solemnly. Jack poked her and she rolled her eyes. "I like strawberries."

Holly laughed. "I don't like salad either."

"Then why did you bring it?" Gavin asked. They were all crowding around her, little bouncing bundles of curiosity, and she wanted to eat them up with a spoon.

Ryan swooped in, taking the bowl and giving his kids a

glare, which she also thought was pretty cute. "Okay, that's enough rudeness for one dinner. Can you guys say something nice to our guest?"

"Thank you for coming to dinner, Holly." Gavin said it totally straight, his deadpan delivery cracking up his siblings.

Ryan just shook his head as he pulled a plate of raw burgers from the fridge. "I'm going to put these on the barbecue." He gave her a warm look as he slid past, murmuring something about good luck under his breath.

I don't need luck, she thought. She already had something in common with the kids—she was a big fan of their dad. And despite the teasing, she could see how attached they were to Ryan. "I bet your dad's a good cook, huh?"

"He's okay," Jack answered first. "But he doesn't bake. Those muffins you gave us were awesome."

"I didn't bake them, either. It was a stretch of my cooking ability to make this salad."

"Which you don't like."

She grinned. "I like that it's good for me. And it's not awful. I hope. Don't tell me if it's awful, okay?"

Gavin nodded. "We wouldn't, anyway. That would be rude. My dad said we had to be on our best behaviour or he's going to tell Uncle Rafe that we're allergic to pizza."

"Wow, that's some stiff penalty. Did you guys all go to school today?"

"I go to pwe-school," Maya said, twirling in a circle.

"That sounds like fun." Holly dropped down, squatting so she was at eye level with the tiny dancer. "Do you dance at school?"

"Uh huh."

"I sometimes dance at work."

"My mommy used to dance with me. She's dead now."

Maya kept twirling, oblivious to the stunned expression Holly was trying to wipe off her face.

"I know, sweetie. I'm sorry," she whispered, blinking back unexpected tears.

In her peripheral vision, she saw Jack leave the room, and her heart clenched. Had she done that? She glanced up at Gavin, who just shrugged. "He gets sad when Maya says things like that. She's just little, she doesn't know what that word feels like here." He pointed to his chest.

"Should I get your dad?"

The seven-year-old shook his head, wise beyond his years. "He'll be okay. He needs a minute. Maybe tell Daddy later. He doesn't like secrets."

She'd already learned that lesson. "Okay." She gave him a small smile. "You're pretty brave."

He shrugged. "I get sad, too."

"Of course. I'm sad about it, and I never got a chance to know your mom." She stood up. "Do you have any pictures of her?"

Gavin took her hand and led her into the living room. On the wall was a matching set of black picture frames, laid out with deliberate care in pattern on the wall. Holly blinked back more tears. Before Ryan's wife was killed, she was a woman who danced with her daughter and carefully organized family pictures with pride. Anything else she'd heard about Lynn Howard faded away.

"Where are you?" she asked Gavin, her voice catching with emotion. "Oh, there you are!"

He was smaller in the picture hung in the middle of the wall, and Maya was a baby. The only formal photo of the entire family, it was taken at the lake. Holly recognized the railing as being Lynn's parents' house. Ryan held a gangly little Gavin in his arms, Lynn—a beautiful woman, taller than Holly, with long blonde hair—had baby Maya in hers, and Jack stood proudly in front of them.

"And that's my hockey picture from last year, and this is when we went to Canada's Wonderland, and that's Maya's first birthday."

From behind them, Maya whizzed past, leaping onto the couch beneath the pictures. She jammed her hands on her hips and started singing a song about cake, and how much she loved it.

"We get it, Maya. You love cake!" Gavin said, getting exasperated. "Her birthday was a couple of months ago, but she's still kind of obsessed."

Holly laughed and wiggled her hips to Maya's tune, only to be interrupted by Ryan clearing his throat from the doorway. She spun around, cheeks flushing. "Dinner time?"

"Almost," he said quietly, his gaze unreadable. Did he hate her being in this room? Had she overstepped by asking about the family pictures?

"Do you need help?"

He shook his head. "Jack's setting the table."

She nodded, her pulse skipping uncomfortably in her throat. "I'll toss the salad?"

"Okay." He stepped back as she walked toward him, but when the two kids sprinted past, heading to the kitchen and out of sight, he moved back into her path, blocking her in the living room. His chest rose and fell in front of her, and she took her time looking up at him, nervous to see his face up close. He was so skittish, and even though he said he wouldn't run again, she couldn't be sure he really knew that about himself.

When she met his gaze, she didn't see nerves. The pain on his face was a million times worse.

"Hey, it's okay," she whispered as her stomach twisted in knots. He *so* wasn't ready for another relationship. "Let's go have dinner."

"I..." he started, then trailed off. She wanted to kiss him, but that might not make him feel better. All the little muscles in his face worked hard as he looked down at her, tiny twitches all over the place as he worked to keep control of the reaction he was having. When he spoke again, though, he was calmer, and the storm clouds in his eyes cleared. "I can put the kids to bed early, if you can stay. They all had a busy day, they'll be tired."

"Sure." She smiled. "I'll go after dinner and come back once they're asleep."

"You don't need to."

"But I will." She reached out, squeezing his forearm. "At your speed, and on your terms. And just between us, I promise."

Slipping past him, not wanting him to see the heartache mirrored on her own face, she joined the kids at the table. He went out the side door to the barbecue, returning a minute later with a plate of burgers.

Dinner sped by in a flurry of questions. Why didn't Holly eat bread? Were tomatoes a vegetable or a fruit? What was her favourite hockey team, and then why didn't she know that the Kings were *not* the team to cheer for? Before she knew it, they were clearing the dishes and Ryan was making threatening noises about homework and bath time. She thanked the kids for having her over, gave Maya a hug, and took her almost empty salad bowl back to the house down at the lake.

She left her heart behind in that kitchen.

And as she put the small leftover salad away in the fridge, she thought for a second that she might not go back for it. *You have no place barging into their life,* she told herself. *They're just surviving, and you could break them all just by being there, and then gone.*

If Ryan asked her to stay, she'd find a way. She had a film shoot scheduled for the fall, but it was just six weeks. And after that…

But she'd always be coming and going.

And she'd always be a secret.

How Lynn died…Ryan would never want his children exposed to the scrutiny of Hope Creswell's world, where paparazzi would go nuts for the tragic death of a woman in the wrong place at the wrong time. Then the sordid details of her marijuana use would come out. And the whispers of a secret disease she'd kept from her husband.

It wouldn't take long for paparazzi to wonder why she was lingering in the small Canadian town once filming was over. Even though she wasn't high-profile enough for TMZ to hound her regularly, she'd rate enough for *something.* Ugh. Another reason for her agent to start pursuing New York stage options for the next year. She loved acting, but being a celebrity was entirely overrated.

She avoided Emmett, or maybe he avoided her, and when Ryan texted that the kids were in bed, she slipped out again, meeting him on the porch.

"Do you want to come in?" he asked quietly after kissing her hard on the mouth. There was a lot poured into that kiss, and she couldn't unpack it—didn't want to try, lest she get something wrong. Get her hopes up. Or have them dashed. Both equally bad.

She was walking a tightrope over a pit of snakes, it felt like.

Didn't stop her from closing the gap between them and

hugging him tight. But it did prevent her from accepting the invitation to be somewhere more private.

"It's nice out here…" She pointed to the steps. "And that way we might actually talk."

"That's not nearly as much fun as what I was thinking," he muttered against her temple, and she grinned.

But when they sat, he was the first one to launch into it, and he didn't hold back. "I'm sorry about earlier. Somehow you being here at night is different than during the day, with my kids." He took a deep breath. "You're good with them."

"They're fun."

He laughed. "That was them being on their best behaviour, if you can imagine."

"I can. I was a kid once, remember. Although I missed out on the sibling fun."

He laughed. "I was the middle of five kids. It was a bit chaotic."

"Wow." A small pang of envy twinged in her gut. "Are you close with them now?"

He shrugged and nodded. "Yeah. My brother and I are pretty tight. My sisters…they're sisters." His quiet laugh warmed her as she watched him think about his siblings. "And now they're all mothers, including the youngest one, who's still practically a kid herself. I mean, she's the same age I was when I had Jack, but that was somehow different. Sometimes I feel so old."

"You're not." She nudged his shoulder with hers. "Or if you are, you're super cute for an old guy."

He shot her a disbelieving look.

"What?"

"I have trouble wrapping my head around that. You thinking I'm…"

"Cute?" She grinned. "So cute. Also handsome, rugged —" He laughed, interrupting her, and she giggled before continuing. "When I first met you, I thought you looked like a lumberjack. But cute."

"There's that word again."

"You're totally lumbersexual."

"What the hell is that?" He dragged his lower lip between his teeth as he pulled her close.

"You know, like metrosexual? But the opposite. Lots of plaid, rocking a beard, knows how to handle an…ax."

"Jesus," he growled, cupping her cheek. "You make it sound dirty."

"If I'm lucky," she whispered, parting her lips for him. Their tongues tangled, breath rushing faster as she rose onto her knees, her fingers sliding over his stubbled cheeks. She clung to him as he deepened the kiss, but pulled back when he tried to tug her into his lap. "Wait…"

His chest shuddered as she slid back to sit next to him, and he didn't say anything at first.

But she didn't say anything, either. She didn't want to put into words why she'd thrown on the brakes again. *You might think you're the needy one, Ryan Howard, but I've got you beat.*

"You deserve more than this," he finally said, his voice thick and heavy.

What? "No…" God, that was so not what she wanted him to think. She was scared of being hurt, but he was still the best thing to happen to her heart, ever. "I don't expect anything, Ryan."

"You keep saying that. No expectations." He cracked his jaw as he worked it from side to side, clearly considering his next words carefully. She was glad—this felt precariously close to the last two times they'd slid apart. "But you *deserve* more."

"You're the nicest guy I've ever kissed, Ryan. If we can only have a secret fling, or whatever this is…I'm never going to say no to that. I'm not saying no right now. I'm just…nervous, maybe."

He nodded a few times, but she got the feeling it was more a processing nod than one of agreement. "I've never done the casual sex thing," he finally said, his voice low. "Before Lynn, I had two girlfriends, not serious, but steady."

Steady. Such a sweet word. She had no idea what it was like to trust someone enough with her insides to go steady. Until now. Oh, the irony.

And she wanted to trust Ryan, and would, even knowing the risks. But there was a strong chance that he was going to break her heart. Maybe knowingly, maybe not. Either way, falling for him meant willfully dodging around a dozen warning signs. *Construction Zone. No Traffic Allowed. Beware of Emotionally Locked-up Men. All Hearts Past This Point Belong to Someone Else.*

It was the last one that she thought of, constantly. She felt no jealousy toward Ryan's wife. The poor woman died far too young, and her family was struggling because of it. Holly's only thought about Lynn Howard was that she'd been blessed with a beautiful family.

She traced a circle on his knee, her index finger rubbing against the worn denim, faded white. "I've never really had serious relationships, not like a marriage, but I've never done the casual thing, either. Seven. That's my number. My longest relationship was almost two years, and only that's because we were both working so much on opposite ends of the globe that we never spent enough time in the same place to realize we weren't a good fit."

"How many of those guys treated you right?"

"They all treated me better than most men treated my mother," she whispered. "I've had a fucked-up model to follow. And my standards are both low and high at the same time."

"If you don't want to do this…"

"I do. But maybe not like this. Not when your kids could wake up." She kissed his cheek. "I don't want you to ever regret what we do." *I don't want to be the cause of your regret.*

"Okay." He laced his fingers through hers and looked up at the stars. "My in-laws will be back soon. They'll be staying with us. I might be able to get away at night then. We'll see."

Lynn's parents. The weight of that landed squarely on her shoulders, pushing the last trace of arousal out of her body.

"I need to tell you something," she said quietly, leaning against his arm. "Before dinner, while you were grilling, Maya brought up Lynn, and Jack got upset."

"Ah." He cleared his throat. "I'm sorry."

"Nothing to be sorry about. I'm just telling you because…" She laughed a little. "Gavin said I should, to be honest. He said, 'Daddy doesn't like secrets.' And I know that's true. So I thought you should know. It wasn't a big deal, really."

"Okay, thanks."

She sat up and turned toward him. He was staring into the distance again.

"Can I ask about her?"

A guarded expression dropped onto his face, but he nodded slowly. "Sure."

"There are rumours. I try not to listen to them."

Like shutters slamming closed, he dropped his gaze to the floor. "Most of them are true."

"She was sick?"

He nodded jerkily, and her heart stung like she'd just been whipped.

"I'm sorry. I don't want to bring up anything that's too upsetting."

"What do you want to know, Holly?" He blinked up at her, his face pale now, and she inched closer again. Not too close—just friendly-like. *I'm on your side, Ryan.*

"Nothing. I just…she was your wife. And the mother of your children. If you ever want to talk about her, talk about the good things…" A few unexpected tears slid down her cheeks. She was mortified that she was crying, because this wasn't about her. She took a deep breath and tried again. "I'd like to hear about her. That's all."

He shook his head, not looking at her. "It's too hard."

"Okay, forget I said anything." She swallowed hard, trying to get ahold of her reaction. Exhaling roughly, she changed the subject. "Are you going to come to the bonfire this weekend? Olivia said she'd invited your family."

He nodded. Acknowledging the invitation? Or would he actually come out?

"It should be…well-catered." She couldn't bring herself to say fun. It wouldn't be, not really.

He huffed a humourless laugh. "That sounds like code for no marshmallows."

"Probably not."

He shook his head, laughing more freely now. "Okay, we'll bring our own."

CHAPTER FIFTEEN

THEY SHARED a few more kisses that week, and a lot of fleeting looks as their paths crossed, but he didn't invite her over again and she didn't wander up the lane. There was an unspoken agreement that they needed to pace themselves, because it wouldn't take much to have them rutting on the floor of his kitchen like animals.

Holly's pulse thumped hard in her neck as that visual burned itself into her brain. Ryan, shaking with need, holding himself above her. How wet she'd be for him, welcoming him into her body. The weight of him as he'd thrust into her, claiming her.

Her cheeks heated to a million degrees and she twisted her face into her pillow. It was late, and she'd had a long day. Joshua had been a toddler on the set, throwing tantrum after tantrum. She needed to sleep. Her personal trainer's voice echoed in her head. *We age while awake. Divas get their eight hours.* It was so unfair that men looked better and better with age.

Another image flashed in her mind. Ryan with greying temples. Still big and broad. A few more eye crinkles. She pressed her legs together and swallowed a moan. She needed to get laid. They needed a night together, but she couldn't ask him for that. Her nipples hated her for not skipping up the lane and knocking on his door.

Turning out her lamp, she rolled onto her stomach, sliding her hand between her body and the mattress. She rocked her pelvis, lightly teasing herself as her fingers danced around her clit. Already she was breathing hard and soaking wet. It wouldn't take much, and she wanted to hang on to this moment, this fantasy of Ryan in all his different possibilities.

When her phone vibrated on the nightstand, she almost didn't roll over. *Leave me alone*, she thought, thinking it must be Liana or her mother. But at the last minute she reached for it, and then her heartbeat picked up even more.

Ryan: What are you doing?

She bit her lip as she re-read the words.

Hands shaking, she dialled his number.

"So you're not asleep." His voice rumbled in her ear, making her chest all tight and achey, and deep in her belly, her womb clenched. The effect this man had on her was lethal.

"Not exactly, no." Her words rushed out of her on a single breath and she closed her eyes, every part of her hanging on for his response.

"Where are you?"

She smiled. "In bed."

"Me too."

Oh, goodness. Heat swirled through her like the liquid wax in the top of a candle. Burning hot, freezing into a solid at the edges. She felt brittle and melty at the same time. *Fuck it*, she thought. "I'm naked."

Rough breathing sounds were his first response. They worked for her. She trailed her free hand down her stomach, pausing just above her sex. His next question, low and urgent, almost made her pass out. "Are you touching yourself?"

"I was. I was thinking about you, and how close we've come a few times..." She sighed, pressing the heel of her hand low in her belly to keep from stroking lower. *Not yet.* "How good you'd look above me."

"I have a fantasy about you, too," he said, and the hitch in his breath as he admitted that made her dig her heels into the bed, tensing up all over. "It's the middle of the summer and you're spread out on a blanket in a field somewhere. Naked. You're gorgeous."

Middle of the summer. She'd be gone by then. She closed her eyes again, refusing the tears that prickled there. "I can feel you, pressing my thighs open."

"Are you wet for me, Holly?" He exhaled, then groaned. "Touch yourself for me."

"I am," she whispered as she gave in to her need, sliding her fingers through her folds. "Are you...?"

"Yeah. I wish this was your hand jerking me off."

"It is." She allowed herself a small moan—as much for him as herself—and arched her back, straining her nipples against the cool top sheet above her. "And you're touching me. Fingering me."

He groaned in her ear. "I want to feel how tight you are. Hot and wet for me."

She rolled her hips up, tilting her pelvis so she could follow his instructions. "I am." The admission was freeing. "Just for you."

"I want to taste you." He was growling now, his words fast and hard in her ear. She could picture his hand, pumping up and down his shaft as he worked them both toward their release. "Lick you up until you scream."

"Yes…" she whispered, panting as she rolled the pads of her fingers over her clit, imagining they were his tongue.

"Suck on you as you come—"

He kept talking, dirty words that enflamed her senses, but she was already orgasming, her sex spasming against her hand, fresh floods of moisture proof of his effect on her. *Oh. My. God.* She struggled to catch her breath as her limbs twitched, and she pressed her face into the phone, desperate to hear Ryan losing it. He grunted in her ear, then let out a long, low, strangled sound. *So that's what he sounds like when he climaxes.* She pressed her lips together, happier than happy with that secret knowledge.

Together, they took long, shaky breaths. Then Ryan cleared his throat. "I was kind of expecting you to not respond until the morning or something. But…that was really, really nice."

She laughed, pressing the phone tighter to her ear. "Yeah."

"I can't wait to do it again, maybe in the same room."

"Same."

He took a deep breath. "You're going to sleep now?"

Definitely. "Uh huh."

"Sweet dreams, then."

"Oh, you can count on that."

"Me, too. See you tomorrow night. Try not to blush too hard."

Impossible. "I can't wait."

————

"IS it time for us to go to the party yet?"

Ryan's kids had been perched at the kitchen window for thirty minutes, watching the stream of vehicles come in the lane. They were parked almost all the way up to his house now. *Definitely enough people so we can blend into the crowd.* After the scorching hot phone sex the night before with Holly, Ryan was more than a little nervous about sharing the same space as her, and people who knew him —like Olivia.

She was going to know in a split second that something was up.

Like his dick.

He needed Prozac to get through this party. What he had instead were three unbelievably excited kids. That was probably karma hard at work.

Not that he regretted last night—after Holly pulling back a few times, he wasn't sure where she was at, and he wasn't in a position to push her if she didn't want to take their physical relationship to the next level. When she sucked in that little quick breath, then spilled out those two magic words—*"I'm naked"*—he'd done a fist pump like a giddy teenager.

Now he just needed to keep a lid on his reaction to her, and make sure nobody fell into the fire.

"Yep, it's party time. Everyone remember the rules?" He opened the door and they all filed out onto the porch. "Keep an eye out for cars. Keep to the side. No touching the fire. Ask for someone to help with the—"

Crap he almost forgot the marshmallows. He darted back inside and grabbed the party-sized bag. He handed it to Jack to carry, then they were off.

As they neared the gathering of cast and crew and locals, he caught sight of Rafe and Dean Foster, heads bowed. They were talking shop, no doubt. Part of him wanted to slide on over there and find out what was up—either cop talk or Army talk, and he'd know the players in both conversations. But that stuff was never kid-friendly, and it wasn't like he had someone else to hand the munchkins off to.

And as Maya slide around his leg, hiding from all the faces she didn't recognize, he couldn't begrudge his Non-Stop Dad role. They needed him, and he needed to be needed. It gave him a sense of balance—he'd never get over feeling like he'd failed Lynn somehow, but he wasn't going to fail their kids.

"You want up, baby?" He stroked her hair as she shook her face into his thigh. *Nope.* "Okay. Hey, I see food. Who's hungry?"

He navigated his tiny clan toward the buffet. Still no sign of Holly, but Olivia was talking to the pretty woman who was staying in cottage number four...*Parvati.* The name slipped into his mind from a conversation with Holly. An actress, and the director's wife. Ryan lifted his hand when Olivia caught sight of him, and she waved them over.

"You came! Hi, guys." She got down to his kids' level and leaned in, lowering her voice. "There's so much good food. Would anyone like a fruit kebab? Or maybe a sausage on a bun? Tiny quiches?"

"We brought our own marshmallows," Jack said, holding out the bag. Olivia winked at him and whispered that he could hide it under the buffet so they'd be all theirs once the bonfire really got going.

"I want Holly," Maya whispered, tugging on Ryan's hand.

Olivia shot him a confused look, and he took a deep breath, hoping she just hadn't heard Maya use Holly's real name. "Have you seen Hope?"

"I think she's inside with James and Joshua, they'll be out in a minute." She glanced back to Maya. "You like Hope, eh? She'll be out soon and I'm sure you can get a picture with her."

Ryan's chest squeezed tight. This was just his friend, and he already couldn't handle it. His arms burned as he kept them loosely at his side, feigning a casual presentation he didn't feel in the least. "Come on, let's go find a strawberry."

"Holly likes strawberries," his daughter said, tugging him in the direction of her grandparents' house. Where his almost-lover was, but she'd be wearing her celebrity hat and he didn't want to see that. Didn't want anyone to see him seeing her and not being able to touch her, because nobody could know what she was to him.

Which is what, exactly?

He shoved that question away. He had to focus on the more immediate problem—what she was to his children, and how to manage that. "Hang on there, boo. Remember that the movie people are working today, too, even though it's a party. We can't just barge in. Let's go find one on the buffet."

And have a private chat about maybe not using Holly's real name in public. Convincing his kids to go home for popcorn and a movie in his bed would probably be a hard fail. He shrugged at Olivia, ignoring the still confused look on her face as she returned to her conversation with Parvati. At the buffet, he gave each boy a plate to carry. Maya could share his. He didn't feel like eating, anyway. Swallowing around the massive stress lump in his throat would be impossible.

"Hey, three pieces of cheese is enough, kiddo." Gavin grinned up at him as he glowered. It was a really impressive spread. He didn't even know there was this kind of catering available on the peninsula. "Okay, where should we sit?"

"Can we go down to the dock?" Jack asked. Where Gavin and Maya took after Lynn, social butterflies when Maya wasn't being typically pre-schooler shy, Jack was exactly like Ryan. *Can we get away from these people, please?*

"You bet. Come on."

But before they could step away from the group, a cheer went up. He knew why before he even turned around, but that didn't change the punch to his gut any less. Bracketed on either side by her director and co-star, Holly glowed on the steps of the deck in a blue sundress and white heels, her hair done up and face professionally made-up. She looked slim, confident, and unbelievably beautiful. Way out of his league, and she was, at the moment. That was Hope Creswell, A-list movie star, in her element.

From the back of the crowd, with three kids banging into his legs, juggling a plate of food and a metric ton of emotional baggage, Ryan watched as the woman he was undeniably hooked on lifted her hand and said a few lovely words of thanks to the crew, and the local community for their hospitality. She looked around as she spoke, seemingly making eye contact with everyone.

But she didn't look at him, not until the end. And when she did, she stopped scanning the crowd.

James Spencer also spoke, but Ryan didn't hear

anything the director said. He was too tangled up in Holly's gaze, locked on him, and the warm little smile playing out on her lips. *I was thinking about you, and how close we've come a few times...* Nope. Couldn't think of that, not right now.

Couldn't really think of anything *else*, either.

He needed to get her alone. Alone alone, not with his kids sleeping upstairs.

Maybe if they slept together, he'd be able to function in her presence.

Probably not. But it was worth a shot.

———

HOLLY MOVED AROUND THE PARTY, talking to people she knew and taking pictures with those she didn't. The whole time, she felt Ryan looking at her. Watching. Wanting.

It burned her up inside, being this close and not being next to him.

"Holly!" She turned as she heard her name, but it wasn't Ryan. He was moving toward her, but his attention was focused lower—at the three-foot level. *Maya.* The little blonde head bobbed through the crowd toward her, and she lifted her head to tell him she could see his daughter. The tight, anxious look on his face pulled her up short, and she just waited until they both arrived at her side.

"Hi," she said quietly, smiling.

He gave her an absent-minded smile in response, but his focus was all on the four-year-old. "Maya Howard, there's no running away from me."

"Daddy, I just wanted to see—"

"You can't bother Ms. Creswell..." He kept talking,

quietly lecturing Maya, but Holly's head went fuzzy hearing Ryan refer to her in a formal, distant way. Blood rushing through her ears, she tried to rewind the last ten minutes. She hadn't been imagining the look they'd shared.

But of course things were different in public.

And they were very much in public. Not just people he knew, but a lot he didn't, and all of them knew who she was. She'd gotten lost in the fantasy of being an ordinary girl.

No freedom for you, Holly Cresinski. You gave that up a long time ago.

"It's fine, I was looking forward to spending some time with Maya today," she said smoothly, her voice bouncing lightly over the family disagreement. Inside she was still reeling from the sharp reminder she was Ryan's little secret—not new information, but it still smarted. "Did you get something to eat?"

"I have strawberries for you," Maya said, pointing to the plate in Ryan's hand. Sure enough, almost half of it was covered in fat, red berries.

"They look great, thank you."

"Can we sit and eat them?"

"Absolutely. Give me two minutes to say hi to a few more people and then I'll meet you at the logs by the fire, okay?"

"Okay." Maya slid her hand into her dad's and tugged him away. Holly waited for Ryan to catch her eye as they turned away, but he didn't.

That stung too, but she knew she was being silly.

It was another ten minutes before she made it over to them. Ryan had securely surrounded himself with kids, so she sat next to Maya and they ate berries together. Slowly other people joined them, then Greg and Trey from Dance-light Productions, one of the producing companies of the film, got up and gave a big speech of thanks to the community. They'd done this once before, at the start of the film, and they'd have another big shindig for the wrap party, but this smaller bonfire for the community members directly involved—local police and park rangers who were doing off-duty security, all the food service and site maintenance crew, right down to the eternally helpful and chipper Olivia Minelli, who knew everyone and everything, and could make anything happen, all you had to do was ask her.

Despite Parvati and James snapping at each other and Joshua acting like a baby, the film was getting made on schedule and close to budget. And she'd met the Howards. So the biggest one couldn't look at her in public. Maybe that was because he'd jerked off in her ear the night before. Never before had grunting been so sexy. Now if he made those sex noises in her ear, she'd need to change her panties.

"Rumour has it that some of the kids here today brought their own marshmallows," Greg said, winking at Olivia.

"That was us," Gavin called out.

"Good idea, son." Greg nodded at him. "You want to get those and pass them around? A little bird might have given us that heads up, so two of Bruce County's finest, Rafe Minelli and Dean Foster, spent most of the afternoon finding good marshmallow roasting sticks. We'll pass those around..."

Even with Maya sitting between them, she could feel Ryan laughing quietly. She slid him a sideways glance. "What?"

He didn't look at her, but his lips curled up a bit. "Can't believe Rafe and Dean had to find people sticks."

"It was my idea!" she hissed under her breath, but now she was grinning too.

That made him laugh harder. Okay, so maybe people could have just found their own. They were surrounded by brushy forest, after all.

"I also had them pick up marshmallows in case you forgot."

"Yeah?" He made this little *well all right then* chin lift that warmed her to her core.

"Daddy, can I have a shmarshmallow?" Maya asked, leaning into Ryan's side.

He wrapped his arm around her. "Sure thing. Can I roast it for you?"

"I don't like it roasted. I like white."

He took one from the bag as Gavin slowly walked past them, carefully holding the treats out so each person around the fire could take one if they wanted.

Holly took hers, thanking the seven-year-old as he moved past her, then slid it onto the end of her stick. To actually roast it on the fire, they had to get up from the logs used for seating, and as she stood, Jack jumped to his feet. "Can I roast yours for you?"

"Sure." She grinned at him then sat down again. She settled her hands on the log, on either side of her hips, and leaned forward to watch her mini-chef prepare her treat. Around the fire, people were making new friends and having fun, and nobody was paying any attention to the fact that she was sitting with the Howards.

Nobody except Ryan. Her heart skipped a beat as the side of his hand rubbed against hers. He was cuddling Maya close to him, and his eyes were on his sons, one at the fire, one still making a polite circuit through all the party attendees, offering marshmallows for roasting. Ninety-nine percent of his attention was on them. But one percent had found a way to hold his daughter in a way that he could also stroke Holly's fingers ever so gently with his. She held still and just let the tingles creep up her arm and into her heart.

This was hard. But it wasn't impossible.

No, impossible would be not having Ryan at all. If she only got a sliver, that would have to be good enough.

CHAPTER SIXTEEN

RYAN PARKED his truck two spots up from where the street was barricaded off.

He was definitely going to hell for this. But when he woke up that morning to a phone call from Dani, offering to take his kids to church, and then a message from Holly saying that she was on set all day but not busy, if he wanted to stop by for a visit…it was like the universe was telling him to seize the day.

Not God. God would want him to go to church, but he and the big guy hadn't exactly been on speaking terms since Lynn died.

Which he felt guilty about, enough to send the kids off with Dani, but not enough to keep him away from Holly.

They were shooting on Main Street today—Sundays were a quiet day in downtown Pine Harbour anyway, most of the stores closed or only open for a few hours in the afternoon. Holly had told him they would start early, ready to get the first shots as soon as the shadows stopped being obviously long. He stood on the sidelines of the action for a few minutes, watching as Joshua tried to kiss

Parvati and she shoved him away. When James called "Cut!" and had them retake their marks to do it again, Ryan slid his phone from his pocket.

Ryan: I'm here. Where are you?
Holly: Trailer in the parking lot behind the bank. My name is on the door.

When he got there, he followed the row of trailers—five of them—and found hers at the end, tucked back against the buildings on the far side of the block. He knocked quietly and, after flashing a quick look over his shoulder at the empty lot, stepped inside when she opened the door.

She was wearing tiny black shorts and a sweatshirt, and her face was make-up free, like she'd just scrubbed off her character. Gorgeous didn't do her justice.

"Hey," he said quietly, reaching for her, gathering her in his arms, relieved that she came easily. "We're all alone."

Nodding, she stretched inside the sturdy circle of his arms, rubbing up against him. "I sent Emmett back to the cottage for the day. I told everyone else I'm having a nap until after lunch."

"I sent my kids to church so I could be alone with you." He grinned down at her shocked expression and kissed the end of her nose. "I know. I've already processed it in my head and I've decided you're worth the risk of eternal damnation."

"Pretty sure God is more forgiving than that." She kissed the corner of his mouth and when he smiled, she licked along the curve of his lips until their faces aligned. "But that's very sweet."

"And how about you?" he asked softly, moving his lips against hers, unable to pull away, even as they talked. "How forgiving are you?"

Wrinkling her brow, she pulled back to look at him better, but he caught her by the back of her neck and brought her mouth back to his. "What do you mean?"

"I was…brusque yesterday. I thought the bonfire might be fun, and my kids had a blast, but it was harder than I thought to pretend not to know you."

"When you touched my hand," she breathed against his skin, "all was forgotten."

Hot relief pulsed through him. He'd known it—they'd sat together for more than an hour, quietly talking, brushing arms and fingers, and sharing glances. But he'd left with his kids while she was busy, and they hadn't talked again. The lane had still been full of cars when he'd fallen asleep. And then her message this morning hadn't promised anything.

Hadn't stopped him from stuffing condoms in his pocket, though. She turned him into a nineteen-year-old again.

But the ease at which she bent for him—further and further, like she was unbreakable—it worried him. Because everyone had a breaking point. He'd fallen right through his over the winter. He didn't want to be the cause of heartache. Didn't want to take advantage. "You shouldn't forget, Holly," he said roughly, gripping her tightly. Holding her to him as he dragged the truth in front of her. "I'm selfish and thoughtless and can't offer you much. You should be wary of me."

"I am," she said, so soft it took him a second to process that she'd agreed with him. Her eyes, half-hooded with unmistakable desire, crinkled at the corners as she smiled languidly at him at the same time as she leaned into his body, tucking her hips into his. His hands went to her ass as if by automatic command, hungrily stroking over her lean but curvy muscles there. "I know better than to fall for you, Ryan Howard. Even though you're so…very…cute." Punctuating the last word with a kiss, she shook her head at him. "But you're a better guy than you think. I know what we're doing here, and I'm not scared."

Something flickered in her gaze. Maybe a silent *anymore* that she didn't want to say out loud.

Well, two could be brave. "I'm scared." Admitting it felt good. Freeing. "This feels like madness, what we're doing."

Her face lit up at that, her reaction tugging his arousal to the forefront. "I know. But we're doing it together. It's our secret madness. And I might not know how you'll react to me any given day, but I always know you'll keep my secrets."

It pissed him off that she didn't seem to have that in anyone else. Her best friend was traveling around the world—a musician, she'd said—and her mother…Ryan couldn't go there. Not without losing his shit. And they only had a few hours.

He coasted his hands over the skin at her waist, smooth and soft and taut, then up the inside of her sweatshirt. Up, up, up. His mind blanked a little when he realized she wasn't wearing a bra, but then his inner caveman took over, hauling her in for a desperate kiss as he cupped her hot flesh and rolled her tight nipple between his fingers. His mouth watered at the memory of how good she'd tasted, and he kissed her hard, demanding more and more until they were clawing at each other.

"Wait," he burst out, remembering what he'd practiced on his drive into town. "I want to ask you out. On a date."

"Huh?" She nosed along his jaw, her fingertips working at his belt buckle. Her breathy sounds and cool, questing hands were distracting him again. "In public?"

He cleared his throat. Yes, damn it, in public. It was hard to think with her so close to him, but he wanted to do this the right way. "Maybe not at Mac's, but yeah. I thought we could take a drive somewhere. My in-laws will be back soon, or I could ask someone to babysit."

"Do you want to bring the kids? I mean, if you want to, that's okay—"

"I don't want to." He shook his head. "I love my kids, and I love that you like them so much. But we've only got a few weeks left, and I want some time alone with you. I'm not going to get greedy. But one night, just you and me."

"A boy and a girl on a date," she whispered, her eyes bright and her lips soft.

"Yeah." He leaned in and tasted her again, sucking her lower lip into his mouth before realizing he might have given her the wrong idea. "In case it wasn't obvious, I don't want to wait for a real date to…you know. I should, that would be the right thing to do—"

"You know?" She laughed and flicked her gaze past him to the door. "There's a lock on that. The right thing sounds terribly overrated. Let's have sex. Right now. Let's just…be mad."

In a stride and a half, he had the lock flicked, and when he turned back, she had her shirt off.

"Wow," he breathed, taking her in. She was all limbs and shadows, willowy and soft. Her breasts looked better each time he saw them, and now he could actually take his time… "Bed? Couch? Wall?"

"Yes, yes, yes."

He advanced on her, telegraphing his intent to lift her up, and she leapt into his arms, sighing as he pressed her against the floor-to-ceiling cabinets. She wiggled her hands over his shoulders, shoving his buttoned down shirt down his arms before tugging his undershirt up his mid-section. Which made kissing her a challenge, because she'd effectively handcuffed him with his shirt. Leaning over, he laughed as he shook it off, then pulled off his tee. Two of them could play the naked skin game, although hers was infinitely more attractive.

But she thought he was *cute*. He'd work with that.

———

IT WAS REALLY unfair how good Ryan smelled. Holly breathed in the warm, sweet scent of his skin. *A full-bodied masculine aroma, with undercurrents of laundry detergent and a high note reminiscent of Irish Spring bar soap.* She tried to laugh at her inner funny, but she was too turned on, so it just came out as a breathy sigh as he loomed over her. He was doing it on purpose, being all big and lumberjack-y. He knew what that did to her.

And now that he was half-naked and right in front of her, she needed to touch him. She spread her hands across his chest, achingly aware of her upper arms rubbing against her bare breasts. His smooth skin burned her fingertips, stretched tight over his flexing muscles. She traced down the narrow path of hair down to his belt, twisting as she tugged them together to make sure her breasts were free for him. *Touch me.* Why she didn't just say it out loud, she didn't know. Not shy, just…now that she was touching him, and they were really going to do this, the flirty fun was fading away—something even better, headier, was replacing it. Her pulse beat confidently as she worked his belt open, then the button at the top of his jeans.

His breathing changed, too, and she looked up at him.

This was big for him, too. *Bigger, you idiot. The last person he had sex with was his wife.* Swallowing hard, she tightened her grip on his waistband and, slow as molasses, pulled him hard against her. She didn't go for his fly yet. She could feel his erection straining, knew he wanted her. She needed to show him first that it was okay. That she wanted him too, that he could trust her to give him this.

This wasn't a game. It was real and awesome and yes, frightening. "Okay, I'm scared, too," she whispered, pressing her mouth to the side of his pectoral muscle, twisting and sliding between his body and the wall so she could always see his face as she kissed his body all over, loving the way he shuddered under lips and hands and breath. "But I want you. I want you inside me, and on top of me. I want this. You and me. Just for us. Just for today and this month, our little secret." She exhaled as she let go of his belt and wound her arms over his strong, broad shoulders and wrapped them around his flexing neck. "So you can have me wherever you want me. Bed's through the door. Couch is fine. Or this wall—"

She squeaked as he spun them around, pointing her backwards to the bedroom. Finding her feet beneath her, she laced her fingers through his and guided him there, her eyes on his the whole way. As soon as they were through the doorway into the minuscule bedroom, not much bigger than the bed itself, his hands were on her hips, then his fingers were under the fabric of her shorts, shoving them down.

Yes. She wanted to scream it from the roof, but that would violate the promise she'd just made him, so she hollered it in her head instead. *Get me naked, mister.* Dipping his head, he kissed her neck, then along her collarbone. Rough and hungry, he licked and sucked and swirled his tongue along her skin as her shorts slid lower on her ass, then off. She reached for him as he slowed down. She wanted his pants off, too, but before she could snake her fingers between his jeans and his yummy skin, he grabbed her wrists. His breath was coming faster now, ragged and heavy. *Please don't change your mind.*

"If you touch me, I'm gonna blow," he said, his words unexpectedly interrupting the loud thud of her heartbeat. "And I wanted…I promised…"

Ever so slowly, she twisted her wrists out of his grasp and kicked her shorts off her toes. Naked, she crawled backward and stretched out for him, letting him look his fill of her. Under his hot, hungry gaze, she felt radiant. Between her legs, she could feel the evidence of how he affected her, and when his eyes lingered there, she slid her thighs apart, just enough for him to see her slick, pink skin.

Drunk on desire, she wiggled her fingers at his pants. "You don't need those, either."

He pulled some condoms from his pocket—*thank you thank you thank you*—and pushed the jeans down, then cursed because he was still wearing his boots. She giggled, rolling to her side as he sat, swearing a blue streak as he shoved everything off except his boxers.

Just regular boxers. *I'll get him some boxer briefs. Black ones. Snug,* she thought, then… *No. Let him be different. Let him not give a fuck about Calvin Klein, because he's cute. And rugged. And—*

"Stop thinking, woman," he growled, as he tipped her onto her back again and covered her body in his, his mouth demanding entry to hers that she gave him immediately. His tongue stroked into her like a promise. *This is how I'll fuck you.*

She wrapped one of her legs around his hips, the soft cotton of his underwear a delicious contrast to the crispy hair on his thighs, teasing her calves as she stroked her other leg up and down his.

Leading with his hands, he moved down her body, loving her neck, then her breasts, and her belly, before settling between her legs. He kissed the insides of her thighs, back and forth, back and forth, working his way higher until her legs met her pelvis. The first feathery brush of his lips against her labia made her jump, then sigh. And blush, but he kept going like he didn't know he was torturing her in a wonderful, dangerous way. Kisses turned into licks as he made her bloom for him. She dug her heels into the bed and rocked up to meet his mouth, and he laughed as he slid his fingers through her slippery pussy, holding her open so he could enter her with his tongue.

"Don't laugh at me," she murmured, watching through lust-heavy eyes as he thrust slowly, each wet plunge lifting her higher and spinning her faster. Vaguely aware that her legs were starting to shake, the muscles burning, she tried to relax back against the bed, but that wasn't what she wanted. Curling up, she propped herself up on her elbows, the sight of Ryan's head between her legs just as hot as the magical things he was doing with his tongue. And his lips. *Oh God.* He covered her entire sex, kissing her now, sucking on the lips and circling her clit with the tip of his tongue, then sucking *there*, too. She threw her head back, the electric tug sending a bolt through her entire body. Her legs now twitched out of control, and she collapsed, wrapping her thighs around his head—*try not to kill him, Holly, you're going to want him to do this again*—as she catapulted into a stunning climax, complete with fireworks behind her eyes and a sexy, muscular man to catch her as she floated back down to terra firma.

Ryan slid up her body. He kissed her after she caught her breath, then rolled onto his back, pulling her with him. She braced her hands on either side of his head as he cupped her breasts together, kissing her nipples, then sucking one deep into his mouth, leaving it wet and hard and ready for more when he licked across to the other. More came in the form of his thumb, stroking around the wet peak in a lazy pattern that worked a direct current straight to her core. She rocked against his thick, muscled middle, an ache building inside her. She wanted to be filled by him, stretched to her limits.

She wanted him inside her.

Lifting her hips, she rocked down his body, her naked centre finding his tented boxers. He groaned as she ghosted over him, a desperate feeling she recognized in herself—every muscle and cell in her body was crying out to submit to this man, let him claim her in the most elemental way. Working her way down between his knees, she grabbed his boxer waistband and stripped him bare, getting her first look at his cock.

Thick, long, and curved, his erection bobbed in the air, leaning toward his left hip. Dark curls surrounded his sex, but his balls were mostly bare, and all of his most sensitive skin was a dark, dusky pink and beautiful. She circled his shaft with her fingers, loving the way he gasped as she started to stroke him. The crown of his penis was exposed, glistening with pre-come, but as she jerked him she realized he must not be circumcised, because his foreskin slid effortlessly up the head with the movement of her hand.

Blinking ever so slowly, she found his gaze, burning as he looked at her looking at him, and she smiled and licked her lips.

RYAN WANTED to freeze time and stretch out this moment in Holly's trailer as long as he could. She was sitting between his legs, curled up on her hip, one hand bracing herself next to his thigh, the other wrapped about his cock like it was an ice cream cone she was about to lick.

When she did, he was going to do his damnedest not to come all over her face.

His pulse was rocking, wild and out of control, and his mouth was dry and hot as he stared at her. Her cheeks were flushed, her lips wet and swollen, and they both smelled like sex. *Private madness.* He wanted to preserve this moment forever.

As she twisted onto her knees, her ass rising in the air behind her, her golden hair falling to the side, he fought to keep his eyes open. Too easy to give in to the feeling and rut against her hot breath, find her lips and slide into her hot little mouth.

That would feel too good. Too much. Too perfect. And he'd be lost. So he held himself back and let her set the pace. Slow. Teasing. Her tongue met his cock softly, licking beneath the head, then around and down, circling like her fingers had. Her hand slid lower, squeezing him at the base. He flexed into her touch and she made a pleased sound.

"You're so beautiful." He reached for her head as he said the rough words, and she leaned her cheek into his touch before lifting up and taking just the head into her mouth.

He'd been wrong. There was nothing too much about this. It was just right.

But he couldn't keep still. His hips jerked, driving his shaft between her lips, and she gobbled him down, their urgency apparently shared. Moaning around him, she bobbed her head, his shaft slick now with her spit. She wasn't working him too hard, wasn't trying to make him come. It just felt good. Amazing, really. He sank into that feeling, letting himself enjoy what Holly was giving him.

The gift of happiness. Of pleasure.

He hadn't known it could be like this again—although this was different, too. Special in its own way, uniquely made from the two of them. Memories hovered in the background, but there wasn't room for anyone else right now.

He'd deal with that thought later. Right now, he was all Holly's.

He wanted to touch her. Spin her around and have her sit on his face. Fuck, they didn't have enough time for all the ways he wanted to worship her body. Stroking his hands over her shoulders, he tapped her side and she looked up, her mouth sliding off him with a wet pop.

He'd meant for her to twist to the side so he could finger her or something, but the wide-eyed, wet-mouthed, sloppy-happy-*fuck me* face she gave him was too much.

"I need you," he said hoarsely, then they were kissing and spinning and grinding, the world all upside down and crazy and perfect he just couldn't handle it.

"Condom," she gasped, and he found one blindly with

his right hand as she sucked his tongue into her mouth, refusing to let him go even as he sheathed himself.

Once protected, he hovered over her, one hand next to her cheek, the other fisting himself between them. "Ready?"

"Oh God, yeah," she whispered, lifting her hips in invitation. Her softness brushed his tip and he pressed in, just a bit. Just enough to seat himself in her entrance. Already she felt snug and hot, and as he stroked in a bit, she cried out, tightening her hold on his torso.

She was so tight, it felt like he must be hurting her, but she rocked and ground against him, welcoming each gentle thrust. "Okay?"

"Soooo okay," she panted, grinning up at him. "It's just been a while."

"You feel incredible." He lowered his weight onto her, pulsing gently with his hips as she slowly stretched around him, taking him fully into her body. Kissing her softly, their lips lingering together, he pulled almost all the way out, dragging his length out of where it wanted to be, so he could thrust deep again. Worth the aching loss of her heat to feel that clutching sensation as she tightened around him.

Over and over again, he pistoned his hips, surging into her, and she met him on each stroke, fucking him from below. She circled her hips and rocked her pelvis, finding all the spots where they rubbed together just right. When she gasped at the same time as something perfect rubbed against the sensitive spot right behind the head of his dick, they both froze and looked at each other, not wanting to lose that connection.

"Is that good for you?" she breathed.

He huffed a laugh. "Oh yeah."

"Keep doing that. Yeah, just…Oh, God. Ryan!" She went wild beneath him, writhing as she found her pleasure from where he was buried deep inside her. His balls were already tight, ready to explode as soon as he picked up the pace.

"Hold on," he grunted, and he wasn't sure if he was talking to himself or her, but she wrapped tight around him as he let himself fly, carrying her with him as he chased the best feeling in the world. Higher, faster, *right there*. Their bodies moved as one, Ryan thrusting hard into Holly as he braced his hand against the wall to keep her head from slamming into it. Her heels dug into his ass, her teeth grazing his pecs as she shuddered beneath him, seizing. And inside, she squeezed him hard, once, twice, three times before devolving into fluttering little clutches that milked his own release deep inside her.

CHAPTER SEVENTEEN

LIMBS ENTWINED, they lay together in her cozy trailer. Ryan had rolled away long enough to deal with the condom, then pulled her close again, and she pressed a line of soft kisses down his arm. It had been so good.

And not nearly enough. When Ryan rolled her onto her stomach, kissing his way down her back, she readily lifted her hips so he could enter her all over again from behind.

She was coming practically from the first thrust through her sensitized folds. When he realized she was already there, he gripped her hips and powered into her, taking his own pleasure rough and fast before collapsing beside her again. She grabbed his fingers and kissed them breathlessly. "Wow."

"That was a bit wild that time."

She just smiled. "Wild is good." No, he deserved more than that. "Or so I'm discovering." She rolled her lower lip through her teeth, still feeling that hum of arousal coursing through her blood. *Really? After three orgasms?* "I've never had sex quite like this before."

He'd shifted away to get rid of the second condom, and

now whipped his head back, looking at her incredulously. "What?"

"You know… all reckless, wild abandon and that kind of thing." Frowning a bit, she reached for the right words. "It takes a level of…trust. Like I said, I trust you with my secrets, Ryan."

He relaxed into the pillow next to her as his gaze searched her face. "Why me?"

"Because…" She shook her head. "It's hard to explain."

He shrugged. "Try me."

"Being famous…it doesn't make it any easier to date. That sounds so sad panda of me. God. I'm not complaining about my life. I'm blessed with a wonderful career that allows me to escape from my mother as often as I want, but still support her with ease because I'm pretty sure that's why I was put on this earth." She groaned. "But it doesn't make it any easier to find the handful of people in this world that I just *click* with, you know? I don't have more friends than other people. If anything, I have fewer, because there are all these other layers that I need to wade through to know if I can trust someone. So take that and add in the intimacy of sharing my body and my heart…it's…"

She rolled her face toward her pillow, running out of words and feeling embarrassed. Her hair draped between them, and Ryan didn't push it out of the way. He just skated his fingertips down her spine, leaving a lazy trail of awareness in their wake. He stopped in the small of her back and started drawing circles there. "I think I get it. I'm the same way now because of how Lynn died. I feel exposed and wary, I guess."

It was a small window of opportunity, and she didn't know if the time was right, but she was going to try and squeeze through it anyway. "This was your first time since she died, wasn't it?"

He was nodding slowly when she twisted onto her side and looked at him. "Yeah."

"Was it okay?" She said it earnestly, and when he started laughing, she scowled at him. "Not like that. I know it was *good*. You rocked my world. But I mean… emotionally. Are you okay with it?"

He just looked at her, but his eyes didn't go cold and his lips stayed soft. *He's really giving it some thought. And not running scared*, she realized with relief. She gave him a small smile and waited, quietly tugging up the sheet they'd shoved down the bed in their exuberance. Maybe best to be covered for moving the conversation from sex to emotions.

But as she wrapped the lush Egyptian cotton around her, he reached out and pulled her close anyway.

"I've been worried since I met you, about disrespecting Lynn's memory," he started, his voice quiet. "I've gone to a support group, a bereaved spouses thing. And we've talked about moving on, but it's…different in theory than in reality. There's this guilt. And I don't feel it all the time, but then it tugs at me after the fact."

"I'm sorry," she whispered, an ache building in her chest.

"No…I don't feel it right now. And I don't want to feel it anymore. That might be easier said than done, but—" He tensed, and she froze, not knowing what to say or if there was anything she even *could* say. "I don't want to say anything that might make this awkward for you."

"Hey, I'm pretty boneless right now. How about you trust me to know that your feelings are complicated and that's okay?" She kissed his chest. "You still love her. If she hadn't died, you'd still be happily married and I'd never know how good you are at all of this naughty stuff. That's okay. It's all true. Not saying it doesn't make it disappear."

"It's not all true." He inhaled roughly. "Yes, I loved her. Always will. She was my wife, and the mother of my children. When she danced with Maya, I thought my heart would explode with happiness. But we weren't happy. And that's my fault. I should have done something. Counselling, a weekend away, try to reconnect with her. I don't know. And I don't know why I'm telling you this, because you're right. If she was still here, I wouldn't have...we wouldn't have talked. I would've noticed you from afar as the pretty movie lady and moved on with my life."

She nodded, trying to process that at the same time as giving him some space to do the same. When it was clear he wasn't going to say anything else, she spoke quietly, choosing her words with care. "You know I've got issues with my mom. And they don't compare or anything, I'm not saying that. But I tried a lot of different therapy once I was a grown-up, and the advice that helped me the most was a Buddhist quote. 'Forgiveness means letting go of the hope for a better past.' You won't be able to forgive yourself for not doing things differently until you stop wishing things were different."

"I can't," he said, his words strained. With a jerk, she looked up at his face, and he twisted away, like he didn't want her to realize he was close to tears. "I'll always want things to be different for my kids. They deserve their mother."

"I can't argue with that. I don't want to. But they've got an awesome father who stepped up to the plate, Ryan."

He snorted, his face still tipped up to the ceiling. "So awesome that I ditched church with them to have sex."

"Were you going to church otherwise?" She'd known him for almost three months, and never once had he gone before. He carried enough guilt, he didn't need to add that to the pile.

He closed his eyes, a wry smile curling up one side of his mouth. "No."

"Then shut up."

———

HOLLY LET him use her shower, then dried his hair for him, making an actor joke about continuity errors as she restored him to his pre-fucked look.

On the inside, though, he was permanently altered—both by the amazing sex, and the unexpectedly emotional conversation afterward. When they kissed goodbye, he poured all the gratitude he could muster into it. Words wouldn't do his feelings justice.

After she peeked outside and confirmed the coast was clear, he took one last firm taste of her lips and headed for his truck, going the long way around the block to avoid anyone he might know.

He grinned to himself as he steered his truck out of town, past the home of Colonel Foster, father of Dean, Jake, Matt and Sean. Their old man did the parenting thing on his own, and his kids turned out all right. Even Sean had buckled down after a rocky couple of years at the end of his teens. Baby Foster was now gearing up for his overseas tour as a lieutenant. Had to fucking salute him and everything.

Jake had tried to tell Ryan that it would work out, months ago. He hadn't been ready to hear it.

Now he still didn't want to hear it. Wasn't ready to

accept that he was all his kids had. But Holly was right. Wishing it was different wouldn't change anything.

By the time he pulled into the driveway for a different Foster—Jake, and by extension, Dani—he was feeling something that felt a lot like calm. Settled.

He wasn't the only guest for a late post-church lunch, it looked like. Rafe's truck was parked in front of the garage, and Matt's was around the side of the house.

Inside, he found almost the entire Minelli and Foster combined clan. Apparently Sean and Dean had hopped in Matt's truck, and Tom had biked over, and they were all crowded into Jake's office at the front of the house with Rafe, listening to sports radio and yelling about something.

Ryan did a quick count. The only one missing was Zander. The older generation were also absent, but with the noise level his kids were generating, that probably wasn't a bad thing.

"What the heck is going on in here?" he asked as he strolled into the great room. Living room at one end, eat-in kitchen at the other, the room was both a shining example of the high-end construction Jake was capable of, and a comfortable family-centred space.

And with the hand print artwork Dani had taped to the walls, courtesy of his monsters he was sure, it tilted a bit heavier to the latter right now.

Jake paused mid swing, his hands still around Gavin's ankles. Ryan stared at his friend, and his suspended in mid-air seven-year-old.

"I'm a clock," Gavin said, giggling.

"All right, carry on." Ryan scooped up Maya, inspecting her hands for paint, but he didn't find any. "Did you do art work with Aunt Dani?"

"Last time. Today we went to church."

"And was that fun?"

"Mmm-hmmm. I went to Sunday School and made a spring basket to put prayers in."

Ryan was pretty sure something was lost in the translation there, but he nodded and smiled as his daughter wrapped her arms around his neck and squeezed, still telling her story about the teacher and the prayers and thinking of others. It all sounded pretty good in Maya's sweetly squeaking voice. "That's great."

"Do you want to come next week, Daddy?"

"Maybe, boo. Maybe. Where's Jack?" He'd heard his oldest crowing about something when he came inside, but now that he'd covered most of the main floor, the nine-year-old was missing.

"Dani's teaching him to cook." Maya leaned, pointing to the kitchen, and sure enough, there was his kid wearing an apron and proudly waving a spatula on the far side of his friend and former co-worker. Across the room, Olivia waved at him as she glanced up from typing something on her phone.

Still carrying Maya, who was now squirming, he walked into the airy, gourmet kitchen space and used his free arm to hug Jack as he peered into the frying pan. "Sweet potato?"

His kid grinned up at him and nodded. "Salmon cakes! Yeah, with sweet potato and green onion and an *egg*! I know, it sounds gross—" Dani interjected a weak protest but Jack kept going "—but they taste amazing! And I'm cooking them!"

Huh. And here he'd been making mac and cheese like a chump. "They look great."

"We made a sauce for them, too."

"Really?" Ryan couldn't get over seeing his son cooking lunch like a man. "Tell me more about the sauce."

"We started with mayo…" Jack listed off all the ingredients, then told him how they put the lemon in the microwave to make it warm first. "So the juice comes out better."

"I can't wait to try it. Do you think you could make it again at home?"

"Maybe if Aunt Dani writes down the recipe for me?"

"I can do that," Dani nodded. "Hey, Ryan, can you grab the salad and put it on the table?"

"Sure can." He set Maya down and opened the double-wide stainless steel doors. "You've got enough food for an army in here."

"Well, yeah. I've got an army in my house, literally."

"And you love it." He winked at her as he carried first the salad bowl to the table, then the trays of cold meat she'd already prepared.

"Yep." She grinned back him.

He left her to the final preparations, and followed Maya back into the living room.

"Okay, everyone to the table!" Dani hollered a few minutes later. *Oh yeah, the mother gene is strong in that one,* Ryan thought. It reminded him of how Lynn used to call everyone to the table, Maya hanging off her leg. *You made them eat their veggies, baby. How did I forget about that?*

Everyone swirled past him, heading to the big long table in the kitchen, and Ryan just stood in the living room, alone with his…*not guilt.* No, what he and Holly had shared wasn't wrong. But that was just for him. That didn't change *this,* the big family gathering where he was reminded that he still had a big hill to climb, parenting-wise. As he watched his kids clambering onto seats next to their adopted aunts and uncles, finding an adult to glom onto, he missed Lynn so much it hurt.

But there was also something new in his heart. A longing to share this with Holly, an aching wish that he hadn't crept out of her trailer, that she wasn't working today, that she could squeeze in between Gavin and Jack and help them fill their plates with salad and corn bread.

Did she like to cook? Would she help Jack and Dani, or would she be in the living room with Jake, twirling kids around in circles and laughing her beautiful laugh?

Don't wish things could be different. Isn't that what Holly had said just an hour earlier? He was being an idiot.

He reached for the cucumber salad, taking a big spoonful before offering some to Maya, who said no until Tom told her he loved cucumbers and then she wanted some. Always the way. Ryan shook it off and lost himself in the conversation and food, trying desperately to just enjoy what he had.

As they ate, talk turned to the church service and where everyone parked because Main Street had been closed off. The church was a few blocks away, but didn't have a huge lot.

"Hey, what were you doing in town this morning?" Matt reached across the table for the bread basket as he nodded absently at Ryan. "I thought you were sleeping in."

"Nah, I just stopped to see the film shoot after dropping the kids here," Ryan said, his heart pounding.

"He went to see Holly," Gavin said with a grin at the same time as Maya spilled her cup of milk and Dani leapt up, and for a second, Ryan thought maybe nobody heard him.

That would be too lucky.

How the hell did he know that? Ryan thought as his neck began to prickle, and he turned reluctantly in Olivia's direction, his head swivelling as if pulled by an invisible rope of doom. She was looking at him far too knowingly. "Holly?" she mouthed, her eyes twinkling.

Eyes wide, he made sure that Dani had the spill under control before shoving up and out of his chair. "Hey, Liv. I almost forgot, I've got that baby stuff for you in the truck!" So what if he sounded like a panicky girl? That's how he felt inside.

A few adult heads popped up, looking at him curiously, but Olivia made some similar noises, letting him drag her away. Lunch was almost over anyway and Ryan didn't really care.

Smirking, his friend followed him outside. As soon as the door clicked shut, she dropped her jaw. "Holly? As in *Hope Creswell* Holly?"

"Don't make a big deal," he said gruffly. "And you can't tell anyone."

"Tell them what?" She crossed her arms over the slight swell of her baby bump. "I mean, if I knew *exactly* what I shouldn't say, I could probably keep my trap shut."

"She's leaving at the end of the film shoot." He was reminding himself as much as Olivia. "We're just friends."

"Friends that…" She trailed off and if she said *fuck* he was pretty sure he'd die of embarrassment, but at the last minute she smiled and added, "Skip church together?"

"I wasn't going to church anyway. And she was working."

"She didn't have a lot of scenes to shoot today."

"You're super annoying. And why aren't you at work?"

"Union rules. They're filming right through the weekend but us little people need days off. And *you* are the annoying one. Holding out on me. I *asked* you! In the diner! I didn't know that Holly was Hope's real name then, or I'd have figured this out sooner. Oooh, Ryan, this is fantastic! She's so lovely and—"

He held up his hand. "She's leaving. And she's famous. I can't do that."

Olivia frowned at him. "Can't do what?"

Can't fall for a woman who's so far out of my league it hurts. Can't expose my kids to the painful scrutiny of the world. "Holly's leaving in three weeks, six days and approximately twelve hours."

"Pretty sure you're not just friends if you've got that countdown going in your head. She's a wealthy woman, Ryan. You don't think she can fly back here for the occasional booty call?" He reared back as if Olivia had slapped him, and her eyes immediately softened. "So it's not just sex. Or you haven't had sex yet."

"I'm not having this conversation with you."

"You should tell her how you feel."

"Stop!" He didn't feel anything. "She knows I'll miss her when she leaves. We're friends. Leave it alone."

"How did you…" Olivia tilted her head to the side. Did she see the panic on his face? He couldn't have this conversation with Holly, or himself. He sure as hell wasn't ready to start having it with all his friends. "Well, okay. I think it's great, because she's great, and you deserve good things in your life. Don't be a martyr or anything."

"I'm not doing anything of the sort. It's not just as easy as snapping my fingers and anything being possible." He dragged a breath into his burning lungs. "Please don't tell anyone."

"Do you actually have baby stuff in your truck?"

"No." He winced. "What do you want? Name your price."

"Lynn raved about the baby swing."

"It's all yours. I'll drop it off tomorrow, and throw in a bouncy thing-a-ma-jig, too."

CHAPTER EIGHTEEN

HOLLY JOGGED the last few hundred yards to the cottage, cooling down after a long trail run. It was almost dusk. She glanced at her watch. An hour or so until the kids were asleep, and she could slip over to Ryan's house like she'd done every night this week. They were going to talk about maybe getting away for that date, either the next day or the following weekend.

Tomorrow was the start of a two-day weekend. If they didn't get away just the two of them, Ryan had made some noise about maybe doing something with the kids.

She'd been topless at the time, sitting on his lap in his living room while he lazily played with her boobs. A shiver went through her at the memory.

"You wanna do something fun with the kids this weekend?" He lifted her breast enough so he could kiss the plump swell spilling over his palm.

"If you can keep your hands to yourself, definitely." She gently cupped his jaw and brought her mouth to his for a soft kiss. "I kind of like making you hold it in until we're alone. Delayed gratification and all that."

"Wind me up tight and take advantage of me, okay, I see your play there." He nipped at her lower lip before sliding his hands down her body to her hips. She loved the feel of his hands there—everywhere—branding her with a possessive heat.

"It's good for both of us."

And it really was. Their chemistry was crazy, both playful and intense, and each time they came together, she just wanted more.

Don't think of saying goodbye.

Now she could only think of a good stretch, a hot shower, and being back in Ryan's arms for another night. Part of a night. She couldn't sleep over, and she knew that. Actually sleeping with him would be such a luxury.

So distracted was she by her thoughts that she almost missed the clink of wine glasses from inside the lake house before she opened the screen door. She didn't hear it in time to run away, though, so when she froze in the doorway, Emmett saw her.

"Ahh, there she is!" he exclaimed, his eyes wide.

Oh, shit. "Liana. What are you doing here?"

It took all of her inner courage to step into the house and plaster on a smile. There was no way she'd escape to see Ryan tonight. Or maybe ever again.

"My bestie!" Liana Hansen cried out, putting down her wine glass and rushing across the room. She stopped short of throwing her arms around Holly. "Oh. You've been exercising."

"Yep, just got back from a run."

"Is that allowed? What if you twisted an ankle?"

Holly rolled her eyes. "Well, I'm playing a woman in a wheelchair, so I'm sure it wouldn't be a problem."

"Ooh, right, I forgot!" Liana squealed and threw her

arms around Holly's neck, clearly forgetting that she thought the sweat was gross.

"So…why are you here, sweet pea? I'm happy to see you, really, but I'm working. And aren't you on tour?"

"Tiny break! And I had to see you. You sounded so sad when we talked."

They hadn't talked, just exchanged some text messages, but that didn't seem worth pointing out now that her best friend was here.

"I won't stay long, just the weekend. Emmett says you've got two days off! I'm so excited! I love you!"

Holly laughed at the quiet stream of words in her ear and squeezed Liana all over again. "I love you, too." She stepped back and pointed at Emmett. "Wine me up. I'm going to take a two-minute shower, then we can catch up."

She pulled her phone out of the armband holder as she trudged up the stairs.

Holly: Came home from my run and found a surprise visitor. My friend Liana. Might be able to sneak out later, but not any time soon.

Heart heavy, she hit send, then clicked on Ryan's name to look at his photo. She'd taken it on Wednesday. Two days earlier, and all of a sudden it felt like a lifetime. He was scowling because he wasn't ready for the picture, but a ghost of a smile played at the corner of his lips and his eyes were all soft. The sexiest scowl ever.

Ryan: No worries. Bedtime tantrums here. Might fall asleep in a pile of kids, but I'll wake up if you end up getting away.

She didn't get away.

When she woke up, slightly hung over from too much wine and too much Liana, there was a sleepy selfie of Ryan sent at half past six in the morning, Maya photobombing him over his shoulder.

Holly: OMG, so much cuteness.
Ryan: I know, I'm adorable.
Holly: I meant Maya.

She went into the bathroom as she began her day. She climbed into the shower, then hopped out again and grabbed her phone.

Holly: This is what I'm doing right now.

Rule number one of being a celebrity—no naked self-ies. So she covered up the good bits and went for mood over content, taking a picture of her bare shoulder and smiling lips, barely parted, with the steaming shower in the background.

Her phone rang immediately. "Yes?"

"Okay, that was good. Great, even. I feel suitably punished for being cheeky."

"What are you doing?" She reached into the shower and turned off the water, then crawled back into bed. Getting ready for the day could wait.

"Making breakfast." He sighed. "And I got a phone call from my in-laws. They just crossed the border at Port Huron. They'll be here in four hours."

"Oh." Damn double damn. "Well, that's sucky timing."

"At least we're both dealing with visitors at the same time. And I think they're going to only be here for a few days, then they're going to go visit Lynn's sister until the movie's done filming."

That was something. "Well, I'll miss you this weekend."

"Maybe we can steal some kisses." Like they had been until the week previous.

"Definitely. I'll meet you by the woodpile."

He rumbled a warm laugh in her ear at the same time as someone knocked on her door.

"I gotta go. Hostess duties call."

"Okay. I…I'll text you later."

"Can't wait."

She hung up the phone and pressed her hands over her face. The knock sounded again. "Hang on!"

Grabbing her robe off the hook, she covered up and opened the door. When she saw it was Liana, she waved the tiny brunette into her room.

"Who were you talking to?"

"None of your darn beeswax." She threw herself onto the bed. She actually wanted to tell her best friend every last detail, but she'd keep the sharing to an acceptable-for-everyone level. "It doesn't matter, he's going to be busy this weekend anyway."

"He?" Liana joined her, sliding onto her side and giving Holly a gleeful look. It wasn't fair how pretty her friend was after a night of wine, although maybe the latter had only been Holly's burden to bear. "You didn't tell me about a *he* last night."

"I know. I was hoping he'd stay a secret," Holly said pointedly.

"We have no secrets, silly."

"Okay. I've met a boy." She could feel her face softening as she said it. "And he's lovely, and not really available, not for the long-term, but he's just…nice and handsome and *good*. He's a good guy, not in the industry at all, and I can't get enough of him."

"A local?"

Very local. A few hundred feet away. "Yep."

"So why isn't he available? He's not married, is he?"

Heavy emotion lurched through Holly's gut. "No. But it's complicated in other ways. He's not comfortable dating someone famous, with the scrutiny that brings. Plus he's got kids, so traveling to L.A. or wherever I'm filming isn't an option. And I get it. But I wish things were different."

"Do planes only fly in one direction?" Her friend scooted closer and wrapped her arms around Holly. "Anyone who puts that look on your face is probably worth flying back to Pine Harbour for, at least between movies. You hate the city."

"I don't." It sounded weak, because yeah, she did. She loved big skies and coyotes in the distance. Her heart skipped a beat. She loved plaid shirts and work boots. But they didn't love her. They liked her—a lot—for a safe, guaranteed-to-end private fling. "And even if I didn't like it, that's where a lot of my work is."

"That's what the Internet is for. I've been on tour for almost a year, and I'm still able to do deals and collaborate with people, from wherever I am in the world. It's the same as when you're on a film set. You don't feel like you need to be in Los Angeles then, right?"

That was true. But Emmett lived in L.A., and while he was happy to travel with her, he wouldn't move to Pine Harbour… "Oh my God," she groaned. "I just thought, 'But how would I convince Em to move here?' How out of touch with reality am I?"

Liana laughed and squeezed her tighter. "You can hire a local assistant, honey. I'm sure there's a miracle worker here who can coordinate with him. He can be your California boots-on-the-ground warrior."

"I don't need an assistant."

"Now you're just talking crazy. Do you think Emmett will make us smoothies?"

"Yep. I'm going to have a shower, I'll be down in a few." She grabbed her best friend's hand as Liana slid off the bed. "Don't tell Maggie, okay?"

"Of course. You just remember that life is too short for regret, got it?"

Holly totally got it. She just wasn't sure what she'd regret more—not taking a chance, or overstepping the bounds of her relationship with Ryan.

———

RYAN WATCHED his kids pile on their grandparents, then he moved in and gave big, welcoming hugs to Mike and Gloria Fenich. If he was only half-way happy to see Lynn's parents, he buried that deep.

"Mom, Dad, glad to have you back."

"We're happy to be back, although we had a wonderful time down south. And we brought so many presents, our suitcases are *bulging,*" Gloria said loudly, winking.

Ryan just laughed and shook his head. His kids didn't get spoiled that often. His parents loved them, but they had half a dozen other grandkids as well, and were four hours away. His three kids were the only grandkids Mike and Gloria had, and all five had missed each other something fierce.

"Come on in, I just put on a pot of coffee. Tell us about

your trip. I've shown the kids some of your pictures on Facebook..."

An hour later, the conversation finally turned to the cottages. Gloria had taken the kids upstairs to put Maya's new stuffed animal down for a nap, and Mike gave Ryan a stern nod. "Everything okay with the movie people?"

"Yes, sir. They seem happy with the accommodations. They'll be gone in a few weeks. You can sleep in Maya's room until then, when you're here."

"We'll try to stay out of your hair as much as possible. The Minellis invited us to stay with them, if you'd rather."

If it was Gloria, Ryan would have protested, worrying the question was a trap, but Mike was always straight with him. "Stay here tonight. But you might find it a little less noisy over at Anne and Alessandro's after that."

And if Ryan wanted his own privacy...well, there was that, too.

"I might just take a walk down to the house, do you think they'll mind?"

"Um..." There was no good reason for his father-in-law not to visit the lake house. *His* house. "Probably not."

Mike stood and clapped Ryan on the shoulder. "I'll take the kids."

Oh fuck. "They're probably having fun with Gloria..."

It was too late. Mike strolled to the bottom of the stairs. "Who wants to take a walk down to Grandma and Grandpa's house?"

A chorus of "Me!"s came blasting down the stairs, followed quickly by a herd of excited children.

Ryan barely had time to send a warning text to Holly before he was following his family down the secret path between the houses, a terrible sense of impending doom twisting his guts into knots.

The boys were walking on either side of their grandfather, and Maya was hanging onto Gloria's hand, skipping along in excitement.

Of course she's excited, she's going to see Holly, who is made of light and magic because she's a fairy. He couldn't disagree with his daughter's assessment, either, but the thought of his in-laws scrutinizing how close his kids were to the woman he was secretly sleeping with made him want to blow something up as a distraction.

If only his demolitions certification hadn't lapsed.

And all the nearest C4 explosive was at the base in Meaford, a solid hour away.

Toss in the live grenade of being a criminal act, and it wasn't his best coping strategy.

So he grit his teeth and hung back as their little parade came out into the clearing…and stumbled onto a tea party.

Jesus Christ.

Holly gave him a wide-eyed look as she glanced up from her phone, obviously just getting his text message right now. She was sitting on a blanket spread out on the grass with two other women, Parvati on her left, and he assumed the smaller, dark-haired woman with big lips and an even bigger voice on her right was her friend Liana.

"Hi folks," Mike said in that booming voice of his, honed from decades spent running his own construction company. "Mike Fenich, nice to meet you. No, don't get up, sorry to interrupt. We're just going for a walk with our grandkids. We're the property owners, actually, but we're happy to stay out of your hair while you make your movie. The wife and I were just down south for a while, and our son-in-law there says all has been quiet here, which is great. We just missed the place a bit, thought we'd walk around."

Holly got up anyway, because she was awesome that way, and she could probably tell that Maya was four seconds away from joining them. "Would you like to join us? We could move onto the deck. I'm Hope Creswell, by the way, and this is Parvati Spencer, and—"

"Liana Hansen on a blanket in my backyard, oh my word," Gloria breathed, fluttering her hands. "I have to tell you, Ms. Hansen, I am just such a fan, and your newest album is a work of art."

Ryan breathed a sigh of relief as his mother-in-law and the country music singer started talking. Good. Maybe the veil of celebrity would mask the inappropriate level of heat that simmered between him and Holly.

"Hope's secret name is Holly," Jack said not so quietly to his grandfather, and Holly laughed.

"That's true. You can call me whatever you want. Would anyone like tea, or can I get you beer or wine?"

Maya tugged Gloria over to the blanket. "We want tea, right Grandma?"

"Well, yes, I think I'd love a cup of tea."

Like he'd been watching all along, Holly's assistant Emmett appeared with a tray. More mugs for tea, and two bottles of beer. He handed one to Mike, and the other to Ryan—with a look that said he knew this must be awkward. Great. So that made Olivia and Emmett and probably their respective spouses who knew their secret. Add in Ryan's kids, who probably hadn't guessed the kissing part but definitely knew Holly was a special friend, and their secret didn't feel so safe anymore.

Ryan downed half his beer right away, then took a slow turn around the yard, keeping an eye—and an ear— on his kids. His initial assessment of Holly's friend was that she was lovely and gracious and more than a little overwhelming. Plus obviously high-maintenance, which didn't matter to him, but it was quite the contrast to Holly's natural appeal. As the impromptu party continued and everyone moved onto the deck for munchies, he had the misfortune of being trapped in conversation by the woman.

It didn't take long for him to realize that *she* knew their secret as well. And she was very excited about it.

Holly rescued him, somehow conjuring Joshua Pearce from thin air, and Liana moved on to bat her false eyelashes at the actor. After making the introduction, Holly drifted back in Ryan's direction. He watched as she did it, with subtle misdirection, talking to Gavin about Minecraft as she backed up against the railing right next to Ryan.

This woman can do anything she puts her mind to, he thought. He was a lucky asshole that she put her mind to him.

"Having fun?"

"Kill me now."

She just smiled, looking out over the gathering of people. She watched her best friend like he watched the kids. "You don't like her."

"I don't know her." He wanted to choose his answer carefully. "She loves you, and so I like that about her. But she's…intense."

Holly laughed quietly, her shoulder shaking against his biceps.

He resisted the urge to turn and just watch her be happy. "You're very different."

"I had a lot of different influences in my life. I've learned to look below the surface of people. Under all of that, Liana has a heart of gold. And when I met her, I realized…this is what it is to have family. To be loved, unconditionally."

With a start, Ryan realized that for all the *poor me* sobbing he'd done to Holly about his kids not having their mother, she'd never once pointed out that she'd done just fine without a father, and really, without a caring mother, too. *Shit.* "I think you should get a lot of credit for finding her and making yourself a family. You probably should get credit for raising yourself," he said gruffly. "You're pretty amazing."

She didn't say anything, just smiled again, but her shoulder pressed against his arm again, and this time she didn't move away.

———

AFTER DINNER, Gloria asked if she could help the kids with their bath and bed routine. Ryan waved her on upstairs, fully expecting at least Maya to want him there at the end, but for now, they all looked happy with Grandma being in charge.

"You got any scotch, my boy?" Mike asked once they were alone. Ryan nodded and went to the cupboard.

"You got me my first bottle of this stuff," he said as he slid the finger-and-a-generous-half across the table.

Mike just nodded, then tipped his head to the porch. "Let's go outside. I want to smoke a cigar with this."

Shit. That meant he wanted to talk. But Ryan couldn't very well dodge a conversation his father-in-law deserved to ask him for. "Sounds good."

It didn't take long. "So Hope Creswell's quite pretty."

"She's kind and thoughtful, too." If he was going to be taken to task, it wasn't for being a randy teenager.

"I can see that." His father-in-law lit up, dragging a few deep breaths through the cigar before continuing. "The kids seem like they've spent a lot of time with her."

"Some. They'll be sad when she leaves."

"Few more weeks, eh?"

Ryan nodded, ignoring the stabbing pain in his chest. That was the price he had to pay.

"You going to keep in touch with her?"

"I don't know." He honestly didn't know if he could—or if he could not. "Probably not."

It was the more likely outcome. At first they might exchange emails, but over time…And when she started dating someone else, he wouldn't be able to handle it. He knew that without a doubt.

"I gotta say, it was a surprise to see you cozy up to her on the deck like that."

Ryan clamped his jaw shut, biting back the none-of-your-fucking-business response that almost spilled out. They'd been completely appropriate today. As they always had. "Do you have a problem with something I did today, Mike?"

His father-in-law shook his head slowly. "Don't put words in my mouth. We're more concerned about what you have to say about it than anything else."

"To you? Or to her?" Ryan clenched his fists at his sides, then relaxed his fingers, wiggling out the tension. "First of all, to my family her name is Holly. She knows about Lynn. She knows how much I loved your daughter, about the life we built here. How private I am about how Lynn died, and how I'd never do anything to expose my children—"

"Okay." But the harsh tone didn't match the agreeable response. "It's just hard to see."

"I can appreciate that." That hurt to say. He hadn't asked to lose his wife. Hadn't asked to be alone. Hadn't asked to meet someone else, someone famous, someone incompatible with life in his sleepy little town. "You're not going to see anything else."

"You sure about that?"

"With all due respect, Mike, I'm not sure what you're asking me." That was a lie, and they both knew it.

"You look like you're falling head over heels in lust with the woman, Ryan." As Mike talked, his words pulled tighter and tighter, revealing just how angry he was. "It's embarrassing. And if it's obvious to me, then it's obvious to the kids."

"No!" Ryan snapped. "You see something because you've come back after being gone for three months, and when you left I was a sad sack of shit and now I'm happy again. Barely happy, I might point out. How about you ask me a different question? Ask me if I still miss Lynn. Because I do, every minute of every day. Even when I'm with Holly, *talking at a party.* You didn't see anything inappropriate today. And the kids have seen me pull out of my shell because of a friend. They've done the same. Our fleeting acquaintance with her will end. It has to, because we exist in different worlds. But we'll forever be better for knowing her, and I'm not going to apologize to you or anyone else for being *happy* about that." He'd probably gone too far, said too much, but it didn't matter. It was done. Without looking at his father-in-law, he nodded at the dark. "I'm going to go in and check on the kids."

CHAPTER NINETEEN

HOLLY WAS REACHING for her phone, to text Ryan that the coast was clear for a late night visit if he could get away, when he knocked quietly at the sliding door.

She hopped up and let him in, giving him a quick hug. "I was just going to invite you over. Is everything okay?"

"I had a fight with my father-in-law," he said with a groan as she led him to the couch where she curled up next to him. "Before the kids went to bed, although they were inside and we were outside…Then we made nice for a bit, but once my mother-in-law went to bed, I told him I was going for a walk. Pretty sure he knew I meant I was coming here since walking into town would be stupid."

She wrapped her arms around her knees. She wanted to wrap them around him, hold him tight and tell him it was okay, but she wasn't sure it was. "Did you tell him…"

Ryan shook his head. "Yes and no. He guessed." His gaze was pinned to the floor. "I told him it was none of his business."

"It's not." She gently bumped the back of her hand into

his arm. "What we're doing is just between us. If he saw it, he had to have been looking pretty hard."

"I'm sorry that I'm keeping this a secret."

"It's okay." It really was. She didn't have any right to ask for more, knowing it would hurt him. "Do you want to come up to bed for a bit?"

"No." But he pulled her in close, his lips playing against hers, lightly at first, then harder, more insistent. When his tongue hit hers, and she could taste his need, she pulled back and grabbed his hand.

"Come on."

"Holly, I don't want—" She stopped and looked at him, and he flushed. "I don't want to use you for sex."

She was speechless. Ryan using her for sex would be awesome. Lips parted, she just gaped at him for a moment, then laughed. "Come on, my lumberjack."

"Where's your friend?"

"Liana's gone over to Joshua's cabin for drinks. I'm sure she's going to violate him in ways I don't want to think about." She laughed as she led him up the stairs. Emmett's light was already out, but the master bedroom was at the end of the hall, around a bend. It was pretty private.

As they entered the room, she realized he knew this house better than she did, although the furniture was all rented—a rider demand her agent insisted on when they rented accommodations for her. It had always felt silly in the past, but she was insanely grateful at the moment that this was, for all intents and purposes, *her* room she was welcoming him into. On the walls were generic rented art, and a picture of her and Liana she took everywhere with her. Nothing to remind Ryan of his wife or his in-laws or anything other than losing himself for an hour or two.

"So," she said, spinning in his arms as he tried to kiss her neck. "You want to use me for sex, huh?"

"That's not what I said," he murmured, brushing her jaw with his lips. "Get back here."

"Nope." She planted her hands in his chest and shoved him away with a smile. "Go sit on the bed."

He laughed and stepped right back into her personal space with a single stride. "Not a chance. I want my hands on you. I want to make you scream."

Her breath caught in her throat. She wanted that, too. But they needed to be quiet. "Someone might hear me."

"Maybe I don't care."

"You do." Sighing as he wrapped his arms around her, she melted into him. He held her in place as he loved her neck, then took her mouth again. This time she gave in to the passion between them, sliding her fingers through his hair as they clung to each other, hungrily kissing while moving in the general direction of the bed.

He tugged her t-shirt up, and her sports bra down, kneading her breast, each roll of his palm over her nipple making her insides tug in a filthy way. She reached for him, too, getting his belt open and his fly down, his jeans slipping low on his hips as she fished his erection out of his boxers. His hand splayed wide in the small of her back, his fingers tucked into the waistband of her yoga shorts, he pulled her against him, her fist caught between their bodies.

With each slow pump of her hand, he squeezed them tighter, until she couldn't move at all, but she still pulsed her grip around his swollen length.

"I can think of a way to keep me nice and quiet," she whispered, teasing the tip of her tongue along his lips.

"Stuff my mouth with something. Maybe something big and hard."

Laughing, Ryan released her. "Be my guest."

She stripped off her t-shirt first, then dropped to her knees on the plush rug beside her bed. Ryan's erection bobbed in the air in front of her, and she immediately ran her nose down the shaft, pressing a kiss to the taut skin of his lower abdomen, right above his dark curls. Licking her way back up to the wide crown, she kissed him again there, a tiny peck that made him flex.

"Lick it again," he groaned.

She did. Over and over again, until he was throbbing in her hand, pre-come leaking from the tip, and his hand had snaked into her hair.

When he growled for her to suck on him, she did that, too, but not before issuing an invitation for him to finish in her mouth.

He did.

She pressed her face to his thigh, waiting for him to catch his breath. He smoothed his hand over her hair and she leaned into him, and as soon as his thighs stopped shaking, he hauled her up and tossed her onto the bed.

Crawling over her, he kissed away her laughter, consuming her mouth until they were both breathing hard all over again. Then he traced the outline of her bra, his finger dragging along her skin, raising a line of goose-bumps in his wake. "I'm going to forever get a hard-on when I see a running magazine now, you realize that, don't you?"

She arched into his touch as he peeled down her shorts. "You know...I was on the cover of *Runner's World* last year."

"I'm going to need a copy of that." He sucked on the soft spot just inside her hip bone.

"Pretty sure the pictures are online."

He shook his head, his breath now nearly where she wanted him the most. "I can't..."

"What?" She reached down and touched his cheek, stilling his progress. "You can't what?"

He glanced up, and the look on his face—sweet, slightly embarrassed, totally honest—blew her away. "I can't Google you. I don't want that part of you. Not when I've had this."

"But a magazine would be okay?" She grinned. "I'm not complaining, that's the sweetest thing anyone has ever said to me."

"Yeah." He nodded slowly, biting his lower lip in thought. "It's different somehow. At least if I have a copy of the magazine, I've got you in my hands. And that's you, on your own terms, I guess. I don't know what people put on the Internet. I might see something you don't want."

"You've already seen all of me," she whispered. "You might be the only person who ever has."

He smoothed his hands down the back of her thighs, lifting her knees and spreading her wide as he glanced back to her face one more time, his gaze dark and intense. "Good."

That heavy, possessive stare stayed with her long after he lowered his head, after he parted her sex and used the tip of his tongue to stroke around her clit. As she closed her own eyes and threw her head back, that feeling of being Ryan's made every lick and suck that much more intense.

She had no secrets from this man. He knew what made her tick, what made her scream. Even what made her feel sad and small. *I think I love you*, she wanted to say. So maybe she had one secret, after all, because she couldn't. She knew she couldn't, and the cruel irony was enough to make her cry, but Ryan was making love to her with his mouth and she needed to cling to that instead.

Feel what he's doing to you, her inner voice of reason promised. *That's love, too.*

He was stoking her fires, that's what he was doing. Not teasing, exactly, because it was damn satisfying, but he wasn't in any hurry for her to come either. He was taking his time, alternating between long, lazy strokes of his tongue and wiggly little twists with just the tip, exploring her most private places until she was panting and blushing and out of her mind with desire for him.

And then he slid his fingers inside her. First one, then two, and when she started begging for more, three thick digits squeezed inside her, making her burn.

Inside, he stroked his fingertips against her hungry walls, and his mouth kept working hard, too, as he lapped at her clit and the lips stretched wide around his fingers.

She panted his name as her hips started jerking of their own accord, rocking against him as she started climbing the ramp toward a climax. "Sooo close," she moaned, ending on a squeak as he closed his mouth around her swollen clit and sucked.

She didn't scream, because she'd twisted her face into the pillow, but inside she was throwing a ticker tape parade for Ryan and his talented mouth. Aftershocks ricocheted throughout her body, nerve endings firing at random as he slowly slid his fingers from her body, squeezing her entire pussy gently as he moved back up her body, pulling her tight against him.

She burrowed deep into his side, and they lay there, just holding each other, for quite some time.

But it couldn't last…she knew that. They probably had less time than when she walked up the dark lane to his place. "You have to go, don't you?"

He nodded in answer to her quiet question, then kissed her forehead. "Soon."

They hadn't even gotten all the way naked. Her heart squeezed. "Okay."

"But not yet," he promised, his voice rough, rasping in the quiet. She didn't look up at his face. She didn't want to cry. "I'm not done with you."

She wanted to read so much into that statement. Too much. *I'm not done with you, either.* But she couldn't say it, because she meant it in a way that Ryan couldn't.

CHAPTER TWENTY

WHEN RYAN SAW Dani and Matt Foster climbing out of their ambulance at Mac's on Tuesday, he knew it was a sign. His in-laws were heading out of town on Thursday, Holly's guest was gone…life was back to the weird new normal, and he wanted to take her out on a date.

But he needed a babysitter first.

He parked in the gravel lot and jumped out of his truck. "Hey guys!"

They turned and waved, waiting for him. As he approached, Matt's phone rang. Serendipity.

He waited until Matt headed around the corner, then he turned to Dani. "I have a favour to ask you."

"Shoot."

It required telling her *something*, but he didn't need anyone else in on his secret. "I need a babysitter for Saturday night. In return, I'll make sure Matt doesn't book any strippers for Jake's bachelor party."

She rolled her eyes at him. "I can do that all on my own. And why do you need a babysitter?" She punched him lightly in the upper arm. "Is it a hot date?"

"You think Matt's going to be honest with you about his stripper plans?"

"Nice distraction technique. Tell me more about this mystery woman. Is she nice? Pretty? Easy?"

"Um…" She started laughing as he gave her a helpless look. "I know I've been asking you for a lot of childcare lately."

"Oh, shut up. I love your kids and they love me. But we're putting in a dock on Saturday…"

"Really? You're doing that?"

"Okay, I'm watching Jake put in a dock on Saturday."

Ryan winced. "Please don't tell me that I'm interfering with your plans to bone your fiancé after watching him be strong all day."

"Then don't ask me to babysit on a Saturday night. Or any other night." She laughed at the pained look on his face. "No, it's fine. He'll be zonked anyway. It's a massive dock. But I'll come to your place, okay?"

Ryan's heart thumped at the promise of this plan actually working out.

"So a date, huh?"

"No comment."

"You're really not going to tell me who it is?"

"Nope."

"Okay." Just like that. He had the most amazing friends. He'd forgotten that in the haze of grief. It was time he started appreciating them more.

"Hypothetically… would that be weird?"

"You dating someone? I think you're the only one who can answer that."

"It feels strange to say it out loud."

"Bad kind of strange?"

He thought about that for a few seconds, searching

inside himself. "Nope. Good." Really good. For all his early concerns, Holly had bent over backwards to protect his privacy and be together on his terms. They weren't great terms, he knew that, and there weren't enough words to properly express how much he appreciated her. *And she's leaving.* Maybe that was why he was doing this—no risks. *Other than your heart.* But that was so damaged, what was another ding?

HOLLY GREETED him at the door of her trailer on the set—at his request, because picking her up at the cottage and then driving past Dani and the kids felt a bit weird—and he almost staggered backward at the sight of her.

"Wow," he said slowly, raking his eyes over her. She was wearing a little black dress that ended at mid-thigh, and tall, strappy sandals. It wasn't the first time he'd seen her dressed up, but it was the first time she'd dressed up *for him*, and it took his breath away how drop-dead sexy she was.

From the flash of diamonds at her ears to the perfume she'd put on—heady, rich, probably laden with unicorn pheromones—she was a living, breathing fantasy woman. *His fantasy.* He leaned and kissed her gently, deepening the kiss when he realized she wasn't wearing any lipstick.

"Nice touch with the bare lips," he murmured, rubbing his thumb at the corner of her mouth when they broke apart.

She winked at him. "I have big plans for more of that all night, lipstick would have been silly."

"Smart girl."

He helped her into his truck, glad he'd driven down to

Wiarton on Thursday to get it detailed. The carseat and booster in the back still knocked his cool factor down a few pegs, but luckily Holly didn't seem to care about that. "I made reservations at a steakhouse Olivia recommended, but there are other options. What do you feel like?"

She slid her hand over his, a warm press of bare flesh. "Totally up to you."

Jesus. He had to bite back a suggestion of burgers right there at her trailer.

But that would be a waste of what might be their only opportunity to do this right. "You know what I want?"

She shook her head, smiling slightly. "What?"

"A giant steak. With mashed potatoes."

"Then let's go get *that*."

He laughed as she winked again, the tip of her tongue poking out between her teeth, and he turned left at the highway, leaving Pine Harbour behind. She kept touching him, stroking her hand up and down his arm as they drove north to Tobermory. Pine Harbour didn't have any restaurants fancy enough for a first date, but even if it did, he still wanted privacy. When she left, he didn't need his entire town knowing his heart was broken.

Olivia had suggested a new fancy-pants grill pub, close to the marina, and the parking lot was nearly full. He squeezed his truck into the back corner, then hurried around to Holly's side and opened her door.

"Thank you," she breathed, her eyes glittering. "I forgot to tell you that you look amazing tonight, too. I think I got distracted because you kissed me like crazy."

He did it again, then glanced down at himself. Light blue dress shirt that he'd bought new for tonight, his best jeans, and combat boots because they were the only black shoes in his wardrobe. He wasn't sure her praise was substantiated by the evidence, but he'd take it.

Offering her his arm, he led the way to the restaurant. A crowd of people blocked the entrance, but he steered her around them, finding the hostess. He gave his name and she promised their table would be ready in a minute.

"Guess I'm not fancy enough to justify actually saving a table," he said, smiling down at Holly as he backed up against the wall, protecting her from the crush of people coming and going. "I can't get over how busy this place is."

She played with the front of his shirt, stroking her fingertips through the gap between the buttons to the light t-shirt underneath. "This is what it's like most nights when I go out in L.A. Except there's also paparazzi outside and dinner starts two hours later."

He couldn't wrap his head around that. He thought seven was already plenty late enough—he was starving.

"I like this. That wasn't a comparison."

"I know." Someone bumped into him and he braced his hand on the wall beside her, closing their little world in even smaller. "Listen—"

"Table for Ryan Howard," the hostess called out, and he turned in acknowledgement.

Holly squeezed his hand and followed as they made their way to a table along the wall. He held the chair for her, then took his seat on the banquette across from her. He sat looking out the restaurant, but he only had eyes for the woman across from him. Which was why he didn't see Faith Davidson until she was standing next to his table, an older woman waiting for her a few feet away. "Ryan!"

"Hey, Faith!" He did an awkward half-attempt to get up, but she waved him down. "Nice to see you again."

"Same. I won't interrupt, I just wanted to say hi. You were missed at the meeting on Thursday."

"Yeah, I'm sorry about that. Been busy. I'll be back. Scout's honour."

"Really? Because I'm not above tracking you down like a creepy stalker."

"I know. I'll come next month. Promise." He slid his gaze from Faith to Holly, unsure if he should introduce her, and if so, how. He went with a leading intro, hoping she'd take care of it for him. "Faith, this is…"

"Hope." She gave Faith a dazzling smile. "I'm a friend of Ryan's."

"Faith. I'm his stalker."

Ryan choked on the sip of water he'd just taken.

Faith groaned and wrinkled her nose. "Sorry. That sounded funnier in my head. We know each other through a parenting thing."

He took Holly's hand. "Faith leads a bereaved spouse support group. But she's not kidding about the stalking thing."

Holly laughed. "Gotcha."

"Have we met? You look really familiar." Faith turned her attention to Ryan's date.

"I get that a lot," Holly said with a smile.

Faith's eyes got really big and she whipped her head toward Ryan, then back to Holly before lowering her voice. "You're Hope Creswell."

"I am." Holly whispered the answer back with a polite smile, but her eyes were dancing.

"I knew you were in the area filming a movie, but I didn't realize it was right in Pine Harbour."

Ryan cleared his throat, and Faith nodded. "Right, I'll leave you to your dinner. It was nice to meet you."

"Thank you." Holly reached out and touched Faith's forearm. "It's a bit of a secret dinner, okay?"

"Lips are sealed." She grinned widely. "It was so awesome to meet you. Seriously. Major fangirl moment here. Oh crap, I almost kept that inside."

"Bye, Faith," Ryan said drily, this time waiting to take a sip of water until they were alone again.

Holly looked at him for a long moment. "I like her."

He laughed. "Yeah, I do, too. I'm glad she lives in Tobermory, though. She's a little intense for Pine Harbour."

"Do you know her well?"

"Not really. Just through the support group." He shot Holly an alarmed look. "We've never—"

"Oh! No, that wasn't what I was asking." She pressed her lips together. "Although thank you for saying that, because I can get just as jealous as the next girl. I was wondering more about if she's likely to tell anyone about seeing us together."

He sighed. "Ah. No, probably not, she seems pretty considerate. I think she'll keep the secret of how much I like you."

"You like me?" Her eyes crinkled.

"Yeah. I like you." *So much it hurts.*

"Then maybe I'll let you buy me dinner." She picked up her menu and flipped it open. "And if you're really nice, I'll let you feel me up on the way home."

"Funny, I was going to say the same thing to you." Under the table, her foot hooked around his ankle, and behind his zipper, his dick swelled a bit. He'd let her do anything she wanted to him.

When the waiter arrived, Ryan ordered a striploin with mashed potatoes and green beans, and Holly nodded.

"Same for me. Make mine just an eight ounce steak, please."

"Do you want wine or beer?" the waiter asked.

"Just water for me," Ryan said, shaking his head, and Holly asked for the same. He wanted to be fully sober for the entire night, and he got the feeling she shared the desire not to miss anything.

While they waited for their food to arrive, they talked about everything except the fact that she was leaving. He told her about the summer camp he'd signed the kids up for, as if she'd still be around then, and she confessed that after her next film, scheduled for shooting in the early winter, she had no clue what her next career move was.

"My agent keeps asking if he can send me scripts. I've been telling him I don't want other stories in my head while I'm working, but the truth is, I'm terrified that I'm not going to like any of the projects available to me."

"Has this ever happened to you before?"

She shook her head, and the lost look on her face made him want to pull her around the table and into his lap. He settled for squeezing her fingers.

"Can I confess something terrible to you?"

Her eyes twinkled. "Of course."

"I don't think I've ever seen any of your movies."

She laughed, a rising tinkle of wind chimes. "Yeah?"

"I mean, I'd have to Google you to be sure, and you know my stance on that. Not going to happen. But…yeah. I don't watch a ton of movies, and I don't remember your face, not like that."

"I like that, actually. I'm just Holly to you."

He tugged her fingers across the table a bit more so he could stroke her entire hand. "Never *just* anything to me."

"I like that even more."

He took a deep breath. "So…that's why I'm not sure what to say about the script thing. Trust your gut, I guess."

"You think that's a good idea?" She gave him a sideways, curious look.

He held her gaze as he nodded. "Always."

When their food arrived, they both dug in, and Olivia's recommendation had been bang on, because it was amazing. They slowed down after the first few groan-inspiring bites, but they both cleared their plates.

After Ryan paid and they made their way out the door, Holly rubbed her tummy and giggled. "I ate too much. I'm totally going to get yelled at on Monday for being bloated."

"Send them my way, I'll pound them for you. You're beautiful." He wrapped his arm around her waist, not caring if anyone saw them.

She stroked his middle as they swayed slowly to his truck. It was almost dark, but the parking lot was surrounded by trees, making it seem like the middle of the night. "This was really wonderful."

Sliding his hand up the outside of her body, he tried to tamp down a tremor of anxiety threatening in his gut. It had been wonderful. And they still had hours. She could come over after Dani left. Maybe they could sleep together in Maya's room.

Maybe not, but the thought pushed the anxiety away. He wasn't ready to be done with her. And the countdown to the end of the movie was marching in lock-step with his ever-increasing attachment to this woman. The thought that they'd never share a full night together bothered him for reasons he couldn't really put his finger on.

He wove his fingers into her hair, tipping her face up to his for a quick kiss, then a longer, deeper one as they stopped in front of the truck. By the time they got around to the passenger side so he could open Holly's door, he had a thick erection straining at his fly and a warm, willing woman in his arms.

It was going to be a long-ass drive back to Pine Harbour.

He pressed Holly against her door and leaned into her, hips to hips, chest to chest, lips to lips. She rocked against him, finding his cock with the heat between her legs—her dress and his jeans were no match for their need for each other.

Drunk on lust, he speared his tongue into her mouth as he groped her, each touch feeling rougher and more desperate than the last. Under his hands, she writhed with the same urgency.

Panting, she wrapped her arms around his shoulders, trying to climb his body. He didn't have a problem with that plan at all. For all the people traffic inside the restaurant, the parking lot was quiet, and they were hidden behind his truck.

"Do you have protection?"

Oh, shit. He did. Could they? He might have a problem with *that* plan. Except his dick didn't. And his heart didn't. *Two votes to one, head. You lose.* "This is crazy."

"We'll be quiet." She grinned and tugged his shirt out of his waistband.

They were good at that, at least—swallowing each other's moans to keep the secret. He lifted her onto the running board and reached up her skirt, finding a skimpy thong. She was already soaked for him, and she shivered as he pulled the underwear down her leg, bracing her hands on his shoulders as he shoved it in his pocket. Looking around, he confirmed they were completely alone, and it was dark enough in the shadows that he couldn't see her that well, let alone be spotted by anyone else. They worked by touch, him undoing his belt, her teasing fingertips finding his lips, then his neck, her mouth soon following the same path.

"Get in me, Ryan. Now. I need you."

Fumbling in his pocket, he managed to grab the emergency condom he'd brought because he wasn't stupid, and in a few short seconds, he was sheathed first in latex, then in Holly. She wrapped her legs around his waist as he held her bottom, pressing her against the truck as she adjusted to his girth. Spreading his legs wide, he rolled his hips, fucking her slow at first, then faster, the weight of her making each thrust intense. Perfect.

"I'm not going to last long," he groaned, and she cupped his face, kissing him.

"Same," she whispered, whimpering as he hammered into her, making her bounce between him and the truck. She took his lips again, this time harder, sucking on his tongue like her pussy was consuming his cock, and he chased that feeling, giving himself to her completely.

With a choking sound, she tightened her legs around his waist, locking them together as she ground her pelvis against his, and he took three final, jerking thrusts in the tight confines of her body, following her over the edge.

They both started laughing as soon as the rush of their orgasms faded.

"Uhm, so…yeah." Holly pressed her forehead into his neck. "I can't believe we just did that."

"It's not my fault," he whispered, grinning into her hair. "You're really pretty and you made me do it."

"I accept all blame," she said breathlessly.

"No, it's our shared madness, sweetheart." He drew a

line along her jaw with his knuckle, tipping her chin up so he could kiss her. "And I loved it."

"Me too."

They drove back to Pine Harbour, holding hands. Holly's thong stayed in his pocket. When he drove back, he took her all the way to the lake house and walked her to the door.

"Thank you for a lovely dinner," he said quietly, kissing her chastely.

"My pleasure," she said, cheeks flushed. "Thank you for the quick fuck against your truck."

"My pleasure. Come over after Dani leaves," he whispered against her mouth. "I'm not ready for this date to be over."

CHAPTER TWENTY-ONE

HOLLY TURNED the details of their date over and over again in her head as she waited for the all-clear. The crazy sex against the side of his truck. Ryan telling her to trust her gut. *It's our shared madness, sweetheart. And I loved it.*

She was twirling as she shimmied out of her black dress and pulled on yoga pants and a t-shirt, then a sweatshirt. She left the diamond earrings in for a bit of sparkle, but the fairytale portion of the night was over. For what she wanted to do next, it was important that she be as ordinary a girl as possible.

When her phone beeped, she sped up the lane. Ryan was waiting at the door, and he swept her off her feet as soon as she stepped inside, carrying her into the living room. She wiggled her legs in the air, giggling quietly as he lay them down on the couch together.

"Hi." She stuck her tongue out at him and he swiped at it with his own.

"Tonight was fun."

"It was." She touched his face, still in awe that they'd found each other. That she was lucky enough to have this man. She didn't know how they'd make it work, but they were meant for each other. And she was positive he felt the same way. Everything had changed.

"What are you thinking?" He flicked his gaze over her face, a lazy, happy smile playing on his lips.

"So much. All good things."

"I'm glad," he said quietly, kissing her softly.

They cuddled, kissing and talking, for almost an hour. When they settled into a comfortable silence, she knew the moment was right. Her pulse skipped in her throat, giddy at what she was about to share.

"You're the best, Ryan."

"I try," he teased.

"No, really. You're so special to me. I…" She smoothed her hand over his chest and wiggled her head into his shoulder. He was so warm, so comfortable. So perfect. "I love you."

"What?" The word dragged out of him, raw and extra long. She'd really surprised him.

She grinned. "Oh come on, you know I do. You light up my entire world."

Under her hand, she could feel his heartbeat, pounding faster and harder than a second ago. More seconds passed, and he still hadn't moved, or said anything. He just stared at her.

"Ryan?"

"You don't mean that, Holly."

"I do." She pushed herself up, scrambling to her knees in the narrow space on the couch when she saw the stricken look on his face. *Oh no. No, no, no.* "I don't say it to stress you. Hey, it's okay."

"It's not okay."

"It will be," she said, pain lancing through her chest. "I

know that's a big thing to hear, and I don't expect you to say it back. But I do love you, Ryan Howard. So much."

"I'm going to hurt you." His voice was sharp and cold, a heavier weapon than anything she could've imagined. "And you're leaving."

"You couldn't, and I don't need to, not forever. I can come and go—"

"No." He shook his head, but she couldn't see what was in his eyes, because he'd turned away from her. Her hands shook as she moved to touch him, but he jerked away before she got there, jumping to his feet to pace.

"You're just freaking out," she pleaded.

"I'm not *just* anything," he said, a cruel echo of what he'd said to her over dinner. "And if that's what you think, then you don't know anything about me."

It was like a physical slap. She jumped her own feet, keeping her voice low because there were children asleep upstairs. "I *do* know you. I know you've been hurt. I know you've lost a wife you loved and a future you'd counted on. So I know this is scary, but—"

"You think I'm just scared about *you* hurting *me*? I am, but that's not the worst possible thing that could happen, Holly. *I'm* going to hurt *you*. I've already done it." He twisted to face her, his entire body shaking. "I lost Lynn *three times*. The first time, she pulled away from me and I couldn't reach her. Then she was killed, and I thought my life was over. And then I found out that she'd been living with the diagnosis of a debilitating illness for more than a year, and I'd failed her. I lost her three times too many, you hear? And I'm not sure that each one of those times wasn't my fault. That I wasn't a good enough husband. Most of the time, I'm sure of that. And the rest of the time? I'm angry. I'm so angry at her for leaving me."

"That's okay. I get that. I'm not pressuring you."

"I'm a *mess*, Holly, inside and out. This? Us? We were a *vacation* from the mess. You don't want any part of that. I like you. So much. But I'm never going to be able to love you. I want to. God, you have to believe that. You're the most wonderful person. You've brought me back to life. And yet…the tiny bit of my soul that is capable of love is busy being a full-time parent to three kids who half the time just hate me for not being their mom."

The words she wanted to say—that the kids didn't hate him, at all, that she'd love him, no matter what—died in her throat, blocked by a massive lump she just couldn't get around.

On the coffee table, her phone vibrated. She ignored it. This was too important. She should have known this would be a hurdle for them. Maybe she should have known he'd run scared—because no matter what he said, that's what this was. Fear was zinging off him in all directions.

But she'd believed him when he said he wouldn't push her away again. Trusted him when twice before he'd given her ample reason not to.

And she'd still fallen in love with him.

She'd do it all over again, in a heartbeat, because loving Ryan was wonderful, even when it was hard. Even when he hurt her. Her therapists would have a field day with that, but she didn't care. She had faith that he'd realize how special their connection was. He just needed some space to freak out.

"Your phone is going crazy," he muttered, still not looking at her. But at least he hadn't kicked her out or stormed upstairs.

"I don't care," she whispered.

"It's the middle of the night. What the hell are people doing texting you at one in the morning?"

"It's only ten on the west coast," she snapped. What did it matter what her phone was doing? She grabbed it off the table just to turn it onto airplane mode, but the text on the screen made her blood run cold.

Emmett: Why aren't you answering your phone? Photo of you and Cute Dad on the Internet. Questions galore.

"I need to…" She couldn't form the words. Her mouth was too dry and her tongue had stopped working. She swallowed hard and tried again. "I have to call Emmett."

Ryan crossed his arms, still seething. *Why hadn't he kicked her out?* It was a moot question. She scrolled through the messages, trying to figure out what exactly was going on before she called her assistant. It wasn't good.

Someone at the restaurant had taken a picture of them while they waited to be seated, and posted it to *Please Patty*, an extra-awful celebrity gossip blog. She was pulling at the front of Ryan's shirt, and he was leaning over her. The photo was taken from the side, showing a lot of her leg and enough of their faces that there was no question of identity.

Hope Creswell's Gone Country! **The pretty blonde actress, currently filming in the northern Canadian town of Pine Harbour, might not be known for dating, but anyone who had bets on her batting for the other team can send their pennies to Patty because she was super cozy with an unknown local man last night.**

It didn't matter that the date had been Ryan's idea. She should have known better. Hot, fat tears started rolling down her face as she held out her phone. "I'll find out more in a minute, but you need to see this."

He stalked across the room and grabbed the phone. His expression didn't change as he read it. He didn't blink, or swear, or do anything. Just stared at the screen for a minute or two, long enough for her to die a dozen deaths.

"You need to leave," he said coldly, handing the phone back.

"This isn't over," she said, shaking as she stood. "We've done this before, right? You just need some cooling down time."

"And then what, Holly? We can have a nice family picture taken for *People* or *US Weekly*?"

"Of course not." She licked her lips. "This will go away. I have a publicist and they're very good at their job—"

"One date," he said, his voice quaking with cold fury. "And our secret was busted wide open."

"I didn't think I was your dirty little secret anymore." Her voice was raised as much as she could without yelling. "There's a difference between discreet and shameful, Ryan. Which hat do you expect me to wear?"

"Neither. I never expected anything of you, except to respect my privacy. And while I get that you didn't do *that*," he snarled, pointing at the phone. "It was still *done*."

It was true. He'd never led her on. She'd fooled herself because of some good sex and quiet moments. And she'd lost her heart to him. If anything, he had to know that. She furiously wiped away her tears. "I love you. No matter what, I love you."

"You should go," he said, turning his back to her again. Not responding to her last declaration, because it had already been addressed. Repeatedly, although she'd been slow on the uptake.

Maybe she should.

The only other option would be to stay and beg him to love her back. And she might be a fool, but she wasn't an idiot.

Slowly, she got up, staring at his back as she made her way to the hallway. It took her too long to take the next step. Long enough to hope that he'd turn around, and realize that he wouldn't. Long enough for her heart to break all over again.

CHAPTER TWENTY-TWO

SHE MIGHT NOT HAVE drunk anything the night before, but this was the worst hangover of her life. At least she didn't have to work. She wasn't getting out of her bed except to pee and find more tissues.

Her phone had beeped a few times, but she ignored it when she saw the messages weren't from Ryan.

Finally, Emmett knocked on her door.

"Go away," she called weakly.

"Can't. Let me in."

"Fine, whatever. I don't get my way anyway."

He cracked the door, and when he'd ascertained that she wasn't going to throw something at him, came in and climbed onto the bed next to her. "You have a million messages."

She knew. Her agent, Liana, someone from her publicist's team. "I turned my phone off in the middle of the night. Still no comment beyond what I told the publicist last night."

"Okay. I'll handle it."

She took a deep breath. "Can you loop Olivia Minelli in

on it, too? Tell her it's…in the past, now, and that I'm sorry."

"You shouldn't be sorry for going on a date."

Nope. But she was. So much it hurt.

The gossip piece didn't matter. They were over—a single date wasn't worth any future press. But the real threat that it posed, that Ryan had predicted all along and that she'd ignored…she started sobbing all over again as she realized he was right.

She'd put his kids in harm's way, all for a hopeless crush.

No, not hopeless. Loving Ryan hadn't been a mistake. She hoped that in time he appreciated their relationship, too. She'd been his rebound fling. At least that was something.

An awful something. God, she couldn't stop crying. She didn't want to be his rebound. She wanted to be his forever.

After Emmett left her alone, she grabbed her phone. She couldn't leave it up to Olivia to tell Ryan about the next story that would come out.

Holly: I know you don't want to talk to me. I just wanted to let you know that my publicist has arranged for what's called a "re-direct". Something big to distract the press. At some point in the near future, you'll see a story about me and a famous actor dating. It won't be true, btw.

She re-read it three times before hitting send, crying harder each time. It didn't say nearly enough, but it was still the longest text message she'd ever sent.

His response was painfully short.

Ryan: Thx for telling me.

And that was that. She typed a counter-response many times over the course of the day, and the next day—after sobbing her way through showers and mindlessly eating smoothies she couldn't taste, after being reprimanded for her red eyes, before and after filming. By the time she crawled into bed the next night, exhausted even though it was barely dinner time, she was all out of potential words.

Because there's nothing to say. Not really.

She just needed to move on.

————

IT TOOK until the end of the week for Emmett to convince her to take a call from her agent, and she only did so after she was reassured that it wasn't about Ryan.

"Hi Walter, what's up?"

"You, my darling!"

"Oh yeah?" She picked a piece of invisible lint off her knee. "Tell me more about that."

"The studio is very happy with what they've seen so far."

"Seriously?" That wasn't the impression she'd been getting from James, but it was her first time working with him. Maybe *asshole* was just his strategy.

"On my mother's grave. I know you guys still have some sound-stage shooting to do in Toronto, but provided that all goes well, they're planning to push this out before Christmas."

"Oh my God." Holly didn't need her agent to explain the importance of that. A pushed release to keep it in this calendar year...they wanted to do a run for the big awards. "That's amazing."

"There's a condition, though. They want you to sign a deal for three more films."

"What? Why?"

"Joshua's...not a great bet right now. Parvati looks good in this film, but they're concerned about her range. You're going to be the star. If they throw the money at a bid for an Oscar, they want to be able to leverage that back into new projects."

Leverage her. A week ago, she'd have told them to stuff it. She wasn't anyone's puppet.

But work...throwing herself into new projects sounded like exactly what she needed right now. "Tell me about the movies they want me to do."

"You'd have some choice."

"Some?"

"There's one they already have in mind. The other two would probably be up to you, especially if this next one goes well. But you might not like it."

She'd find a way to like it if it kept her distracted. "Send me the script."

———

"DAD, do you think the lake is warm enough to go swimming yet?" Gavin asked.

"Not yet, bud." Ryan set the bowl of fresh strawberries on the table.

"Nummy berries, Daddy." Maya grabbed the biggest one and smelled it before taking a bite. "Holly likes strawberries. Can we take some to her?"

"She's busy with the end of the movie, baby."

"I'm not a baby, I'm Maya." She grabbed another strawberry and climbed off her chair. "I'm going to take this to Holly."

"Maya, you can't." Ryan took a deep breath. He'd been avoiding this, but he needed to tell them. "You guys know that Holly lives in California, right? She was only here to make a movie. She's going home soon."

"She's going away?" Maya frowned at him, and his chest pulled even tighter than it had been.

"She was always going away. She's a big movie star, remember?"

"Can we have a party for her?"

"I think she's too busy for a party." He took a deep breath. "But you guys could write her a card? And Aunt Olivia could pass it on."

"She's staying in Grandpa's house. Why can't we just go see her?" Of course Jack would ask that question. It was logical and rational and Ryan didn't have a good answer at all.

"I don't want to see her if she's going away." Ryan jerked his head toward Gavin, shocked at the emotion in his middle child's voice. The boy's eyes were full of tears, and he shoved away from the table. "I'm not writing a stupid card."

"Wait, Gav—" But it was too late, his son was already sprinting up the stairs, and Maya and Jack followed him, making comforting noises.

Fuck.

———

AS THE FINAL week of filming drew to a close, talk starting buzzing about the wrap party in the centre of town—which Ryan had every intention of avoiding. Not just the party itself, but any talk of the party, and all posts about it on Facebook. He stopped going online completely, moving through his days like a zombie.

It didn't mean he actually escaped anything. Everywhere Ryan turned, people had opinions, because no sooner had he blown up his relationship with Holly than the secret slipped out. Jake and Rafe told him he was an idiot and left it at that, but Dani was slower to forgive his secret-keeping. At least the fact that she wasn't speaking to him meant there was one fewer voice telling him what he should do.

And as the cherry on top of the Nosy Parker parade, Faith just showed up at his house.

"This is probably an invasion of privacy," he groused as he let her into the kitchen.

"I'm a big Hope Creswell fan," she said instead of addressing his completely valid point. "So it's a really creepy small world situation that you were dating her."

"Do you want coffee?" He wasn't going to talk about Holly with Faith or anyone else.

"Sure. So like I was saying—"

"Don't. You can come over here and make sure I'm okay, but we're not talking."

"It wasn't me, by the way. I wasn't the person who shared the gossip about her being on a date with a local guy."

"Didn't think it was. If I did, I wouldn't have let you in."

"I don't think you understand just how visible she is. Probably half that restaurant recognized her. And the way social media works these days…nothing stays a secret."

"So I'm learning. And it's a non-issue now." Which was

for the best, because if that was truly the case, he couldn't be a part of Holly's world. No matter what his heart or his dick felt, he couldn't expose his children to that scrutiny.

"Which is why I'm here. Because the chat rooms are humming about how she's broken-hearted."

He closed his eyes, glad he was standing at the sink, filling the coffee pot, and Faith couldn't see his face. He didn't need to hear that. *You already know she's broken-hearted, you ass. You did it to her.*

"So I thought maybe you might be kind of torn up yourself, and need some moral support or something."

"What part of we're not talking don't you understand?"

Instead of being offended, she just laughed. He really needed to work on his growl. "Okay. I don't know anything about anything, except that keeping stuff inside is deadly."

He nodded absently. Anything to change the subject. "How's your kid?"

"Ready for summer vacation. School's been a challenge this year. Yours?"

Not enough of a subject change, apparently, because his children were broken-hearted, too. "Coffee'll be done in a second."

––––––––

HOLLY SAID and did all the right things at the wrap party, but seeing all of Ryan's friends was hard. So too was realizing this would be the last time she'd see this small town she'd come to love almost as much as one of its most loved families.

After delaying all week—and hoping Ryan would

come around, find her, beg forgiveness or at least let her yell at him and point out how moronic he was being—she gave Emmett the go-ahead to book her flight home.

Home. Los Angeles would never feel like home again. Now she knew what a true home felt like—hamburgers for dinner, bedtime routines complete with songs and stories and tickle fights, and friends that kicked your ass if you didn't go to support groups that had nothing to do with sex addiction and mommy issues.

She'd be back in Canada soon enough anyway. They only had a week break before they re-camped in Toronto for the last phase of principal shooting. She hadn't decided what to do after that. Joining Liana in Nashville, and then for the last leg of her Asian tour, sounded like a really good idea. Planes, trains, and no more lumberjacks.

"Hope?" Emmett poked his head into her room. "Almost packed up? You've got a visitor."

She *hated* the way her heart leapt at that. "Oh?"

"It's Olivia Minelli."

"Ah." Okay. "Send her up."

Holly carried her larger suitcase into the hallway and was just hefting the smaller one off the bed when Olivia came in. "Hi, Hope."

"Olivia..." Holly took a deep breath. "Is everything okay?"

"Yes. Well, no. I mean, I'm not sure." The other woman screwed up her face and groaned. "I'm not great at this."

"How about you start by telling me what *this* is." Holly leaned on the end of the bed and crossed her arms and watched as Olivia twisted her fingers together.

"I don't want to meddle. Really. But I thought I should offer myself as a point of contact. For here, I mean. If you might visit in the future."

Holly shook her head. "I don't plan to come back."

"I don't know what happened. But Ryan's been through so much. He's probably prickly."

That hardly touched the level of hurtfulness he'd exhibited. But she knew Olivia was right on at least some level. "Look, I care about Ryan. And that's why I'm going. It's just not the right time. He's not ready for a relationship."

"Please keep in touch. If anything...just keep in touch. I'm not sure if there's anything I could do, but we all care about him, and by extension, you. I mean, I care about you, too. On your own. Oh, jeez, I'm bungling this. But you were good for him. We all saw a change, and we didn't know what the cause was. And now it's like he's right back—"

Holly held up her hand. She couldn't be responsible for how Ryan was now. He was a big boy, and she wasn't dead. If he wanted to make things right, he could reach out to her. "Between you, me, and the walls, I love Ryan Howard with all my heart. But he's not ready. At all."

"Tell him that," Olivia said more urgently, her voice pleading now.

Holly winced. Time to bare her soul. "I did. That's the problem. And now that's enough of that. But I will keep in touch." She smiled and pointed at Olivia's growing belly. "I want to know all about that little one."

Olivia took a deep breath. "Okay. I also have something to give you. From Maya."

Holly hadn't been prepared for that in the least. "Oh?" she asked, her voice thick and her eyes wet.

Olivia pulled a bright pink envelope from her purse. "Here."

Holly waited until the other woman had left to open it.

As soon as she did, she had to close her eyes and let the sobs just wrack her body for a few minutes before trying to read it. Ryan had obviously helped her write it, and that he would do that for his daughter but couldn't do it for himself made her so angry and sad at the same time.

Dear Holly,

Thank you for the strawberry salad. Good luck with your running and movies. We will miss you so much.

Your fairy friend,
Maya

Below that, Gavin and Jack had written their names, and added, **Her Brothers.**

"Emmett," she called out. "I need paper and an envelope!"

CHAPTER TWENTY-THREE

SHE'D REALLY LEFT.

He'd told her to, so he didn't know why he was surprised. *Did you expect her to wear a hair shirt and beg you to take her back? What sort of backwards fucking world do you live in where you get to treat a movie star—or any woman—like shit and still keep her in your life?*

He deserved the pain of walking through his in-laws' empty home, waiting for movers to bring back their furniture. Restore the lake house to it's pre-Holly look. Standing in the master bedroom, remembering how he'd made love to her and how she'd fallen asleep in his arms. How he'd held her and wished for exactly what she'd turned around and offered him a week later, and he'd lost his mind.

That bed was now gone, and the room was scrubbed clean of her memory, as if she'd never been there. Never marked him irrevocably.

A loud knock on the door downstairs broke him from his misery.

It wasn't the movers, though. It was Jake.

"Hey, man." Ryan scrawled a note. ***Door's open, bring***

stuff in. He stuck it on the sliding door and tipped his head up the lane. "Let's go back up to my place. I'm tired of waiting down here."

"That's where I parked."

They fell into step together, and Jake launched right into why he'd stopped by. "I know you're not looking for full-time work, but I've had a couple of things come up recently. Repeat clients asking for help with little tasks, and I end up losing one of my guys for half a day or more for what is basically a handyman visit. On the other hand, I want to protect those client relationships, so I don't want to pass that full cost of that guy's entire daily wage on…so I was wondering if you'd take those jobs—if your schedule allows."

"Be a handyman?" He was a trained paramedic and soldier. He didn't hate the idea, but he didn't love it.

"Be a part of Foster Construction. Do this now, and more later, when you're ready. Taking these calls would be a favour to me."

"I do owe you and Dani an awful lot." Ryan opened his front door and waved his friend inside.

He immediately regretted the decision.

"Owe me enough to talk about your woman?"

"So the job talk was a ruse?"

Jake shook his head. "Nope. I've just got things to say on this front, too."

"I thought you didn't. I preferred it when you didn't."

"Well, bully for you. I've lived it, remember? My dad raised us all by himself."

"I know." Ryan scrubbed his face with his hands. "I do, okay? I'm just trying to keep it together for my kids, so they don't fixate on Holly being gone like everyone else seems to be."

"What exactly happened? In hindsight, it was so obvious that you guys were into each other."

"We were in different places, that's all."

"And you couldn't find a way to get in the same place as her?" Another head shake.

Ryan was so done with being judged. By his father-in-law for falling for Holly, and by everyone else for not falling hard enough. "It's not that easy. I've got kids to consider—"

"It's better to have loved and lost applies to kids, too," Jake said quietly. "I know that's hard to believe now, but you're not doing them any favours by shutting her out of your life. Because you're shutting her out of *their* lives."

"They don't love her yet."

"But you do."

"No." *Yes.* Maybe. Just maybe...he'd walled up his heart enough that he wasn't sure. "No," he repeated, glaring at his friend. "And if I got too wrapped up in her, then that's even more to the point—I don't want my kids to fall in love with her only to have her leave them. And I can't bear to see them lose someone else they love."

"I don't know, the way she looked at you, I didn't think she had any plans to leave."

But she did. In the end, she'd gone without another word. *Because she said the most important words of all and you threw them in her face.*

"Sometimes it's not a choice," he ground out. His eyes were getting hot and itchy and he was done with this conversation.

"Lynn didn't leave you."

"Yes she did. She left our marriage, in her head and in her heart, long before she was killed. And I couldn't get her back. I couldn't fucking reach her."

"You guys had problems."

"I don't want to talk about Lynn."

"Then let's talk about Hope."

"Her name is Holly, and I don't want to talk about her, either."

"You just want to be a miserable ass?"

Yeah. "You know what, Jake? You don't need to tell me how I could be a better father. I don't need that shit from you or anyone else. Don't let the door hit you in the ass on the way out."

He watched his friend shrug and turn to leave. As soon as he was gone, Ryan went to the cupboard where his bottle of scotch had sat untouched for a month.

Pulling it out, he rocked it back and forth between his hands. Then he twisted off the cap, walked over to the sink, and dumped it down the drain.

JUNE HAD FADED INTO JULY. The kids were out of school and into camp, which was a relief, because he wasn't doing a great job of being fun these days, although he was trying.

His friends were still around, hovering on the periphery of his sadness, but they'd stopped talking to him about almost anything that wasn't kid-related.

He'd bought another bottle of scotch. It sat, still sealed, waiting for his father-in-law to ask for a drink.

Mike and Gloria hadn't been over a lot, though. They took the kids a fair bit, but always when Ryan had something to do. He'd been doing odd-jobs here and there for Jake, and ran a short weekend course for the Army.

None of it distracted him from how much he missed Holly.

He'd started a dozen emails to her. Some were complete, others just a random thought. All sat, unsent, in his Drafts folder. He'd deleted her contact profile from his phone, then added it again immediately.

He kept waiting for clarity to set in. Faith gave him a knowing look when he showed up to the July meeting, but nothing new dawned while he sat there, quiet the entire time except for his introduction.

Jake had no more wisdom to share, either.

His friends had all tried. He could feel that in them, a frustration with him that he wasn't getting it, but he wasn't sure what *it* was.

In the end, clarity came in a laundry basket. He'd come home after dropping the kids off. Did the dishes, put on a load of laundry, and grabbed the basket of clean stuff that had been sitting on the dryer for a few days. Carrying it into the living room, he plopped it on the couch and started tossing clothes into different piles. Boys size large soccer shorts—Jack. *Star Wars* t-shirt—Gavin. Maya's new size-five sundress.

Size five, Lynn. Our baby is growing up. He glanced up at the photo array above the couch. Lynn wasn't going to talk back to him, but he wanted to see her face anyway. What he saw instead were babies. *They've all grown up.* There weren't any new pictures to show that, though. The entire wall was a shrine to a time when Lynn was alive.

He needed to let that time go.

He'd been an idiot. Holly had told him exactly that. *Forgiveness means letting go of the hope for a better past.*

Heavy, angry regret pulsed in his gut, and he lifted Lynn's picture off the wall. Cradling it to his chest, he sat heavily on the couch and flashed through fifteen years of memories.

I'll always miss you. Always love you, baby. But it wasn't the same love any more. He could remember the passion that started their marriage. But the special part of his heart that ached for a partner was Holly's now. Cruel irony to realize that four weeks too late.

A knock at the kitchen door interrupted his fugue. "Come in!" he hollered.

Carrying Lynn's picture, he headed into the kitchen, slowing when he realized his visitor was his father-in-law, and he didn't look good.

Ryan took in the drawn expression on Mike's face and rocked back on his heels. "What's wrong?"

"Gloria told me to do this weeks ago, I want you to know that," the older man said, exhaling roughly.

"Do what?" Ryan set Lynn's photo on the kitchen table and crossed his arms.

Mike glanced at the picture, then back at Ryan. Unease was written all over him. "When the movers brought our furniture back, they found this in the house."

Ryan took the plain white envelope. It had his name and the kids' names written in neat letters on the front. His heart pounded in his chest. "I did a walk-through before they arrived. I didn't see anything."

"It was in one of the kitchen drawers. Maybe she didn't want you to find it right away."

Ryan bristled, his fingers itching to open the envelope, but he didn't want to do it in front of Mike. "And you decided to keep it from me?"

"I shouldn't have. I'm sorry. It was wrong."

"You're damn right you shouldn't have." Ryan heard his voice crack; it was like he was listening to himself have this conversation, when in his head he was just yelling *get out get out get out* so he could open it up. "You have no idea what's in this envelope. It has your grandchildren's names on it. You kept it from *them*."

It was lucky for Mike that Ryan was all out of fiery outbursts. He watched with a sense of cold detachment as his father-in-law left, but as soon as he was alone, something inside him snapped and all the fear he'd locked away—the fear that had pushed Holly away—flooded his body. Shaking, he opened the envelope.

Inside was a letter for the kids, thanking them for the card, and promising to always respond if they sent her more. She included her Los Angeles address. Behind that letter was another, thicker one. Ten pages, written on notepad paper, and one short note on plain white paper attached to the front.

Ryan,

This is the first apology note I wrote you, that I didn't give you because it ended up being so much more than just I'm sorry. I should have given it to you earlier. I was wrong when I said we don't know each other that well. I think you know me better than anyone else in the world.

When you're ready, I'm still yours.

Always,
Holly

Blindly, Ryan pulled his phone out of his pocket.

Olivia answered on the second ring. "Hi Ryan, what's up?"

"I need to book a flight to Los Angeles." He could practically hear Olivia's fist-pump in the air. "And I need you to keep it a secret."

"For just you?"

"No, I need to take the kids with me."

"Do they have passports?"

Shit. "No, and neither do I."

"Okay. So the first thing we need to do is…"

———

RYAN SCOWLED at the nail he'd just driven too hard into the drywall. He'd brought home a big painting of a hockey skate to hang over the couch where Lynn had hung their family pictures. He wasn't putting them away—he was moving them to the stairwell, where there would be more room to add photos to the collection. Their kids hadn't stopped growing when she died, and he needed to keep up that tradition.

Across the room, his phone vibrated insistently. He set down the hammer and stomped over to it. *Jake.* Damn it. He'd been hoping it was the post office. They were going to call as soon as the expedited passport delivery arrived.

"Hey, what's up?"

"Got a different kind of job for you," his friend's voice crackled over the line. He was driving and talking through the speakers in his truck.

"Shoot."

"I need you to go take a look at a house for me. The buyer just wants a builder's opinion, not a formal home inspection, but she wants it today."

"Today?"

"It's a last minute thing, no report needed. Just a yay or nay, and if it needs work, how much work."

"Can it wait until tomorrow, because—"

"Sorry, bud. And she said something about the school bus pick-up, if it was in a good spot for that."

"How the hell am I supposed to know that?"

"I don't know, man. You've got kids. I don't. Just go and give it a once-over, okay?"

"That's the thing, Jake. I've gotta pick up the kids from camp in twenty minutes. I'm sorry."

"Take them with you. Please? I'd go do it myself, but this is the only night Dani's got off all week."

"You're whipped."

"Happily so. I'll owe you one, thanks!"

Ryan stared at the phone. He didn't remember actually saying yes, but his friend was gone and…well, fuck it. It was time he got back on the horse, started doing more than odd-jobs. He'd been thinking about going to work for Jake in a bigger way anyway. Better than Zander's security gig—he'd always liked construction. Maybe this was a first step in the right direction.

He grabbed his tool belt from the basement, making sure it had a little notepad and the pens in it still worked. The flashlight's batteries were dead, but he stole two from a toy that made too much damn noise anyway, and headed for his truck.

By the time he had the kids all buckled in after picking them up from camp, Jake had texted him an address just north of town. *Swanky.* The only properties up there were high-end "cottages" owned by people with more money than sense. They'd all be great year-round homes, but the people who bought them only showed up for a few week-ends a year.

At least they provided some employment—part-time housekeepers, landscapers…people like Jake who'd charge five hundred bucks to say the perfectly good house was, in fact, perfectly good.

The address was for the first of the so-called cottages. The smallest one, actually, although it was still bigger than his place. And unlike the others, it wasn't that secluded. Just a short lane, not a long windy road. He thought of one of the questions the new owner had. The school bus would be visible from the house. A short walk if her kids were small, or she could watch from the kitchen if they were bigger.

He unbuckled Maya, and waited for all three kids to line up in front of him before he reminded them he was there to do some work, and they needed to stay close but not touch anything.

"Actually, there's nothing inside. The place is empty," a female voice called from behind him, and he froze. "They can come inside and run around. Go berserk. Whatever they want."

Blinking hard, still speechless, he glanced down at his kids. All three of them were staring past him at Holly, wide-eyed to see their friend again. They didn't know he'd been planning to take them on an adventure to find her— he'd told them the passports were for a trip in the winter with their grandparents. No point in getting their hopes up.

He'd done a good job of that for himself, too. So good that he couldn't turn around, even after they sprinted away and he could hear her let them into the house. As her footsteps crunched toward him on the gravel drive, he stood stiffly next to his truck. Now that the moment was upon them, and it wasn't how he'd envisioned it at all—

she'd come to him, when it was him that needed to beg her forgiveness—he found himself frozen like a statue.

Maybe because if he turned around—if he saw her face —he'd be a goner, and he needed to be sure that was okay. He cleared his throat. "What are you doing here?"

"I thought I was getting a home inspection." She stopped behind him, close enough he could feel her energy lifting all the hairs on the back of his neck. Tugging him back into her orbit.

"So you're buying a cottage?"

"Bought, actually. It's a done deal."

"Not a lot of movies shot in Pine Harbour. Just one that I can remember."

"So I'll have to travel for work."

"Not a lot of agents or movie premieres, either."

"I already have an agent and I've never been a fan of red carpets."

"Cottages are a lot of work. You can't just come and go a few times a year and hope it'll still be in the same condition when you get back."

"What if I spend most of my time with the cottage, and only go away when I need to?"

He felt her hands first, tentatively touching his back, and he stiffened against her as she pressed her face between his shoulder blades. "That's outside the scope of a home inspection report. I wouldn't know."

"I'm not talking about the stupid house, Ryan."

"I know." His voice cracked but he still stood there, an unmoving rock, as she hugged him tighter and tighter, until her arms were shaking and maybe the rest of her was shaking, too. "Don't cry, Holly."

"Is it too late?"

It would never be too late. He'd wait until the end of

time for her, he knew that now. "No." Stupid fucking cracking voice. Now they were both crying. "I was going to come to you."

"I know. That's why I'm here. Your friends don't really believe in secrets."

"Why did you ask Jake about the school bus?"

"I thought maybe it would be easier if I had my own space…give you and the kids some time to adjust to me being around and a part of their lives. But if you all stayed over sometimes…"

"That's not how busses work. There's a schedule. It's not just hop-on, hop-off. They need to be picked up in the same spot every day."

"Oh." Her chest shuddered against his back as she nodded. "Okay. Well, maybe in the future then. If they like me enough…"

He spun around, knocking her off-balance, but he grabbed her by the upper arms before she could stumble. Breathing hard, he searched her face. God, she looked good. Her hair was down, wavy and paler than in the spring, and her cheeks were pink. Her eyes were bright and wide, and he knew he should pay attention to that, but he was running on adrenaline now, need pumping through his veins so hard he couldn't think straight. "Like you enough? They love you, Holly. Don't make them wait."

She blinked up at him, her lips parting as she shook her head ever so slightly. "I won't. I just don't know what the right step is here. I don't want to push too hard and scare them away."

"They're already scared, sweetheart. Scared they're going to lose you forever." He shook his head. "No. That's me. And you're right, they'll need some time. But me…

Holly, I need you now. I don't need time, I just need *you*. I love you. I love you so much it hurts, and if you're really here, I'm not going to let you go again."

"I'm here."

"You took a crazy chance, woman."

"No. Not crazy. I knew you'd eventually see I'm serious about you."

"Tell me more. Tell me how serious."

"I don't know, Ryan. Last time I told you I loved you, you yelled at me."

"That was really shitty of me."

"You had a lot of stuff going on."

"I still do."

"Are you going to yell at me again?"

"Not about that."

"I love you." Her voice shook as she said it. "I fell in love with you months ago, on your porch, looking up at the stars. I didn't know that was what love was, and I'm glad I was in the dark for so long, because it gave me all that time with you. I know you're not ready for more, but I'm here. Whenever you're ready to call me your girl-friend, I'll call you my boyfriend. I want more dates. Just a girl and a boy, getting steak together. I want a lot more of sitting on the porch, looking at the stars."

"The stars up here are beautiful." He hoped she knew he wasn't talking about anything up in the sky. "You're beautiful. And kind. And talented and smart—"

She laughed. "You don't know that I'm talented. You've never watched any of my movies."

"I want to. Unless there are any with love scenes."

"There are a few."

"I want those destroyed, immediately."

She tried to laugh again, then stopped, her eyes filling with tears.

"Hey, I was just kidding." Not really, but he knew it wasn't possible.

"I know. I think you should kiss me now."

With a groan, he did just that, kissing her next to his truck, then again at the door to her new home, where he lifted her up and carried her across the threshold. As he set her down, he stroked her cheek. "I only have one quibble with this plan."

"I'm not sure I can handle a quibble, but shoot." She wrapped her arms tight around him and he kissed her hair.

"I don't want you to just be my girlfriend."

"One thing at a time, my lumberjack."

"Okay. But the next thing is a ring. Because you're mine."

"I am. Forever."

CHAPTER TWENTY-FOUR

RYAN TOOK a deep breath and looked out the limo window.

Beside him, Holly pressed her hand against his arm. "You can stay in the car and go around to the other entrance if you want."

"No, it's okay." And so far, it had been. Their first two months of dating—in public, at least in Pine Harbour—had been completely drama-free. Holly's publicist had done a good job of warning that anyone who wanted an interview with Hope Creswell could ask her about her move to Canada, but they couldn't ask about her personal life—full stop. And she'd put an attorney on retainer, ready to sue anyone who breathed a whisper about his kids.

He still didn't like all this hoopla, but a movie she'd made the year before was screening at the Toronto International Film Festival, and his pride in her accomplishments overrode his discomfort.

The chauffeur opened the door, and Ryan stepped out.

Cameras flashed and people yelled as he held out his hand and helped Holly out of the limo.

She was stunning in a pale pink strapless dress, snug to her hips, where layers upon layers of fluttery fabric floated down to the ground. As they'd discussed, she stepped past him, moving forward on the red carpet. It was exactly as she described, a long tunnel of chaotic noise.

He was used to that, at least.

A woman with a headset bumped into him as he tried to stay the prescribed five feet behind Holly. Far enough back that he was out of the camera shot, close enough that he was there if she needed him.

And so it went, all the way down the carpet.

"Are you having fun yet?" Holly asked, pressing a quick kiss to his cheek as they sat in their reserved seats.

"I think I stepped on Russell Crowe's foot," he muttered.

"Russell's here?" she said, spinning her head around. "I thought he was in Australia right now."

Ryan pointed at a man across the room and Holly giggled. "That's Gerard Butler."

"All those rugged heartthrobs look the same," he said under his breath.

"I wouldn't know, I only have eyes for my real-life rugged heartthrob." She winked at him as the lights went down.

He'd already seen this movie—Holly watched all of her films in private, first, a practice he found fascinating. So they'd watched this one curled up in her bed the week before. The kids had gone to their grandparents' for a sleepover that particular night, but they'd started sleeping over at Holly's place, too.

Slowly but surely, they were finding their way.

In the dark of the theatre, Holly found his hand and laced her fingers through his. She was nervous. This movie was getting a good amount of buzz, and *Unexpected*, the film she'd shot in his backyard, was slated for a Christmas Day release. She was leaving in late October for seven weeks of shooting on another project, and then there would be a press junket for *Unexpected* in the two weeks before Christmas. Her travel plans had her getting back to Pine Harbour two days before Christmas.

They were going to miss her something fierce, but at least they'd have video chats. It would be easier on the kids if they could see her face.

Easier on him, too.

"What are you thinking about?" she whispered.

"Nothing."

"Bull. Your face just got all tight."

She knew him too well. "Just looking forward to Christmas, that's all."

Leaning into him a bit more, she hugged his arm. "You can come visit me. You know that. My trailer is your trailer."

He had a flash of their first time together, in her trailer tucked in the back corner of the parking lot behind Main Street. Best Sunday morning ever.

She laughed at what was probably a stupid cocky grin on his face. "That's better."

Two hours later, the audience gave Holly and her co-stars and director a standing ovation. Ryan stood with everyone else, applauding hard as his sweetheart curtsied and blushed and shone in every single way. A question and answer session followed, then a cocktail reception, and they didn't get back to the hotel until after midnight.

When they let themselves into their suite, Rafe glanced

up from the couch, where Olivia had fallen asleep with her head on his lap. His hand lay on top of her swollen belly. She was thirty-four weeks pregnant, and when she'd told her husband that of course she was coming with them to Toronto—someone had to watch the kids, and besides, she wanted to do big city baby-stuff shopping—he insisted on coming with her.

"Did you have a good time?" Rafe asked quietly.

They started to fill him in, then Olivia roused as she heard voices, so Holly started again and Ryan excused himself to check on the kids. The next day they were going to the zoo, and they were so excited.

"Did they get to bed at a reasonable time?" Holly was asking as he re-joined them.

He kissed her temple. "I was just going to ask that myself. We've got a big day tomorrow."

Rafe laughed. "Pretty sure a night at TIFF would be a bigger deal than visiting the zoo for most people."

Holly just shrugged, and Ryan pulled her close. He was so damn lucky that she wasn't most people.

AFTER SEEING Rafe and Olivia to the door of the suite—the other couple was staying down the hall—Holly flipped the security latch, slipped off her heels, and padded into the master bedroom. She closed the door behind her. They'd open it again before falling asleep, but she wanted a private moment with the love of her life.

She found him in the bathroom, brushing his teeth. He'd taken off his James Bond-esque jacket and shirt, and now stood barefoot, wearing just black dress pants.

"You are a very handsome man," she murmured, cozying up behind him.

"I'm glad you approve." He finished up and they switched spots. She removed her make-up as he unzipped her dress, then carefully stepped out of it and he carried it into the bedroom for her as she finished washing up. When she looked up again, he was in the doorway, watching her. He'd taken his pants off, and in his dark-grey, plaid cotton boxers, he was back to being her mountain man.

She wet her lips and turned slowly as he prowled toward her. "Thank you for coming with me tonight."

"Anytime, sweetheart," he whispered as he crowded her against the bathroom counter.

She kissed his chest, then tipped her face up as he cupped the back of her head and descended, bringing their mouths together.

This fire between them only got hotter and better with time.

"Are you going to marry me when you get back from making another brilliant movie?" he asked as he scooped her up and sat her on the counter.

She spread her legs, wrapping her calves around his waist as he slid their hips together. "One thing at a time. Let's break the news to your in-laws that you're moving first."

"It's only ten minutes down the road. They'll deal." He kissed her neck, then lower, burying his face in her breasts as she leaned back on her hands. Shivering, she lifted her hips into his hands, letting him strip the last scrap of silk from her body.

He stroked between her legs, spreading her arousal around before sliding one finger, then two, deep inside her.

She was more than ready for him. "Now," she panted. "Ryan, I need you."

After shoving his boxers to the ground, he fisted his length and brought the thick crown to her folds, rubbing the head of his cock against her clit and through her wetness before sinking into her, an inch at a time.

He groaned as she squeezed around him, stretching as he filled her up. Each time they did this, it took her breath away how good it was. How good he was to her, how thoroughly he loved her with his body.

Like he loved her with his heart.

They still had some struggles. He didn't like to talk about his feelings. But he wasn't running from them anymore. He was right here, in her arms, and she'd never let him go.

"Take me to bed, Ryan." Her voice hitched as she wrapped her limbs around him.

He squeezed her bottom and hoisted her in his arms, still inside her. "Hang on tight, sweetheart."

EPILOGUE

THERE WASN'T anything in the world Holly liked more than sleeping in.

She hadn't known that would be a thing of the past once Ryan and the kids moved in with her. She wasn't complaining, at all. Just…adjusting.

"Mommy…"

She could feel Maya climbing on top of her, and she smiled at the now familiar name. The boys still called her Holly, and that would always be okay. But for Maya, her Mama was in Heaven and her Mommy was right here. It was an honour and a responsibility that Holly always wanted to live up to.

"Mmm, come cuddle, baby girl," she said without opening her eyes.

"Nope. It's morning."

"Early. Want a show?"

"Nope. I want pancakes."

"Okay, I'll make some soon. Blueberry pancakes?"

"Gavin's making chocolate chip ones."

Well, that sure opened her eyes in a hurry. "What?"

Maya grinned down at her from her perch on Holly's chest. "Gavin and Jack are making us breakfast. Wake up!"

"Oki-dokie." With a groan, she rolled out of bed. Ryan was gone for the weekend, on a winter training exercise. He'd probably been up for hours already. She held out her hand and let Maya tug her insistently down the stairs. "How much of a mess did they make?"

"Big mess," Maya said gleefully.

In the kitchen, that was proven true, but she also found two boys being very careful with the electric skillet. She leaned against the open archway, watching as Jack carefully supervised Gavin pouring batter from a ladle onto the sizzling surface. She resisted the urge to yell for them to get away from the hot appliance—they were fine, and as soon as they weren't in danger of being startled *into* it, she'd intervene.

Ryan was going to kill her.

But then he'd kiss her, and it would all be okay.

———

RYAN YAWNED as he drove past his old house, and took another sip of his takeout coffee. It had been a long, cold training weekend, and he was looking forward to a hot shower, a cuddle with his kids, and going to bed early with Holly. After six months of dating, they'd moved in with her over the Christmas holidays. The family photo wall now stretched up a new stairwell, with room to add more pictures.

Like wedding photos. He had a ring in his pocket that he'd picked up on Friday, on his way through Owen Sound— only in the country did you have to drive forty-five minutes to find a damn jewellery store.

Holly had avoided talk of actually getting married. She was more concerned about offending the Fenichs' than he was. Only a hippie child from California would think living together in sin was less concerning than a widower re-marrying quickly.

But it didn't feel quick. It felt like she'd been a part of his life forever. Part of that was how she treated Lynn's memory. Part of it was how happy she made him and the kids.

He'd talked to all three of them about having a wedding to celebrate Holly being a permanent part of their family, so it was entirely possible the proposal wouldn't be a surprise.

Who was he kidding—Holly knew him inside and out. She knew he wanted her to be his wife.

Just like he knew she'd say yes.

He wanted her wearing his ring the following week when they flew to Los Angeles for the Oscars. Holly was nominated—she kept telling him it was a long shot, but he'd seen *Unexpected*. If the Academy didn't give her that gold statue, something would have to be broken in the system. She shone in that movie—even more than she did in all the other ones, which he'd watched more than once now. Even the ones with the love scenes. That's what God made the fast forward button for.

He turned down the snowy lane, grinning as he caught sight of his family making a snowman on the front lawn.

"Daddy!" Maya ran toward him, her snow pants rustling as her little legs moved faster and faster.

"My baby girl!" He picked her up and twirled her around.

"I'm not a baby anymore," she protested, wiggling her feet.

"You'll always be my baby," he growled, flipping her onto her back, cradling her in his arms.

"No," she shrieked, laughing. "Holly will have a new baby soon."

"Is that right?" He glanced up, looking for his love. She moved toward them, laughing and shaking her head.

"Don't give your dad a heart attack," Holly said, tickling Maya as she reached them.

"I don't know," he said, suddenly full of an unexpected heat. "I kind of like the idea."

He set Maya down and she scampered off to re-join her brothers.

Holly just stared at him. "What?"

"I mean, it's your body. Your call."

"You want to have a baby?"

"I think Maya wants a baby. I was just adding my vote of support to the crazy plan."

"It would be crazy, you mountain man." But she leaned in, tipping her face to his for a kiss, and as soon as their lips parted, he knew she wanted to talk more about that when they were alone. Naked kind of talking.

"Madness," he whispered as she flexed her hips against his. "We'd have to get married."

"Because it would be the right thing to do?"

"Because it's what I want, sweetheart." He dug the ring box out of his pocket and dropped to one knee, right into the snow. "I want you. Forever."

THE END

ACKNOWLEDGEMENTS

aka The People Who Hold Me Up

A year ago I decided to write full-time. The next novel I wrote was Love in a Small Town, Pine Harbour #1, but I wrote that book because of *this* one.

I first "met" Ryan Howard as I was finishing his brother Finn's book, Beyond Love and Hate (Wardham #4), and I knew as soon as I did that I loved him. I also knew his life was about to get complicated and awful, and that made me so sad.

Tragedy is not the best way to start a romance series. So I dug around in his life, and met the Minellis and the Fosters—and there I found a lot of joy. I love big families, and this combined family—combined first through friendship, and then through the love between Jake and Dani, in Love in a Snow Storm (Pine Harbour #2)—is Ryan's safe harbour. They love him unconditionally, and they stick by his side even when he's an ass.

They're the people who hold him up.

I dedicated this book to my girlfriends. They're the

people who hold *me* up. A year after I started writing full-time, they're the ones who took me out to celebrate my millionth word written (that took a heck of a lot longer than a year, of course).

Pine Harbour might look like a book written about a band of brothers, but it's based on my real-life experience of friendship and sisters from other misters.

And my actual sister, of course, gets a huge thank you. She got the first book in the series dedicated to her, and her unwavering support continues to amaze me.

My brother-in-law, who mowed my lawn, and my mother- and father-in-law, who take care of my kids and feed me dinner and are generally the most amazing grandparents a girl could ever want for her family.

Lori, for all your support, and getting why I disappear into my computer for weeks at a time.

My editor on this book, Kristi Yanta, for taking a chance to help a newer author. Dana Waganer, for finding all the mistakes.

My reader group on Facebook, the Wardham Ambassadors, for embracing a lot more than Wardham. Thank for all being so excited about Ryan and Holly's story. Thank you for crying right along with me.

And I said this a year ago, but it's still true: all the readers who have signed up for my mailing list, liked me on Facebook, followed me on Twitter. There are literally thousands of you now, and that just blows my mind. Thank you for believing in second chances, and picking up a book about love in small town Ontario.

I love you all,
Zoe

ABOUT THE AUTHOR

Zoe York lives in London, Ontario with her young family. She's currently chugging Americanos, wiping sticky fingers, and dreaming of heroes in and out of uniform.

www.zoeyork.com

www.ingramcontent.com/pod-product-compliance
Lightning Source LLC
Chambersburg PA
CBHW050829190726
48286CB00007B/2016